EMERALD FLAME

The Jewels Series Book One

Virginia Coffman

This first world edition published in Great Britain 1996 by
SEVERN HOUSE PUBLISHERS LTD of
9–15 High Street, Sutton, Surrey SM1 1DF.
First published in the USA 1996 by
SEVERN HOUSE PUBLISHERS INC of
595 Madison Avenue, New York, NY 10022.

British Library Cataloguing in Publication Data

Coffman, Virginia, 1914–
    Emerald flame. – (The jewels series ; bk. 1)
    1. American fiction – 20th century
    I. Title II. Series
    813.5'4 [F]

    ISBN 0-7278-4890-9

Typeset by Palimpsest Book Production Limited,
Polmont, Stirlingshire.
Printed and bound in Great Britain by
Hartnolls Ltd, Bodmin, Cornwall.

EMERALD FLAME

The Jewels Series Book One

Further Titles by Virginia Coffman from Severn House

The Royles Series

BOOK ONE: THE ROYLES
BOOK TWO: DANGEROUS LOYALTIES
BOOK THREE: THE PRINCESS ROYAL
BOOK FOUR: HEIR TO A THRONE

The Moura Series

MOURA
THE BECKONING
THE DARK GONDOLA
THE VICAR OF MOURA
THE VAMPIRE OF MOURA

Miscellaneous Titles

THE CANDIDATE'S WIFE
HYDE PLACE
THE JEWELLED DARKNESS
LOMBARD CAVALCADE
LOMBARD HEIRESS
ONE MAN TOO MANY
THE ORCHID TREE
PACIFIC CAVALCADE
THE RICHEST GIRL IN THE WORLD
TANA MAGUIRE
THE VENETIAN MASQUE

For my dear sister, Donnie, who said:
"Go on, anyway."

The germ of *Emerald Flame* comes from an event in the life of Jane Austen's Aunt, Mrs James Leigh-Perrot, incredible as it may seem in today's courts. Such near-horrors occurred frequently and often did not have the ending related here and in the life of Mrs Leigh-Perrot.

Virginia Coffman

Chapter One

In the afternoon the two guards delivered their beautiful prisoner from her employer's home to the squire's estate in Bath. They had thoroughly enjoyed their task, only regretting its brevity.

"You'll be here at Squire Blassingame's house, ma'am," the little guard explained, adding, "That'll be 'til the prison warder comes out from London. It's him as gets you to Taunton, for the Assizes. What I mean to say — your trial, ma'am."

With an effort Hester Leland managed to seem confident of the outcome. She even gave him a smile which completed her conquest of the guard. "I didn't think I was important enough to warrant such lofty quarters."

"Oughter take a mighty pretty rope," the lanky guard put in. He caressed her pale, slender neck with his thumb, ignoring her shudder. "Ought to be silk threads and all. Only fitting for a capital offense."

Her two guards, in fawn-coloured pantaloons and black redingotes tightly buttoned up to the throat, formed a barrier on either side of her as she stepped into the elegant hall of the mayor's house.

The guards still looked unsure over their task. They were not often asked to prevent the escape of a respected

1

young gentlewoman, especially one with Miss Leland's physical attributes.

The glass frame around the portrait of Lord Wellington, England's idol since Waterloo a year ago, flashed as the doors behind her closed out the sunlight. Startled by that flash, for an instant Hester did not recognize the face that stared back at her from the glass frame. Her features looked bloodless. The green eyes appeared to be haunted, and the autumn wind had ruffled the fine tendrils of the hair that some admirer, under the influence of the Jerez wine served by Hester's employer, once described as "exactly the colour of pale sherry". He had added the absurdity, "And eyes a lad could drown in", whatever that might entail.

She pushed the tendrils under her bonnet. She should have worn curls or a fringe of blonde hair over her temples, done something with her hair to attract the men on whom her life depended. But she hadn't done so, any more than she had yielded to the jeweller's blackmail attempt, and as a result, her stubborn will brought her to this pass. Despite her high-boned cheeks and the sensuous curves of her mouth, she still looked austere today and, worst of all, frightened. They would surely think fright was a sign of guilt.

She sensed that several people, mostly servants, were peering at her from behind white pilasters or within salons whose doors were all ajar. Obviously, the mayor's dependants and servants wanted to catch a good look at this supposedly genteel young woman soon to be bound over for trial at the Taunton Assizes. She could see the end of that trial now in her mind's eye: the rickety cart, the jeering crowds, and, in the end, the gallows. She had already been threatened with them.

Hester tried to banish this ghastly vision and walked straight ahead, reserving her poignant smile for the little Mayor of Bath. He was an old acquaintance, having occasionally visited Hester's employer, Lady Jerusha Pomfret, with his gossipy wife.

Squire Roderick Blassingame trotted down the staircase and extended his two hands to her. His squeaky, penetrating voice in so small a man always startled people.

"Miss Leland, indeed welcome. May I state that I do not credit the charge for an instant? Pray let us accept this as a social call . . . You, there – " to the guards. "My butler will attend you to your quarters until the escort arrives. You, the fellow on the left, are to be stationed with a view of the forward lawns and the gates. You on the right are to be at watch above the kitchen gardens and the southeast road down into the town."

Hester was grateful to the little mayor when the guards obeyed him. They had clung to Hester like slimy leeches. The leering man on her right, with a body obviously not washed in the recent past, had squeezed so close she sensed that he felt some physical excitement over the contact with her. The other guard, Hobbs, who was a quite pleasant little man and somewhat stout, shrugged at the mayor and edged away, touching two fingers to his forelock respectfully.

"Ay, sir, have it so. Off with ye, Beechum." This to his partner who shuffled away with reluctance.

Hester had stopped, wondering which direction she was to take. The mayor trotted to her and she curtsied.

"Sir, you and Mrs Blassingame have been more than kind. I can never thank you for your faith in me."

In response to her curtsy he had taken her gloved hands and raised her to her true height, but with her

3

hands still in his. He was evasive about another matter.

"Ay, yes, Mrs Blassingame. Yes. I must tell you – that is, Mrs Blassingame asks to be excused. A migraine. She is sorely afflicted, you know."

Hester had not known. Selina Blassingame possessed a constitution of iron and was always in the forefront of activities in Bath, as elsewhere. She was unlikely to recognize a migraine, much less permit one to settle in her sturdy head. But Hester knew the world very well and expressed her sympathy in a brief murmur – Squire Blassingame so clearly wanted to get on to matters of greater moment.

"Lady Pomfret has been most emphatic in your defence. You have a good friend in your employer."

"Yes, sir. I am very fond of her Ladyship."

"She will speak up for you when the counsel is provided for your defence. I understand that Lady Pomfret intends to stand your expenses in the trial."

Hester felt enormous relief. There might be hope in spite of the stern assurances of everyone else who had spoken to her about the shoplifting episode. She had been taken into custody a day after the public accusation on Milsom Street in which the jeweller was supported by three witnesses. Sylvester Girard, who was her chief accuser, had given her twenty-four hours to think over his 'little proposal' in exchange for her freedom.

"I shall be most grateful for Lady Pomfret's help, but even more for her belief in me."

"Of course, as it should be. But do come. I have – we have decided that you must have the bedchamber in the southeast corner."

He offered his arm with a gallant, sweeping gesture.

4

"Permit me. The housekeeper seems to be inattentive and the butler is off showing those two oafs to their rooms. Absurd, in any case. Treating you like a common felon. But I'm persuaded the Taunton High Justice will not let you go to trial."

They were moving up the staircase. She appreciated his effort to make her seem superior to the average criminal caught in the act of High Theft, a hanging crime. But the shadow remained. She only hoped that her fingers, icy within her gloves, did not warn the squire of her terror.

"You are too kind, sir."

"I regret the oafs should remain here at all, but it is only until your official warder arrives to escort you. If they insist that you face that wretched prison while you await trial, then we will certainly keep you here in comfort as long as possible."

"I understand. I depend upon the witnesses. One of them, a boy, seems most unreliable. It is quite possible he may retract his lie."

"Well paid for, I make no doubt," the squire grumbled. "These merchants occasionally bribe likely rascals to testify against innocent persons. It is done, of course, in the hope of the merchants' being paid off by the unfortunate patrons." Paid off in flesh, if not in coin, she thought.

The upper halls of Blassingame House were considerably less opulent. Like a great many other yeomen who had become landowners in this rich, superficial world of the Prince Regent the squire spent freely upon only that area revealed at his lavish balls and receptions.

Hester found the old-fashioned, eighteenth-century aura upstairs more to her liking. She had spent her early years in such an environment, in the house of her soldier-father, a lonely life for the most part, brightened only by her occasional friendships with hired housekeepers and the all-too-seldom visits by her father.

Three years ago in 1813, during the campaign on the French border, her father had received a sword thrust in the vitals while foraging for the First Foot Guards and been invalided home. He was not a sociable man, as his life was bound up in the army. He cared moderately for his daughter but he had no real interest other than the reports of the war. For Matt Leland his death came as a blessing. He could join the only person he had ever wholeheartedly loved in his life, his dead wife Georgina.

With less than two guineas to rub together, Hester had accepted the rough but sincere offer of her mother's girlhood friend, Lady Jerusha Pomfret, to act as that lady's companion. Hester had never been sorry. As for her father, she was quite sure that he and her mother were happy together, at last.

Hester had vowed long ago never to marry for reasons of passion, which had been the great bond between her parents. She could not help feeling, with some bitterness, that such a union excluded the children. There must be marriages that combined both but she had not personally seen them.

Unless, of course, Sir Charles Willoughby, her kind and exceedingly handsome suitor, was sincere in his protests of affection for her. Lady Pomfret thought so, but her Ladyship was an incurable romantic. One of the horrors facing Hester now was the awareness that Sir Charles would lose all respect for her when he heard the charge against her.

Charles Willoughby devoted his life most usefully to

aiding those females who faced the courts on charges of which they might be innocent. But Hester was not fooled by this. He certainly did not regard such women as his equals. He invariably referred to them as 'those poor creatures.' Was the proud and independent Hester Leland now to become 'a poor creature'?

Squire Blassingame left Hester in the care of the housekeeper and went away, evidently pleased with his own broad-minded attitude and the presence of a beauty under his roof. A beauty whose gratitude should be prodigious providing, of course, the lady was found not guilty.

It took very little imagination for Hester to guess his thoughts as he bowed gallantly, lingering over her hand which he saluted with a kiss before departing.

The housekeeper, Mrs Brough, a large woman with a motherly look that Hester soon found deceptive, offered to attend to the guest's portmanteau and her two bandboxes with their worn but cheerful satin bows, one lilac-striped and the other a jonquil gold, the shade of her hair, and her straw bonnet.

"Thank you, you are very kind. But I would not trouble you. Then too, I may be leaving quite suddenly."

The woman had a cold gaze that seemed to dart about as if she did not want to miss anything.

"True, miss. Still, I have been instructed to attend you in any way possible." She was already untying the bow to one bandbox.

"I am most grateful to the squire," Hester murmured, noting the woman's curiosity about the contents, the clothing and books in the box.

The woman corrected her with a snap. "Squire's Lady bade me attend you, miss."

"Very well, then. I'm grateful to Mrs Blassingame. However, I shall not need help at this time." She was certain that nothing but curiosity prompted the woman to persist. "I trust Mrs Blassingame will not be an invalid for long."

Mrs Brough raised her steel-grey head from the band-box. She dropped the untied ribbon of the box with a contemptuous gesture.

"The mistress has never been an invalid. She hasn't had a sick day in my ten years of service in this house." She caught herself. "That is to say, until this very morning."

Hester smiled. "I understand perfectly."

Mrs Brough gave her a quick glance. Then she inclined her head ever so slightly and retreated, shutting the door behind her.

Having no illusions about her welcome in this house, except from the good-hearted squire, Hester unpacked only what she would need within the next few hours. She was preoccupied with the possible journey to Taunton, with imprisonment, trial, and then perhaps an ignominious death. The horror never left her. Even if she should only be transported for life, the prospects were terrifying.

Whatever the housekeeper's feelings about this 'criminal in the house' she knew her duty and had left a delicate porcelain pitcher and bowl on the drop-leaf mahogany side table, the pitcher filled with water, still warm.

Hester removed her gloves and untied the ribbons of her bonnet. Then she turned her attention to the welcome rose-scented water she poured into the basin. Though her fingers still shook a little, her nerves were calmed by the water and the soothing effect of the rose scent.

Around her the household sounds were distant and not

unpleasant. She heard the rattle of dishes somewhere on the floor below and assumed the dining salon must be directly under this room. The view from the long salon windows, including the distant rooftops of Bath and the nearer green copse, must be very picturesque as the family and their guests dined. She had the same view from this room. It reminded her painfully of how little she had appreciated such things before she faced the threat of losing them forever.

Hester dreaded writing to Lady Pomfret about the accusation, remembering how that lady had almost come to blows with the guards and the jeweller Girard, when they insisted on taking Hester away. Lady Pomfret was a formidable personage and not to be trifled with.

In the temporary security of this room, Hester found herself able to rest for the moment. She curled up in the big wing chair by the window, tucked her lavender sprigged skirts under her, and closed her eyes.

When Hester awoke she felt better. After an hour in this position, however, her body was stiff and aching, so she stood up, stretched and walked briskly up and down the room.

How fresh the kitchen garden looked with all its neat rows of planting and the artistic herb garden near the still room door.

Hester looked out enviously. She had always been a brisk walker. She thought nothing would have raised her spirits more than a stroll along those herbal rows and perhaps among the trees bordering the wide back lawn.

She stretched again, then rummaged through the portmanteau for the Spanish lace shawl sent home from the wars by her father and went out into the hall.

No one was in sight. It was the quiet hour of the afternoon, between dinner and whatever festivities were planned for the evening. She went quietly down the staircase, looking over the balustrade to see if there was a way out to the back gardens from the reception hall below. As she had expected, the door was behind the staircase.

One of the young footmen passed along the hall, whistling out of tune. She waited breathlessly until he had disappeared into one of the family rooms. Then she hurried out through what proved to be a terrace door. Once outside, she strolled along the path to the kitchen garden, breathing deeply, enjoying the wondrous freedom of the hazy autumn air.

During the years in London there had never been a place to grow food. Afterward, Lady Pomfret's gardener was as opinionated as his employer. He hadn't welcomed any assistance from a city-bred female like Hester Leland.

There was no time now to linger here. She must be back in her room before the maid brought the tea tray or the family would suspect she was running away from the law. A tempting idea but highly impracticable in her present situation, with nothing but the gown she wore and the fringed shawl to protect her from dangers that beset a hunted criminal.

The chill breeze of afternoon whipped her cheeks and forehead. She remembered how much her mother, long ago, had loved the wind when she walked down a dingy street in the Southwark area of London, hardly more than an alley. She hadn't even minded that the air was thick with sea-coal or that Marshalsea Prison was close by. Only her soldier husband mattered and this was his familiar habitat.

"Dear Mama," she thought, hugging the shawl more closely around her throat and upper arms. "How little you dreamed that your daughter would stand in the dock like any felon bound for Newgate!"

And all because Hester had refused to let those scurvy jewellers blackmail her. But her stubbornness ran in the family. Her father had been even more stubborn, even prouder. He would have understood.

Still, if she had the opportunity to relive the moment of the jeweller Girard's first offer, would she behave in any other way?

Obviously not. Aside from his hint that if she recommended certain jewels for Lady Pomfret's purchase she might find the charge against her dismissed, there had been the even nastier addition: "You might find me a far more generous protector than that clutch-fisted old lady. If you were in my keeping you may imagine what pleasure might lie ahead. Say the word and the charge may be dropped."

His odious sweating hands, busy about her person, so like the guard Beechum, had sickened her even more than the terrible threat of the gallows.

A bird began to sing, unmoved by the wind. She looked around. She could not see the little creature in the vegetable or herb gardens. The bird stopped its song and began to twitter. It was hidden somewhere in the line of willows at the end of the lawn. Beyond the willows was a secluded pond. An ideal rendezvous for lovers, she thought, and remembered her own tentative love affair with something like anguish.

What other woman of twenty-three, with no dowry, was the object of such attentions? In her mind's eye she saw Charles Willoughby, young, devoted, attractive, in

11

every way eligible. Only a month ago he had begun to make casual references to marriage. Such a marriage would have her little world favouring it. Charles spoke of the splendid things they could do together on behalf of the unfortunate, the poor, the 'wretched creatures' in the prisons for crimes of such small nature as to be mere pranks. This unselfish concern of his had mattered to her almost more than his good looks and what she thought might be a sincere affection for her.

He was good to his dependants and spent time and money aiding the less fortunate. Would she now qualify? She closed her eyes to the thought. Yet, if things were otherwise, he would have been a kind, perhaps wise husband, exactly the kind of man she dreamed of. Her relations with him would have been entirely different from the sensual and selfish passion between her mother and father that thrust out all the rest of the world, even their own child.

She had pretended not to understand Sir Charles, wondering if she would be able to live in what she suspected was his elegant little mother's style. But that was several weeks ago. She had thought about him with painful regret during the hours since the criminal charge was laid against her. How comforting it would have been to feel his arms around her in quiet protection, to know he loved her and, most of all, believed in her innocence!

She strolled between the willows and the little dark pool, wondering what her life would be like now if she hadn't been in Lady Pomfret's house two days ago when her Ladyship asked her to have the Pomfret pearls re-strung at the jewellers. It was less than a week before she was to have been taken up by Sir Charles in his new phaeton and been driven around the countryside, though he knew quite well that the sight of her sitting up there beside him would give the females of Bath something to gossip about.

With his gentle smile he had reminded her, "I trust you will become accustomed to the handling of a phaeton. It will be expected of you."

Did he mean "if we are married?" She had let the remark pass.

Too late now. The jeweller Girard had seen to that. Hester always dreaded going to Girard and Hailsham's in any case, knowing Girard's lascivious and pawing ways. She found the sly, thick-lipped, heavily scented Sylvester Girard distasteful in every way. But the Pomfret household knew better than to refuse any of her Ladyship's quick demands.

No matter. Hester was now a prisoner on Squire Blassingame's estate and it was time to return to the house before she was missed. She stopped, turned, and found her way abruptly barred by a strange, theatrical-looking creature in black pantaloons and a tight surcoat that was no darker than his gypsy black eyes. She almost cried out but something about the way his eyes lighted at her reaction put her in mind of Lady Pomfret's remark last year.

Men like this gypsy fellow rode in the train of the handsome Russian Tsar who had arrived in London last year with the other Allies to celebrate the very close-run victory at Waterloo. Every female had noticed the Tsar's good looks. But Lady Pomfret, who had taken Hester to London to see the Allies ride proudly through the streets, was much taken with the Tsar's train of strange officers. She talked most of the journey back to Bath about the fascination of the Cossack riders, the fierce Russian Tartars, and especially the gypsy escort.

"Ah, those gypsies!" she had said and given them a sigh for what she called, "My lost youth. Like your dear mama, I spent much of my girlhood on the Dorset Heath where we were like to see gypsy caravans at all seasons. Romantic devils they were, too."

Just as Lady Pomfret had said, Tartar or gypsy, this creature before Hester would be dangerously attractive to some susceptible females. His almond-shaped eyes and hard, sensual mouth were far from the aristocratic look of men like Charles Willoughby, but there was something about the bronze-skinned stranger that would catch the eye.

Hester pulled herself together, getting up her courage.

"You are in my way, sir." The rogue probably wouldn't recognize a sir, but no matter.

He put out one hand as a barrier.

"A valiant attempt, but foolish. You could not have got far."

His English was commendable and despite an accent, he made himself amply clear to her, and she tried to conceal her haunting fear that this barbarian was somehow involved in her captivity.

"I was not escaping. Anyone but a fool could guess that. I felt the need of a little fresh air before I returned to the house."

He took her upper arm, pushing aside the shawl. His thin, muscular fingers closed around her flesh.

"So it would seem. But come along, we must become better acquainted. I am sent to bring you to Taunton and the magistrates' examination. We wouldn't want to disappoint the magistrates now would we?"

14

"I cannot conceive of anything that would interest me less than the magistrates' disappointment."

He seemed to find this amusing also but, not content with taking her by the arm, he gently propelled her along with his other hand in the small of her back. That was frightening enough – the indignity of it struck her as the worst part – but he raised his voice and called out, "No need to concern yourselves. I have the prisoner. She did not get far."

Hester saw not only Squire Blassingame and his wife but most of the household servants on the terrace, including the two guards who had taken her from Jerusha Pomfret's house. They were all standing there like puppet dolls in a mercer's shop, staring at her.

Mrs Blassingame called out grimly, "Thanks be to heaven for your arrival, Colonel – er – Kirov."

Worst of all, the squire added timidly, "Amen to that, my dear."

There seemed to be no doubt. Like everyone else, her former friend, the squire, also believed she had been running away.

And what was the world coming to, sending Russian gypsy rogues to do the work of good Englishmen?

Chapter Two

The Russian Tartar, or whatever he was, offered Hester his hand, which she ignored. He shrugged, made a gesture permitting her to go ahead of him, and she stepped up onto the terrace, aware that he found her pride amusing in the circumstances.

Then, beside the squire's wife, Hester saw an elderly man with a sharp, pointed nose and a mouth which appeared to have swallowed his lips. He looked dry, businesslike and utterly without mercy. She guessed that she was the object of his visit, and could only pray that he was not a magistrate. He did look like one.

About to pass the squire, she crossed her shawl over her bosom and, ignoring all the others, addressed him. Her pride kept her from pleading.

"Sir, I believed it was permissible to walk in your garden. I am not yet a convicted felon."

"Well – er—" the squire began with an uneasy side glance at his wife.

That lady took over the conversation. "Young woman, it was not through my contrivance that you were brought here, you may be sure. Mr Hailsham, of the jewellers, Girard And Hailsham, is a gentleman of the highest repute. If he states categorically that you are guilty of concealing that emerald on your person, and you deny it, I shall know whom to believe, I assure you."

"Now, ma'am," the gentleman in grey said judicially, "that is rather severe. We do not yet know what the jury will have to say on the matter. One must not make such pronouncements until the judgment has been handed down." He added, quite unnecessarily in Hester's view, "Whatever the conclusions we may have come to."

The servants were now dispersed by Mrs Brough and Hester started into the house, wondering if they were so anxious to be quit of her that the Blassingame family would pack her off to her destination tonight in the company of that terrifying Russian Colonel.

The Russian followed her to the foot of the staircase, looking up into her eyes as she started to climb.

"We're quit of this place sometime after sunrise, miss. Bundle up what you need. I'll have a tray of breakfast sent up to you."

"Thank you." She said it as coolly as she could, but the horror of what might await her in Taunton at the Assizes must have been evident in her low-pitched voice.

He stared at her in silence for a long moment. As she had first noticed, his eyes were strange. They excited her by their dazzling bright light – yet they also alarmed her, because they did excite her. She had the sensation that something inhuman and animalistic studied her.

At this moment in her life he was her most ruthless enemy and enjoying every moment of it. She had begun to understand how a bird might be mesmerized by a cobra.

"Very well. I shall be ready."

"No seducing of your guards, or climbing out of windows or dropping from the roof?"

"Do I look like a stilt-walker at a carnival?"

"Far from it. I've been one, and I ought to know. But then, you don't look like a jewel thief, either."

She picked up her skirts and hurried on to the upper hall, to escape his odious suspicions. She heard footsteps behind her and wondered if they belonged to the Colonel. But he was lightfooted, like an animal.

The sharp-nosed gentleman in grey called to her. "Miss Leland, I am Frederick Iles. Lady Jerusha Pomfret is an old and dear friend of mine. She asked me, as a particular favour, to act on your behalf."

"Thank you, sir." Perhaps he was more sympathetic than he looked. "Where may we talk in privacy?"

He glanced at the various closed doors. He seemed to know the Blassingame house very well. "Shall we try the music room?"

She let him escort her into a small salon done in red and gold. It was clearly not in frequent use. The pianoforte hadn't been dusted and the harp was muffled in Holland covers. There were chairs scattered about, which looked as though the guests had departed pell-mell from a concert, not even waiting to set the chairs to rights again.

The grey gentleman calling himself Frederick Iles drew out chairs for Hester and himself.

"Now, then. You must trust me with the absolute truth. The man who represents you before the sacred Bar of Justice must know exactly what to expect. No unpleasant surprises. No sudden admissions forgotten until the crucial moment."

"I told the Examining Magistrate of Bath, Lord Beverley, the details as they occurred, sir." Her hands were cold again. She sensed the same attitude as that of the Examining Magistrate. Mr Iles wanted her to admit

19

facts that would support the story told by sly Mr Girard and corroborated by Mr Hailsham, who had always seemed so kind and avuncular.

"Yes, yes. You told your tale. Frightened out of your wits, I daresay."

"No, sir. I was not frightened. I am an honest woman and I expected my story would be believed when I told it."

"Possibly." He formed a pyramid with the fingers of his two hands and studied her in a judicial way. "Let us hear your version of the events. All the details, if you please."

Your version. That sounded very like a polite request for whatever tale she had made up to save herself.

No matter. She would tell him what actually happened and only pray that, unlike the magistrate, this man would recognize the truth when he heard it.

It began with her employer, as she explained to Mr Iles. Lady Jerusha Pomfret was a large, lean, imposing female with a distinctly equine face and a salty disposition. When she issued orders people jumped to obey. Those servants who stayed long enough to grow accustomed to her manner remained for life. Hester found her a challenge but soon realized that her gruff exterior concealed a well-meaning, impulsive nature, a defiance of authority and an intense loyalty to those she cared for.

On the morning of the emerald episode Lady Jerusha was supervising Hester's work in the conservatory where Hester pruned the roots of a rose, hoping to finish her work before the temperamental gardener appeared. Her Ladyship startled Hester by the sudden exclamation,

"Heavens! I'd completely forgotten."

20

"Yes, ma'am?"

"That wretched jewellers' shop on Milsom Street. I must have my pearls re-strung for the concert tomorrow night at the Upper Rooms."

Hester, wiping her hands on a cloth, then made the capital error that might eventually cost her life.

"It would be quite simple for me to go. From Queen's Square to Milsom Street should take only a few minutes. I can easily be back to finish the transplanting." So it was arranged.

Hester had washed and changed to last year's neat, jonquil muslin round gown and a bonnet to match. In relating the event to Mr Iles Hester sharply curtailed these clothing details and hurried on to important matters.

So then, there was the elegant little shop on Milsom Street. Lady Pomfret had once quarrelled with Sylvester Girard and sworn not to enter the shop again. However, this had nothing to do with Hester who was always elected to handle any necessities, thus preventing Her Ladyship from breaking her vow.

An obsequious male clerk met Hester and hearing Lady Pomfret's name, immediately turned her over to Mr Girard. Hester remembered long afterward that big, jovial Mr Hailsham, his partner, stood about in doorways, a witness to most, but not all of the proceedings. Mr Girard was unctious in the extreme.

"Re-string these pearls? Yes, indeed, miss. We are always happy to serve Lady Pomfret's household. We only regret that her Ladyship does not honour us with her own custom. Not but that you, my dear, are a charming substitute." He removed the valuable pearls from their soft velvet packet and held them up to the light. "Permit the observation, though. These are not

21

pearls of the first rank. Note the colour." He was very close now, the arm with the pearls rubbing against her bosom as his fingers raised to catch the bar of light through the window.

She shifted away from him.

"Sir, I am in no position to purchase a strand of pearls, whatever the colour."

"Perfectly true." The little man's breath was stale. She turned her head away. He set the pearls on a sheaf of silver tissue and motioned to the shy clerk. "The black velvet case, at once."

Hester said, "I must be on my way. Another time, sir."

"One moment, please. My dear Miss Leland, your employer has a rare taste in gems. Come, see how her eyes will shine when she views this." He took the velvet case from the clerk's hand and set it on the wooden counter. "There, have you ever seen such magnificence?"

"Lady Pomfret collects only amethysts. Nothing of excessive value."

"But she will quickly move on to precious gems when she beholds this. Come closer, look."

The open velvet case revealed several unset stones. To Hester they had unparalleled brilliance: the ruby, deep and darker than blood; the sapphire, a lovely, vivid blue piece of sky. And the emerald: beautiful, fantastically colored, but ominous in some way. Probably the colour itself. She had a sickening vision of her mother's crumpled, twisted body, in the emerald green gown she was so fond of. Long ago in London, a street accident had taken Hester's enchanting mother.

She heard Mr Hailsham across the room. "Are you well, Miss Leland?"

22

"Certainly." She recovered in an instant and pushed the emerald away. "Not that, never."

Girard said, "Fetch Miss Leland a cup of water, Barnes. Or better yet, a glass of Madeira."

"I am perfectly well. Please don't trouble. When will the pearls be ready? She must have them sometime tomorrow."

Mr Girard's insinuating, whispery voice was close to her ear. "Bring in her Ladyship, my dear, and you will find it well worth your time."

She drew back, trying not to show her revulsion. "I am afraid I could not. I have no influence over her Ladyship."

"We hear differently. Think of it, my girl. A nice little bauble for that pretty neck of yours. A pendant to dangle precisely – there."

His moist finger pressed her throat. She flinched away from his touch and took several steps backward, wishing Mr Hailsham had not retired to some secret recess behind the showroom. Her movement brought her hip sharply against the counter. The unset jewels slipped off the velvet pad and two of them fell to the floor. She and Girard knelt to pick them up. Girard rescued both the ruby and the sapphire. She was so anxious to get out of the shop she paid little attention to what had happened to the hated emerald.

"I must go," she said hurriedly. "I shall be late. Lady Pomfret is most particular about the time."

"Just so, Miss Leland," Girard called after her, making no effort to stop her. "Remember our little talk. The profit to you can be considerable."

On the busy street she took her first clean breath and began to walk down to the cross-street where an elderly

23

gentleman in a sedan chair was momentarily stopped by noonday foot traffic. A minute or two later she heard running steps behind her. She stepped aside to let the hurrying man pass her. In doing so, she came face to face with Lady Pomfret's seamstress, Miss Enderby, who looked annoyed as usual. She had long disliked Hester, regarding her as an intruder in the household.

"Your manners leave much to be desired, miss. You nearly trod on my foot."

Hester begged her pardon but had scarcely got the words out when Sylvester Girard came up puffing and panting, to pinch her wrist between his pudgy finger and thumb.

"Miss Leland, I believe you have a property of ours. Perhaps in an absent-minded moment—"

Miss Enderby stared. Her thin lips set tightly. It was obvious that she believed there was something disreputable about a woman she disliked on general principles.

Hester was more angry than frightened. "Certainly not, sir. As you may see." She held out her reticule.

While Miss Enderby continued to stare, Mr Hailsham joined them, likewise panting. He murmured, "Dear me, I am persuaded you must be wrong, Sylvester."

Girard drew the strings of her handsewn reticule and put his fist in. When he drew it out it contained the flashing, dazzling emerald. In the bright autumn sunshine it was like a green beacon of light. Miss Enderby gasped. Other passers by did likewise.

A red-haired youth, perhaps in his early teens, and carrying a package for delivery, had stopped at Mr Girard's accusation. He watched the appearance of the emerald and whistled.

"My word!" Mr Hailsham said. "I cannot believe –

some carelessness. Yes. Absent minded, as you surmised, Sylvester."

"I seen 'er," the red-haired youth put in with an impudent leer. "The lady be a thief, right enough."

"Obtain the names of these good people and where they may be found," Girard said. "Come along, miss. We must discuss this matter."

"There is not a matter to discuss," Hester said coldly. "I did not put that stone into my reticule."

Girard was urging her along, out of hearing of the others. "And how do you think it got there, my pretty?"

"I think you know very well."

He was looking flushed but that might be due to his exertions.

"So that's the way of it. Slander atop of High Theft. There's the gibbet waiting in crimes like this."

They had reached the jewellers' shop and he stopped. His voice lowered, it was oily and insinuating.

"But there are always means of accommodation. You stole a stone worth twelve hundred guineas. If – I make no promises – but if Lady Pomfret were to return to Girard And Hailsham, perhaps making the purchase of several items, it just might repay us our thousand guineas."

"You said twelve hundred."

His mouth curled in a singularly unpleasant smile. "Do not trifle with me, girl. Sit you down. Here, on this stool. I'll give you ten minutes to make your decision. Accommodate me – us, that is to say – or face the prospect of—" He pointed eloquently to his throat, adding, "I will expect your gratitude for my clemency, of course. You would find me a most generous protector. I am said to be quite a favourite among the females. Do you take my meaning?"

25

There was no possible answer to that. If she had agreed to his sordid suggestion so far as Lady Pomfret's patronage was concerned, he would have held her 'crime' over her head forever. But beyond this conniving at a typical servant's trick, she was being asked to become his mistress. Her horror at the idea almost took her breath away. She refused his 'accommodation'. Frederick Iles watched her as she finished. Badly shaken by the memories made vivid in her telling of the so-called 'crime', she said, "That is the story, sir."

She sensed at once that he did not believe her. Or, because the accusation was made against responsible merchants in the city, he did not want to believe her. Her talk of sexual favours bartered was a reflection upon every gentleman in Bath. One knew of them but a respectable young female pretended they did not exist.

Chapter Three

"Your story," Mr Iles repeated. He sucked in his cheeks. "And the story told by impartial witnesses?"

"It was a lie."

"Three witnesses lied, the two on the street and the second jeweller as well as the highly respected Sylvester Girard? Come now, miss, none will believe that a gentleman like Sylvester Girard would be party to such a trick, merely to snare a little extra custom. No, no, no."

"Mr Girard is an odious toad whose private pleasure, among others, is caressing young women foolish enough to bring him their custom."

Mr Iles was shocked. "My dear Miss Leland, I trust you do not bring such sordid charges into the dock. You only prejudice your case. I will allow, ma'am, that you are an extraordinarily beautiful woman. But permit me to doubt that even your charms could persuade a gentleman to behave in so – shocking a manner."

"How innocent you are!"

He looked indignant. And this man is to defend me, she asked herself in despair. Holding tight to a pretense of calm, she said aloud, "Surely, the two witnesses can be questioned, their backgrounds examined. What of their own probity? One of them was a very young man, perhaps easily persuaded."

"And if we should question the other, this Miss Enderby are you of the opinion that she would continue to lie?"

Hester thought of that thin, vinegary woman.

"No," she agreed. "Miss Enderby would not lie deliberately. She saw Mr Girard take the emerald out of my reticule. She could not know that he or Mr Hailsham dropped the stone into my bag in the shop. Or perhaps it was the clerk who works for them."

Probably, like a magician, Girard had slipped the emerald into and out of her reticule in one movement on the street when he ran after and seized her.

But Mr Iles did not believe her. Nothing could be more evident.

If I had anywhere to run to, she thought, I would try escape. Despite that all-seeing, too-clever Russian colonel.

Luckily, Mr Iles could not read her mind. He left a few minutes later, shaking his head but promising her "I will do what is possible for you." It was not reassuring.

No one came to see her until after dark except a fluttering young maid with a tea tray. The girl was fascinated by Hester's supposed background.

"Oh, miss! Colonel Kirov, the strange man sent by the Court, he says you've gone and stole an emerald. Is it the very truth then?"

"The charge? Or the crime?" Hester asked sardonically. She welcomed the tea, but the fresh bread and the iced cakes, even the baked apple, were more than her stomach could take. The horror that lay before her occupied most of her thoughts.

The girl giggled. "You needn't think this is my first

dealin's with a body that's got the law onto him. You'd be that fond of my Jemmy. He stood up a coach once, not knowin' it was the Bristol Mail. They sent him runnin', let me tell you. A musket ball through his breeches. Got away though, my Jemmy did."

"I haven't quite reached the eminence of a mail-robber," Hester confessed. "But who knows what heights I may rise to?"

Nevertheless, in the belief that Hester Leland was a criminal of the highest order, the girl broke into thieves' cant which was totally foreign to Hester. The girl went away in excellent spirits, doubtless boasting to the rest of the household that she had been discussing the lady's deep-dyed criminal past.

Nor would this help Hester's case with her escort, the sinister Colonel Kirov. He had believed her guilty. By this time he must be certain of it, and so was sure to be correspondingly nasty to her.

Meanwhile, there were preparations to be made for the long journey to Taunton, to imprisonment and probably the much longer wait for her trial. Her wardrobe for the interview by magistrates, was satisfactory enough, unlikely to prejudice the jury later by its gaudiness or expense; yet she must not look like a dowd either. Men were men, and they must see her as a genteel, unfortunate female who had been tricked for business reasons by two sharp men of commerce.

God knows it was true! It would have been even better if she could manage a helpless, coy look, but this was impossible to her proud nature. She must make the best of what she had.

In the evening, after a forbidding upstairs maid had lit a candle branch in her room, she was startled when a sharp knock at her panelled white door announced her jailer, the Russian. He had removed his black surcoat and was wearing a black, sleeveless jerkin over a full-sleeved white shirt. High, complicated white neckcloths were apparently unknown to him, no matter how popular they were among his betters. His sinewy dark throat was bare, his shirt unbuttoned lower than would be seemly in a gentleman.

"There is rain tomorrow, miss, and we are for it, but not until noon or later. You'd best go prepared. Do you have pateens for your feet?"

"Certainly."

"And a heavy weather cloak?"

"I shall do very well, thank you."

She had been kneeling over the contents of her portmanteau. Although he was not invited, he came into the room. Without looking up she could see his legs before her. He had changed his boots for exotically embroidered black slippers and the exposed flesh of his calves was hard and muscular. His close proximity made her nervous. She realized how thoroughly she would be in his power on the dreaded journey that lay ahead of them.

A susceptible female might have thought him attractive in his forbidding way. Certainly not handsome like her suitor, Sir Charles Willoughby. (How she wished he was beside her now!) But this fellow was exciting, in a way totally unlike Charles. A dangerous man, one to be wary of.

She wondered what he wanted, standing here so close, with his serpent's gaze, like onyx in a bright light, fixed on her. She said at last,

"Would you please move a little? You are standing on one of my gloves."

30

"Nothing easier."

Instead of a gentlemanly apology, he stepped aside, and still with legs apart, picked up the glove and handed it to her with a flippant little gesture. Then, still watching her, he said,

"You were wise to choose the emerald, it would suit you. The ruby wouldn't have done at all, and sapphires are too girlish for you."

"I did not choose the emerald," she reminded him. "In a manner of speaking, it chose me. I was the victim."

"You aristocrats who have come upon hard times are consistent."

Aristocrat? Hester Leland? She laughed contemptuously at his misreading of her background.

This time he shifted entirely away from the haphazardly stacked clothing. Without looking up she had felt him leave her. Near the door he stopped.

"Incidentally, you have a visitor. You may see her. She does not look as though she is carrying muskets or daggers to free you."

"Thank you." She sounded cold enough to surprise herself and looked around at him.

He added, on a rueful note and rubbing his bare calf, "Although, I will allow, the Old Dragon has the kick of a thoroughbred."

Her depression and her deep fear had lifted.

"Lady Pomfret? Is she really here to see me? How good of her!"

His dark eyebrows went up. "Don't save all your gratitude for her. It was I who gave her permission to speak with my prisoner."

This was too much.

"Your prisoner, be damned to you! I am my own

31

mistress. I always shall be. I certainly do not belong to you, of all people."

He came back into the room, following her in long, deliberate strides. She did not know what to expect and wasn't too surprised when he took her by the shoulders. As he drew her to her feet she wondered if he was about to shake her. For some reason she had infuriated him by defending herself. Or was it another cause that provoked all this commotion?

While she stared at him, her green eyes wide, she tried not to show the uncertainty and fear that had gripped her since the local magistrate explained what her fate could be.

He put one hand out, pinching her chin hard. His tongue flicked over his sensual lips and for a breathtaking minute she thought he was going to kiss her in spite of his anger. It was absurd. But her tangled emotions played on the idea, speculating what it would be like, an invasion of her mouth in that violent, angry mood of his.

He cupped her chin and jaw in his rough hand and studied what he saw there. Gradually, whatever emotion had seized him drained away. He gave her a little push, warning her.

"I know what you think of me, you and all those elegant aristocrats. Well, then, mind this. You are a suspected felon. In my charge. And I intend to deliver you to prison, or wherever else it may be, for your trial. What happens to you after that is in the hands of your *Gaje* friends. You will find they can be quite as nasty as this dirty barbarian."

She had not used the word 'barbarian' aloud. Could he read her thoughts? And what did *Gaje* mean?

He left her there with her mouth open and her eyes wide, staring after him.

She hadn't consciously intended to insult him, but somehow an arrogant belief in her superiority had come through.

So much for my pride, she thought, I have made a dangerous enemy.

A fool's trick. She was both ashamed and disgusted with herself. When the door opened again she was almost ready to apologize to Colonel Kirov, but it was Lady Jerusha Pomfret who sailed in like a full-rigged galleon.

Quite aside from her dead husband's title and fortune, horse-faced, plain-speaking Lady Jerusha held a place in her little world by her own qualities. Her sheer force of personality served her well. Though she was immensely generous and good-hearted, she was known to terrorize the casual stranger.

She barked now. In spite of her looks, she never neighed.

"Your want of conduct is beyond belief. Permitting yourself to be taken up for stealing jewellry, what stupidity! You might have pointed out that for two years you had easy access to the jewels Pomfret left me, and never a one of those disappeared."

Hester could not conceal a smile and her Ladyship, who was removing her gloves, swatted Hester across the shoulders with one of them. "Clumsy girl, you should have spat at that fool Girard."

"I wish I had, ma'am. I truly do."

"So," her Ladyship got straight to the point. "How are we to extricate you from this stupid business?"

"Mr Iles does not believe me, ma'am. There is not one person who believes me, excepting yourself."

Lady Jerusha waved her glove. "That I know. It's my belief that they are all in league. I detest that wretched little man who accuses you. I should have expected better of Hailsham. But the male sex is a weak one at best. And at worst – well, I shan't belabour the point. You must have hit Girard in a sore spot. The rascal is so determined he even refused a bribe. The truth is, we need time. Somewhere, the truth is hidden. That black-eyed creature who guards you, how does he come to be serving the King's Justice? It must be the Russian Emperor's effort to learn British law. This jailer of yours will return home to St Petersburg full of lofty notions."

"Among them the hanging of an innocent female."

Her Ladyship ignored this. She leaned forward. "Tell me, do you think he would accept a bribe?"

Hester laughed. "Not after you kicked him. I'm afraid it won't make him any more susceptible."

To her surprise Lady Jerusha chided her. "That will do, young lady. I lost my temper, I will allow. I should never have done so. I am a woman of amiable temperament and I never permit myself to display bad manners."

This time Hester carefully refrained from smiling.

Her Ladyship sighed at an old memory. "In my girlhood I knew many a creature like this Russian. Played with the young ones on the heath. Dorset, you know. Fell cap over heels in love with one of the roguish rascals. But for my mother, I would be roaming the heath today as a gypsy's woman. However, mama had different ideas, and I ended as Pomfret's wife. Your dear mother, on the other hand, ran away with a soldier and that was the end of her future."

"She loved Papa. They adored each other."

Lady Pomfret shrugged. "Love is a splendid emotion, so I am told."

She looked out the window at the distant willows

blowing in the night breeze. Perhaps she was thinking of a long-ago love with whom the young Jerusha had roamed the heath. This was a new Jerusha Pomfret and Hester looked at her in astonishment. The lady soon recovered, however.

"But neither your mother nor I would like to have you make our mistakes. Sir Charles is a superb prize for any woman. He loves you, and he has Pomfret's background, with a proper fortune and estates. The very man for you, once we free you of this tiresome charge."

"A simple matter," Hester murmured, trying not to sound cynical about the idea.

"No bribe then," her Ladyship said at last, bringing her thoughts back to the present.

"I'm afraid not. My jailer is very proud."

"As a man should be, whether he be barbarian or gentry. Well, what's to be done?"

"I am not very hopeful, Ma'am."

Lady Jerusha said gruffly, "Nonsense. Let me give you my idea. I have a list of inns and houses off the High Road to Taunton. You must make your way to whatever proves to be the nearest of them. I shall have my carriage nearby. We will take you to a very special friend of yours whose Manor House is off the Taunton way. I say no more on that score. You know my coachman, Joshua. A most trustworthy fellow. I rescued him from the gibbet some years gone by. Bought off the judge."

"Really, Ma'am, you shock me." But Hester couldn't help laughing. Clearly, her Ladyship looked forward to snatching another victim from the hangman's rope. Defeating the King's Justice seemed a perfectly respectable object in her life.

"You do agree, girl, that you cannot go to Taunton. You

will be clapped into a Holding-Cell before your friends can free you."

"I hoped the magistrate, or perhaps a trial jury might—"

"With every hand against you? Nonsense. You'll be swinging from a gallows or, at the least, transported for life. Let me tell you, my girl, the hold of a ship, in the company of the worst felons in Britain, is not the place for a lady."

"Yes, but I cannot be running from the law forever."

Lady Pomfret shook her head. "You don't understand. I intend to get the truth from Hailsham, and the Girard man, and that wretched red-haired boy."

"But how?"

"Bribes. Or failing that, threats," her Ladyship explained. "Or even a little of the medicine they tried to use against you. We shall find a chink in the armour, a secret, perhaps a past offence. Something." She added then as a more convincing argument, "Much good it would do you if you were hanged and then we found you innocent."

Hester shivered. A forthnight ago, she thought, I would have said we are both mad. What suggestions! To run from the law. To hide, perhaps disguised, to spend what may be a lifetime in fear of the gallows.

And the alternative? A long wait in prison before her trial, then a quick hearing with every judicial figure against her, even her attorney. And finally, the end.

"I never thought to find myself a hunted fugitive."

"It is better than the gibbet. Mind, now. Joshua and I will attend you along the way without seeming to. We will be ready to take you up when you escape from this jailer of yours. The best chance, I should imagine, will be when you stop to change teams. Joshua knows the road as well as he knows the back of his hand. We will

36

never be far from you, though you may not sense our presence." She rubbed her hands with obvious relish at the thought. "Ah! But this is more entertainment than I have had in years."

Lady Pomfret arose with the heavy rustle of her old-fashioned taffeta gown and petticoats. "Here is the list of possible meeting places, inns along the way, where you may find an opportunity to escape. We will be on the watch. There must be some secret reason why a Russian carrying a military title is involved in the King's Justice. If he has a secret beyond the service of that pretty Tsar we saw parading in London, we might find it useful." She added with another sigh for lost opportunities, "Magnificent lovers, they say. I really do regret that kick I gave him."

Lady Pomfret enjoyed shocking people, and during this visit she had shocked Hester several times. She had also amused her. Perhaps that was her Ladyship's object.

Without looking at the slip of paper thrust into her hand, Hester nodded. She felt as if a veil had been dropped over her head, through whose folds she saw the world and all it contained. She was no longer a part of that free world. She moistened her lips, trying to explain that what this good friend proposed was impossible. She had barely begun to speak when the door latch was lowered sharply noisily. This must be Colonel Kirov's way of warning them that he was about to enter. It was a surprising courtesy.

He came in. "No more time, ladies."

"Remember," Lady Jerusha said.

Hester threw her arms around the older woman, astonished by her own emotions. She did not usually reveal them. Lady Jerusha sniffed, and under the hard gaze of Colonel Kirov, her Ladyship left the room. Hester called after her on impulse, "Dear ma'am, I will never forget you."

Lady Jerusha did not look back but waved her glove behind her, rather like the tail of a noble steed.

Hester turned away. Her throat hurt with the effort to conceal emotions from her jailer. The Colonel said, "I will come for you a trifle after dawn. Be ready."

Hester nodded, thinking that she had no idea what to do. There was Lady Jerusha's preposterous plan which entailed a thousand escapes and hurried journeys, maybe for the rest of her life. Not to mention the serious consequences for her Ladyship. Or there was that other journey, beginning a trifle after dawn, with an uncertain fate awaiting her after prison and her trial.

Chapter Four

She was washed, dressed, packed and ready by the time her jailer came for her at what she assumed was dawn. There had been no sunrise. The sky was various shades of grey that merged into threatening black clouds overhead. And it would be worse as they headed in a south-westerly direction and her trial.

"How appropriate!" she thought. Life had not taught her to be an optimist but it had at least taught her how to accept the evils that lay in wait. She smiled at Colonel Kirov and teased him when he picked up her luggage.

"You are not a very good weather prophet, sir. You said it would not rain until noon. I wager we shall be drenched by nine o'clock."

He stopped to inform her, "Whatever you may think me capable of, I did not arrange the weather merely to make you uncomfortable."

She ignored the snub and the way he had cut off her attempt at conversation. He was evidently one of those people who are always disgruntled at dawn. But at least he had reverted to his unfashionable boots, breeches, high, tight-collared shirt and the forbidding black coat. Those naked calves and oriental slippers of last night had been alarmingly uncivilized.

Holding her luggage he waited for her to leave the

room, reminding her by his close attention that he was still very much an officer and her jailer.

She was aware of the usual heads peering out at her along the upper hall, most of them still adorned by night caps. She pretended not to see them.

At the foot of the stairs Squire Blassingame waited for her. Aside from his hastily arranged neckcloth, he was fully dressed and looked ashamed of himself. As she curtsied, thanking him for his hospitality, he stopped her.

"Please, Miss Leland, do not heap coals upon my head. My dear wife was so insistent. She thought you were running away. But I do not believe it. A misunderstanding all around." He raised his eyes, gave Colonel Kirov a heavy frown. "We all know, ma'am, that you are incapable of such an act." He took Hester's gloved hand and pressed his lips to the small area of flesh exposed above the palm.

"Dear Miss Leland, our hearts go out to you. You must – you shall be acquitted."

"Thank you, sir. Your belief in me is very gratifying."

As they were leaving Blassingame Manor, the Colonel remarked, "I do not see your aristocratic Dragon here to bid you a fond farewell. A pity. I have worn boots in case the lady is on the attack."

At least his disposition had improved if he was now making jokes. She laughed but laid the non-appearance of Lady Pomfret to the early hour. Privately, she wondered if her Ladyship was waiting in her carriage somewhere, bent upon following Hester and her jailer.

Colonel Kirov had acquired a closed carriage and a sturdy, two-horse team for the journey. To Hester's surprise she saw no coachman. She couldn't avoid being sorry for the gypsy when he answered her question by the simple statement,

"It was London's idea. Perhaps you are not considered to be worth a four-horse team and a landaulet. I am the coachman." He added with his dry humour, "Do you think I am not qualified? I assure you, I can tool a team as well as a troika," whatever that was.

"Yes. I understand. But aren't you afraid I will escape?"

He answered this by opening the door of the little carriage and letting down the steps. When he helped her up the steps she realized for the first time that the carriage was not empty. A stout, red-nosed, red-cheeked female in a cloth bonnet, stuff gown and cloak grinned at her from across the coach.

"So here's the pretty thievin' one. Welcome, dearie." Her grin revealed a mouthful of gums decorated by a few scattered teeth.

Hester leaped back. The stench of spirits reached her across the carriage. She glanced indignantly at Kirov. He looked angry as well, but he said, "Nettie Bindle has been sent to act as your companion. It is felt in some quarters that a man alone with you would be unsuitable."

"I must confess, I would prefer almost anyone but a drunken person," she murmured, trying not to be overheard by the woman.

"Shall I accept that as a compliment?" he asked and abruptly left her. He mounted the box and took the reins from the stableboy.

After a hesitant smile, Hester seated herself as far away from the woman as possible, and huddled into the collar of her travel cloak. The tightly closed carriage reeked of liquor. Nor was she free of Nettie Bindle's drunken chatter which went on endlessly. She was so uncomfortable and

41

her thoughts so full of the dubious future that she lowered the window and looked out frequently, while the coach rumbled and swayed into the countryside beyond Bath.

As she had predicted, the skies began to empty over them and in the downpour there was no sign of Lady Pomfret's carriage. This was unfortunate because Hester was now thinking better of her Ladyship's escape plan.

Nettie Bindle chattered on. "So ye snatched an emerald, did ye, dearie? They're mighty fine for squeezing the guineas out. So long's they don't lay onto yer trail, eh, miss? Eh?"

"I did not take an emerald," Hester repeated tiredly. She was certain she had said this before.

"Right as a trivet, miss. Ye've only to tell one and all. And mind, keep to the story. In the end, ye do believe it. Gives ye a bit of what's needed. Ever hear of the Nubbin' Cheat? Me friend Taidje Kirov says that's where ye're bound, dearie."

Hester could think of nothing but to wish the woman dead at the hands of the Nubbing Cheat, or anything else that would silence her.

When they pulled into a country inn yard to rest and change the team, Colonel Kirov opened the door with a vigorous effort. His coat was sodden and his face dripping wet under the pelt of rain. After a look at Hester, he lifted her down to the pebbled inn yard. Her cloak became damp from its contact with his body, but she did not mind that. It seemed a small matter, compared to his condition.

He said, "You look ill, is it the rocking of the carriage?"

"Certainly not. I have never been seasick – or coachsick in my life."

He took his hands off her so rapidly she almost lost her balance.

"My error. I thought you looked pale."

"It is that wretched woman."

As usual, he misunderstood. "Not rich enough company for a lady, I daresay. Old Nettie's company will cure anyone of theft."

"And of spirits."

He turned his attention to Nettie who held her plump arms out to him. "Ye're a handsome divil, Taidje. That ye be, for sure. Take Old Nettie in them strong arms."

Unmoved by her flattery, he took her in a tight grip, holding her wildly dangling feet off the ground.

"You take one more drop on this journey and I'll shake you until your teeth rattle." His voice would have alarmed Hester, but it only brought on a fit of giggles from Nettie.

"Me teeth! Taidje, me boy, always first with the pretty compil – complimen's. Old Nettie with 'er teeth to rattle. How I wish it was so, that I do."

Hester was forced to laugh and she noticed that even the gypsy's stern features lightened.

"Get on with you then, Nettie. Eat what you like but no Blue Ruin. I'll stand the reckoning." He turned to Hester. "That applies to you, as well. I'll see if I can get you the private parlour."

"And no Blue Ruin, I promise."

This time he did grin. "Good. I knew I could count upon you to play the lady."

She was oddly pleased when he took her arm and offered his other arm to the gin-drenched Nettie Bindle. She liked his gallantry that played no favourites. At the same time she was now determined upon escaping. She felt that she herself lacked Colonel Kirov's gallantry. She could not spend what might be her last free hours in the confines of a carriage with Nettie Bindle's drunken company.

Was Lady Pomfret nearby? No matter. She must seize her chance.

The inn was surprisingly sturdy, considering its aged stone exterior and the ramshackle condition of the coach yard. The taproom opened to the left and there was a private parlour on the right.

Kirov managed to obtain it for Hester's exclusive use, which was thoughtful of him but somewhat surprising. She had supposed he would share her noon dinner table. Instead, he went back out in what was now a drizzle to supervise the treatment of his old and new teams.

She had eaten very little the day before and scarcely touched her early morning tea but it occurred to her now that if she intended to carry out Lady Pomfret's wild escape plan, she must be strong. She would force herself to eat dinner. Whatever it might be.

It was less difficult than she had supposed. The fish was local and fresh, though she couldn't identify it. The roast of lamb was both crisp and tender, unlike the usual treatment of lamb in a ragout with little meat and much flour. The greens were fresh-picked. The girl who followed the innkeeper with a forgotten knife and spoon proved shy but unexpectedly helpful.

The grizzled innkeeper on the contrary scoffed when Hester introduced the all-important subject. She had studied the paper given to her by Lady Pomfret and knew that this inn was one of those on the list. There was a Dissenters' little stone church nearby and beside it, her Ladyship had written: "Only a diversion, mind. Do not stop here."

Evidently, she imagined Kirov would believe she had gone there for help.

The innkeeper was on his way out when she asked hurriedly, anxious not to have her jailer hear her, "Does your inn have more than one entrance? It seems so spacious."

The man swiped a hand across his nose and looked her over. "Ay, it's like the law officer said you'd do. Ask another way out. Well, my lass, you'll never find it; so you may as well enjoy my good lamb and be on your way to the Assizes. We've enough thieves running about unhung now. We don't need no more."

He left, slamming the door, but the young girl set the pewterware on the table and leaned nearer to Hester.

"There's a door out to the chicken yard, ma'am. Behind the still room."

"Thank you. It is very kind of you." Hester took out a sixpenny bit from her reticule and put it into the girl's hand. The girl went off with many protestations of thanks while Hester forced herself to eat as she concocted mental plans and prayers for the success of her escape plot.

Colonel Kirov made her uneasy by coming in then, recommending her to eat heartily.

"You'll need it for your battle in Taunton."

"My battle?"

"You don't have the look of a coward. Are you going to make a battle for your innocence?"

She could not guess from the way his eyes studied her, whether he was adding a little gratuitous cruelty.

"I thought you believed I was guilty."

He shrugged. His movement still managed to spatter the area with raindrops from his coat. "My task is to deliver you, not to act as your judge. It is of no account to me

45

whether you are innocent or guilty, but I do not fancy a coward, in the ring or out."

"You need have no concern on that score. I am no coward."

"Excellent, may I?"

He reached for the lamb shank lying untouched on her tray. To her amusement he removed his gloves, took the bone in both hands and began to eat the shreds of greasy meat. How like a barbarian, she reminded herself.

"Heavens! Do your employers starve you?"

"Let us say that since I left the Tsar's service my food allowance is not as generous as it might be."

Yet he had ordered a private parlour for her and given her what, in his eyes, must be a sumptuous dinner. He was a strange man. Like the jewels of Mr Girard, he had many facets. And why had he left the Tsar's service?

She was already acquainted with his pride, and tried to suggest that he share some of the elaborate course provided for her, but he refused.

"We will be on our way when you are done."

Nervous over the prospect of having to escape from him in the next few minutes, she was relieved when the innkeeper scratched on the door and without waiting to be invited in, threw the door open.

"You, sir, there's a female here, bosky as a lord. You'll never get her to her feet."

The Colonel muttered something in a strange language, probably Russian, and then explained, "That will be Nettie Bindle." He rushed out with Hester's laughter in his ears. She had never thought she would be grateful to Nettie Bindle, but the woman's drinking propensities might remove the Colonel from Hester's side just at the crucial moment.

46

Her luggage was still on the roof of the carriage. There would be no chance to reclaim it now. She must make do with the garments she stood in and the past quarter's salary in her reticule, unless she actually found Lady Pomfret.

Kirov had left the door slightly ajar. She looked out carefully, but saw no one. They were all busy across the passage, attending to the violent Nettie who had taken a fancy to toss around any rum mug she could reach on the tapster's bar.

Hester ran down the passage to the rear of the building. The girl had been right: the blackened walls of the kitchen and its big hearth with a turning roast were on one side and the still-room on the other. She dashed into the still room with its shelves of supplies, including baskets of fresh greens and a hanging haunch of mutton. At the far end of the room was the door. Nervous but victorious, she reached it, turned the bolt and swung it open, ready to cross the muddy yard.

She was stopped by the sight of Colonel Kirov, his hands on his hips in what she could only regard as a triumphant pose. Worst of all, though he smiled, the glitter in his eyes warned her that he was not in the best of humours.

"Leaving me so soon? You will not like wandering in the rain, I promise you."

She started to lie, "I didn't – I wasn't—" She broke off, pride coming to her rescue. "I was certainly leaving. Nor can you blame me in my situation."

"And without your guardian angel? Your protector? Myself, in fact? You crush me, pretty thief." Before she could reply to that sarcasm, he prodded her in the ribs. "Back inside. We leave as we entered. No back doors for

47

us. Straight out so that all may see us. The aristocratic lady and the dirty tartar."

Fury came with the sickening knowledge of what her recapture meant. She stopped, raised her hand and slapped his face as hard as she could. The slap may have stung, as it certainly fuelled his anger.

Her bonnet had fallen to the back of her neck and he seized a handful of her hair, pulling her toward him. She screamed, in a momentary fear that he would break her neck. With her pale face close to his he looked into her eyes as he had the previous night, trying to read her real thoughts. Or perhaps inspired by thoughts of his own.

With his fingers still tangled in her hair he brought her so close she felt his mouth on hers. She stiffened her resistance, but he was ready for her. He thrust one leg around hers to prevent her from kicking at him and pulled her face hard against his, crushing her mouth with his, preventing the scream that vibrated in her throat.

There was a subtle change in his violence. With her breath cut off she could make no resistance when his mouth invaded hers with a softer pressure, explorative, arousing in her body tremors of excitement she had never experienced before.

When he released his pressure on the back of her head and she could breathe again she still trembled with the memory of those wild, fleeting seconds.

"Come along," he ordered her.

She took a step, found she had lost her equilibrium and had to grope for his arm to keep from falling. It put a humiliating end to her escape attempt. Gradually, as she recovered her breath, they walked around the inn yard to the coach. She made up her mind to play her cards more wisely. Above all, she must throw off his suspicion before

48

her next attempt. She could not afford to let herself be seduced by either the physical or, more importantly, the sensual power of this barbarian.

The carriage door had been opened for her and to her surprise Nettie Bindle wasn't in it. She was nowhere to be seen. Hester broke the angry silence between them to remark on that woman's absence.

"What? Miss Bindle is not to join us?"

"Nettie will be in London when I need her. It was Nettie who—" He shrugged.

She had no idea what he had been about to tell her. No matter, she still taunted him with the remark, "In short, Blue Ruin seems to have been Nettie's ruin."

She hadn't meant to sound so callous and understood him when he said shortly, "True. She has not had your advantages."

"I beg your pardon. I hope she will be able to find her way home when she wakes – comes to her senses."

"I have her on the weigh bill of the next London Stage."

"I'm glad. I'm sure when she isn't drunk – I mean bosky, she is a delightful creature. She is very fond of you."

Hester wasn't getting very far. He ignored her comment.

"I have two choices. I manacle your wrists or I share this carriage. Jody, the innkeeper's boy, will be on the box." He added with his dry humour, "I promise you, no Blue Ruin."

"I think I prefer the manacles."

He ignored that and started to hand her up the carriage steps. The team lurched forward as the innkeeper's boy climbed up on the box, but Hester avoided his help. Kirov got in after her. He made no effort at conversation but began to stare out the window at the lowering sky.

They started off with the weather providing a little variety. The rain had settled into a foggy, windy afternoon. Looking out on her side, Hester sniffed at the moist air and decided that it was ideal for an escape. She would hardly be seen beyond the first copse of trees, even if he followed her.

The real problem was, indeed, how to get out of this accursed carriage without being stopped by him. He leaned his head back against the rackety corner he was settled in, so that she thought he might be asleep. It was therefore unnerving to find that he had been studying her profile beneath his lashes. She tried smiling.

"I'm sorry you must be at such trouble over me. I should prefer not to have given you any trouble at all."

He stirred a little, took a deep breath, like one tired or bored, and closed his eyes. "You've given me no trouble. You are nothing to the problem I had with a murderer I located last month in Bristol."

She laughed and, forgetting her anger, asked with genuine interest, "Did you succeed in getting him to trial?"

"He was already condemned. You may see his body swinging in chains on the Bristol Crossways."

She suspected he was being humorous in the cruellest way and sealed her lips angrily.

"Don't do that," he advised her, evidently still watching her without appearing to. "It makes your mouth ugly."

Angry and humiliated, she nevertheless opened her mouth and moistened her lips. When she gave him a side glance she saw that he was looking out the window again, his thoughts obviously far away.

As the afternoon wore on, she reviewed in her mind

the next suggestion made by Lady Pomfret for her escape. She must act when they stopped, as they were sure to do at the Ram's Head Inn. She would run back to one of the other places indicated on her Ladyship's paper, either an old miller's house, or the arching stone bridge over a sluggish stream.

Pretending she found the carriage too warm, she lowered the window, looking both ways, sniffing at the fresh, misty air from the stream nearby. In the far distance behind them she fancied she made out a lumbering old coach which would have the crest of the sixteenth-century Pomfrets. She must be ready when Colonel Kirov stopped at the Ram's Head.

It had grown darker, the misty fog shrouding the road ahead as daylight failed. Very soon they would be passing the stone bridge. It was when they drew near this that it all suddenly happened.

With a screech from the youth Jody, on the box, the horses swung off abruptly to the right, and the edge of the carriage itself was slung against the stone abutment of the bridge. In the fading daylight, with only the dimmest of carriage lights to give them leeway, the horses had nearly plunged into the bridge approach.

Inside the carriage Colonel Kirov reached for Hester. The carriage teetered between the river bank and the abutment and Kirov kicked the door open.

"Out!"

The carriage had keeled over about twenty degrees and Hester went tumbling out, pushed by Kirov and falling to the muddy grass. She rolled over, sat up and saw the carriage half-overturned against the abutment, carrying Kirov with it before he could drop to the ground after her. The horses were pulling away, struggling to free themselves. The youth on the box had managed to save himself by jumping before the crash, and he wisely calmed the frantic horses now before he turned his attention to Hester.

She was trying to reach high enough to force the carriage door open for the Russian.

"Colonel Kirov is still in the carriage. The door may be jammed."

"If the carriage goes over he'll get drowned dead for sure." The youth seemed to find this interesting without requiring action on his part.

"Hurry!" Hester reached up over the wheels. She slipped back onto the rain-wet, grassy embankment crying, "Do something!"

Surely, the Pomfret coach should be along soon, to lend help. The most important thing to her now was to rescue her companion. The irony in this didn't strike her for a minute or two. Right now she could only recall that he was a human being, jailer or not.

Hester was still trying to climb up onto the overturned carriage to help her captor when she heard a splintering crash above her. The carriage door flew outward, half off its hinges. Hester was surprised by her own relief when Colonel Kirov appeared in the doorway. He swung himself to the ground lightly and with athletic ease; yet he winced as his left foot touched the grass.

Hester reached out to offer her hand but he refused it, leaning back against the tilting carriage while he massaged his left ankle.

"Is your leg hurt badly, do you think?" she asked. "May I help you in some way?"

He turned this aside. "And you? You seem very much yourself. Are you?"

"Yes. What have you done to your ankle?"

He was surprised by her persistent sympathy and almost reached out to touch her, but quickly changed his mind. He became very official.

"Twisted or strained, I imagine. Nothing serious. Jody! Cross the bridge and run to the Ram's Head Inn. It shouldn't take you above half an hour. Bring back a carriage and team. Tell them it is on the King's business. Give them my name, they're expecting me. And hurry. We are expected in Taunton before the Assizes."

The Assizes, her trial. Hester backed away. The gulf between them suddenly grew much wider than the stream behind them. He was as ruthless and determined as he had been the first moment they met in the Blassingame kitchen garden. So, nothing had changed.

She retreated into herself, beginning to consider the good fortune of the accident. If Kirov needed no assistance, and he certainly looked strong enough, she would concentrate on her escape.

She listened, hoping for the appearance of Lady Pomfret's coach. This time she had no interest in 'rescuing' Colonel Kirov. Beyond the far side of the bridge the woods grew close to the road and the stream bank was covered with bushes and willows. The entire area was dark enough to hide her if she kept away from the road.

With appropriate reticence she suggested, "If I may, I will sit up on the bridge. I feel a trifle unnerved. You should consider it as well. You ought to rest that foot."

He grimaced. "You may be right. But I doubt if I could get that far on this leg."

"With my help?" She returned to him. "Use my shoulder as a cane."

He hesitated, shrugged, and then, his pride having yielded to his pain, leaned on the shoulder she offered. They managed to make the bridge abutment in a few limping, painful strides. Considering Hester's intentions, she found this intimate contact with him troubling to her conscience.

He let her go and boosted himself up onto the abutment, then held out a hand to her.

"Up with you."

She stared at him. She thought he looked as exotic and mysterious as ever in that rolling mist. It was her last chance to behave honourably and not take advantage of his injury, and yet it might also be her last chance for life. She said, "I'm sorry. I don't wish you to see me swinging from the Bristol Crossways or any other gibbet."

For a few seconds he didn't understand what she was saying as he watched her leaving him. She began to run when she heard him drop from the stone balustrade and start after her. Letting out a horrid cry of pain, he muttered something furious in his own language and grabbed at the balustrade to keep from falling.

Hester ran on, hearing the slip-slop of moisture in her low-heeled morocco slippers. To her astonishment a shot rang out. The savage was either actually shooting at her, or into the air, intending to alarm her. She hadn't seen his pistol. He must have concealed it somewhere in the carriage during their ride.

She picked up her pace, though the bullet didn't seem to have landed anywhere near her.

"You devious little bitch! I'll have you back!" he shouted in perfect English. This time, despite his accent, his meaning was loud and clear.

Chapter Five

Kirov had started after Hester again on a long, loping run but couldn't put pressure upon his leg. Under the rain-soaked trees beyond the bridge she stopped to catch her breath. He limped painfully back to the fretting horses, evidently intending to pursue her on horseback, without a saddle.

He must be determined to see her stand trial and all the horrors afterward. His hatred of her at this time logically followed his contempt and dislike of her when they first met: he had never changed.

Hester took a deep breath and made her way through the grassy underbrush, growing wetter by the minute, but she was relieved that the dripping of the trees blurred the sound of her running feet. There was a field beyond and her silhouette in that open space would have been disastrous. She kept to the trees.

With a quickening heartbeat she heard a horse's hooves pounding on the High Road. They slowed to a stop alarmingly near. She remained still, waiting. The horse began to pick its way in the wet grass just inside the copse.

She couldn't help being impressed by Kirov's handling of a carriage horse even without a saddle. She had never seen such control before.

The noise of a coach and horses, probably a four-horse

team, intruded on the individual sounds Hester had been trying to sort out. She moved as quietly as possible to get a better view of the High Road.

The carriage lantern on the right side gave her a brief glimpse of the Pomfret crest. Thank heaven!

The horses galloped along so rapidly she wondered if the Russian had seen and understood the significance of the crest. He made no attempt to stop the coach. Then she caught a glimpse of Colonel Kirov himself on horseback. He was looking carefully into the area she had passed through only minutes ago.

She doubted if the Pomfret coach meant anything to him if he hadn't seen the crest, and that relieved her.

The mist and fog were clearing now, just when she desperately needed them. She retreated, remaining near the road, in the area he had already examined. When he headed his horse on, probably toward the Ram's Head Inn, she crossed the road and hurried in the same direction, careful to remain out of his hearing.

He must have given her up. Or did he expect to meet her when she arrived, exhausted and bedraggled, at the Ram's Head?

She was, in fact, very much bedraggled when she finally reached what appeared to be the abandoned mill, on the branch of a stream beside a water wheel. In the house beyond there were no lights, no candles or oil lamps, and Hester wondered why this had been chosen by Lady Jerusha as a meeting-place if she had passed it without stopping.

Perhaps she and the coachman Joshua had seen the accident at a distance, and intended to keep the coach out of the way while one of them returned to head Hester off to safety. When dealing with Jerusha Pomfret, anything was possible.

A few stars came out, making it easier for her silhouette to be seen. Wrapping her sodden cloak more tightly around her body, she approached the house which was little more than a white-washed Irish coteen. She was still in the shadow of the aged wheel when she heard a peculiar noise like the hiss of a snake.

Trembling with nervousness and cold, she moved slowly, realizing this was a signal, and undoubtedly from Lady Pomfret. Her Ladyship often gave such signals to her riding groom, or even a footman in her house on Queen's Square. But still, it might be a trick, someone imitating her.

In another few seconds a side door opened and Lady Pomfret peered out. She was wearing a preposterous plumed silk turban which apparently struck her as ideal for her present criminal activity.

"Didn't you hear me at the window?" In a hoarse whisper she added, "Come inside, you silly goose."

Hester wanted to laugh. It was half hysteria, and she restrained herself. She stepped inside the little house, unable to see anything but Lady Pomfret's imposing figure, until her eyes got used to the semi-darkness of the room.

Her Ladyship brushed away Hester's trembling effort at a curtsy. Lady Pomfret would have made an excellent commanding officer.

"Able to walk a bit further, I trust."

"Yes, ma'am. But didn't my jailor see your coach? Where is it?"

Lady Pomfret sniffed. "I wasn't born yesterday, let me tell you. When we saw your carriage disaster, I had Joshua deposit me here. Joshua took the coach and team on to the Ram's Head Inn. He hopes to make them believe he is waiting for you. But Joshua will simply say they are bound for London at my order, and I am in London awaiting them. Kirov will not believe it, but what can he do if he doesn't find you? I must say, he is attractive in his barbaric way. If I had been in your place, I might not have been so anxious to be quit of him."

This time Hester did laugh. "Dear ma'am, you are truly wonderful."

"Moderately so," her Ladyship agreed. "I was forced to re-think my original plan when you had that stupid overturn. I will say, this Kirov manages a horse bareback in great style, though. Now, do hurry. He isn't a complete dunderhead and he may retrace his steps, though he already examined this place once."

"Good heavens! Where were you?"

"Watching him from that copse yonder. He limped badly but he seemed a determined fellow."

She led the way out the side door beyond the abandoned fireplace and Hester found herself shivering her way through a ploughed field running thick with mud. Her Ladyship, of course, wore pateens to save her shoes.

The hem of Hester's cloak dragged in the muddy runnels and was soon crusted with mud, adding a heavy, sodden weight to the garment. She forgot this in her terror when she looked ahead, made out the shape of a half-timbered manor house on the horizon and saw a man hurrying toward them.

On closer inspection she was enormously relieved to recognize Sir Charles Willoughby. He ignored the mud even though he was handsomely dressed. She could see the flying cape and appropriate country boots.

Lady Pomfret boomed out, "I'm bringing you a birthday present, Charles."

Sir Charles greeted Lady Pomfret, bringing her hand gallantly to his lips. Then he addressed Hester, taking her two hands in his.

"Dear Miss Leland, what an appalling experience! Her Ladyship sent the message about your predicament. Shocking! She hoped to bring you here. I've been on the watch these past hours." He squeezed her hands. "Come along and my housekeeper will soon have you comfortable. My mother has already retired and begs you to excuse her. She does not sleep well. She suffers from a general weakness, due to her heart, we believe."

Hester had never visited Willoughby Manor and could hardly believe her luck in being rescued by Sir Charles, of all people. But she accepted the miracle gratefully. She saw at once that her Ladyship was taking full credit for the scheme, as well she might, and probably expected a betrothal, at the very least, to come from his gallant hospitality.

"Is it truly your birthday?" Hester asked.

Sir Charles smiled. "Not quite. Not until tomorrow. But I wouldn't dream of contradicting her Ladyship. You are the fairest prize I could receive on the occasion, if I may say so."

"I can never thank you enough for your belief in me."

After a quick, tense look around the field, Sir Charles ushered the two women over the green, watery lawn and across the terrace, into what appeared to be his bookroom. Hester could well imagine how wretched she looked, like a half-drowned cat, in the presence of this handsome, gallant gentleman who had become a hero to her in the last few minutes.

A man in his early thirties, with a fine record of service in the Peninsula, he had always seemed a trifle too courteous, too perfect a gentleman for a woman who recognized that her own position had not made her 'suitable' to him in the eyes of the world.

His clear blue eyes looked into hers and seemed to assure Hester of his faith in her. Although he had dedicated his life to aiding the unfortunate of the criminal class, she wanted no part of that charity. Luckily for her pride, it seemed clear that he knew she was innocent.

"Miss Leland, such events as yours have occurred as long as there have been jewels sold. It is a woman's way. I know you too well to believe the most extreme charge against you. Your intentions I never doubted, dear Miss Leland."

Lady Pomfret ended this moment in her practical way. "You will do Miss Leland a greater service by providing her with a private chamber and a hip bath to refresh herself. Where have you placed the travelling bag of her clothing that I sent to the manor?"

Sir Charles apologized and offered his arm to Hester. While they mounted the heavy, dark, Jacobean staircase, he explained, "My mother suggested the small blue chamber. She thought you would prefer something comfortable and not too grand. It is at the back of the corridor but the view over the fields is inspiring on a clear day."

"Hmph," said Lady Pomfret. "Sounds very like Sophia Willoughby."

Hester was much too grateful to question the motives of her rescuer's mother, and Sir Charles wisely ignored her Ladyship's grumbling.

The stout, tiny housekeeper, a Mrs Jenkins, was

respectful and efficient but like the Blassingame house-keeper, she appeared to be suspicious. She stayed to oversee the preparations for the hip bath, with a servant girl pouring reasonably hot water over Hester's shoulders. Hester was a little hurt, then amused, when she glanced into the pier glass across the room in time to see Mrs Jenkins remove a porcelain ornament from the mantel and surreptitiously hide it in the folds of her black skirt. No doubt she feared their guest's 'thieving ways'.

Hester understood. There were some in the household who believed her guilty. Nevertheless, she was deeply grateful for the warmth and comfort the household pro-vided, the perfumed water for her bath, the tray of food carefully prepared to tempt her appetite. There were, aside from the welcome hot broth, several delicious little pates and the mulled wine which soothed and rested her.

When Hester was sitting, bathed and dressed Lady Pomfret scratched on the door and, being admitted, informed her, "I must be on my way. The small carriage will be by for me at any minute but meanwhile I am to play duenna. Someone asks permission to see you."

He stood in the doorway looking like a radiant Sir Galahad, the man who actually thwarted justice in order to win time to prove her innocent. Surely, that was Sir Charles' intention, how different from that wretched Colonel Kirov who thought of nothing but delivering her to the hangman.

But Hester closed her mind to such speculation. It was an insult to Sir Charles, even to compare him with that other one who had even tried to kill her, shooting at her when she wanted only to save her life and prove her innocence.

"How good you are, dear sir," she told Sir Charles as she greeted him from the big wing chair by the crackling fire, "please forgive my informality." She was wrapped in the robe Lady Pomfret had sent over, a faded blue velvet robe she had worn for years, and her hair, carefully brushed, fell around her shoulders and her back, pulled away from her face by two combs.

Charles was deeply impressed. She knew that the colour of the robe was flattering on her, and her general state of undress must have aroused him to more than his usual daring. He came forward, kissed her fingers and, with his heart in his eyes, murmured, "A goddess. A veritable golden goddess. Would you not agree, Lady Pomfret?"

Her Ladyship snorted. "Pretty, yes. Goddess – no."

Hester laughed. "There speaks an honest woman, Sir Charles. You are very gallant to forget the sight I presented tonight when you first saw me."

"A kitten who needed my care," he insisted. He glanced over his shoulder at Lady Pomfret to get her agreement, then begged her pardon for having ignored her, but her Ladyship was already drawing a milord chair away from the wall. When she sat down she looked like one of fairyland's more wicked queens, properly enthroned. Only her mischievous chuckle hinted at her real self.

"Kitten with claws, I'll wager. Good sort of female, though, in her way. Make some man an excellent wife when we get this ridiculous charge cleared away."

The reminder sobered him. "Yes. That must be our priority. It must be shown that there was no intent to steal the emerald."

"I detest emeralds," Hester put in. "Everyone who knows me is aware that I have an absolute aversion to the colour green."

Sir Charles was eager to cling to any assurance.

"Quite true. I recall a green box of bonbons I brought to Miss Leland. Her reaction was nothing if not decided. Surely, that is an argument in her favour."

"No question of that." Lady Pomfret began to tap her foot on the floor. "But I should be a poor duenna if I permitted much more dalliance tonight. By the by, I sincerely hope Sophia is to be trusted."

Sir Charles' jaw set rather sternly, whether at this implied criticism of his mother, or in loyalty to Hester, she could not guess. "My mother has always followed my advice in matters beyond her own experience. She would never dream of questioning a man's actions."

Hester thought she heard Lady Pomfret mutter, "The more fool she."

Charles asked, "You spoke, ma'am?"

Fortunately, Lady Pomfret arose to her feet at that moment. "I said, 'tomorrow will be – enough to contend with'. Come, my boy. This poor creature must be exhausted."

"Very true. I do beg your pardon, Miss Leland." He hesitated, colouring a little. "I should very much like to call you Hester. May I be permitted that intimacy?"

Hester did not want him to misunderstand their relationship. Obviously, letting him see her *en déshabillé* had rushed their relationship forward, but there had been no gracious way she could avoid this step. In any case, he was the only man she had ever considered marrying. He possessed all the qualities she had dreamed of in her lonely youth. He would make a kind, understanding husband

and father. A companion such as she had hungered for. So much more necessary than passion, which was both selfish and unsettling.

He took her hesitation for maidenly modesty. She found that naïve but delightful.

"Dear Hester! We shall save you, mark me. Meanwhile, until tomorrow." He sealed their good-night, or perhaps more than good-night, by gently kissing her forehead.

In her gratitude she loved him. This room contained the only people in the world who believed in her innocence. It was all-important. She silently blessed him for his faith in her.

He left the room, looking back at her with a smile intended to be reassuring, but she couldn't avoid the feeling that he was badly worried.

Lady Pomfret had no such misgivings. She stayed long enough to confide to Hester, "You've played the game well, my girl. Charles Willoughby believes in your innocence. A man of good heart. Lady Hester Willoughby, it has a ring to it. But I must be on my way. Remember, Lady Hester Willoughby. Even if he has any doubts of your innocence, he will go to enormous lengths for you."

In her rough way Lady Pomfret tapped the back of Hester's hand briskly and swept out, accompanied by the rustle of her taffeta skirts.

Even if he has any doubts . . . had her Ladyship detected a nuance, an indication of doubt, in Sir Charles? Impossible. There could be no future relationship if there were no trust. She banished the thought.

The household was eerily silent. Hester moved her chair closer to the low-burning fire. Although the room was reasonably comfortable, she had never felt so cold. With a stern effort she had refrained from shivering when Sir Charles was present, but her body was tired, her head buzzed with dark fears, and she had never felt more chilled.

She held her hands out toward the coals, scarcely aware of the warmth, while she assured herself that between them, Sir Charles and Lady Jerusha must have enough power to get the truth out of Sylvester Girard or Mr Hailsham.

At all events, she had succeeded in escaping from her captor and the bright darkness of those Tartar eyes. Who knew what calamity would have befallen her if she had allowed herself to be swayed by his kiss?

She must get some sleep. A third night with little sleep would do worse than make her tremble. She dreaded getting into the bed with its icy sheets. Also, since she had lost her freedom, she did not like completely darkened rooms. She crossed the bedchamber and felt for the cords of the dusty velvet drapes.

When she opened the drapes, allowing a bar of starlight to stripe the room, the lawn of Willoughby Manor became visible. Beyond lay the muddy runnels of the ploughed field she had crossed to reach this haven, and they were not deserted.

A man in a rain-soaked black coat made his way across the field. In the starlight his dark face looked pale, but even without the limp she would have known the Tartar gypsy.

Her heart lurched with excitement and fear, and she backed away from the window, huddled against one velvet portière, watching him from her concealment.

He found the white-washed stile and, favouring his left leg, climbed over it and down into the Willoughby lawn. Then he stood staring up at the rear face of the house, undoubtedly studying each window, wondering if she could be here.

Further trying to her nerves, he came onto the terrace. Since he was not likely to enter by that means, she supposed he would limp around to the side and then the front of the manor house. His hand on the front door knocker aroused two women who came out into the hall and headed toward the great staircase.

Hester went to the door of her room, opened it slightly and listened. To her surprise one of the women was Sir Charles' mother, Lady Sophia Willoughby. The other appeared to be her maid. Lady Sophia sounded querulous and certainly no friend to Hester.

"– all the fault of that wretched thieving female my poor boy is so besotted with. Now, we shall have Bow Street Runners and Officers of the Court trampling through the house at all hours."

Someone, presumably the butler, was arguing with Colonel Kirov in the doorway downstairs. Hearing the women go down to meet him, Hester ran to the gallery overlooking the staircase and reception hall. Pressed tightly against the wall to keep from being seen, she had a fair vantage point.

The Russian calmly elbowed the ancient butler aside and stepped into the hall.

"I will speak with your master. Fetch him to me, Crown business."

Lady Willoughby had reached the hall below. A fragile-looking woman who acted considerably more frail than she had sounded to Hester a minute ago, she clutched the collar of an elegant morning robe as if she expected to be ravished on the spot. She spoke to the Russian in a die-away voice.

"I am persuaded you are on a failed mission, sir. I assure you, we Willoughbys do not harbour criminals. Please leave us in peace. Unless of course, you have sufficient written authority to execute your warrant."

"I have, madam, as you see."

He would, of course. He was nothing if not efficient. Hester felt the manacles tightening around her wrists already.

Lady Willoughby recoiled. "My dear sir, you cannot mean it. What – what has the – ah – criminal done? I assure you, we have no knowledge of criminal activities among our acquaintances. We are, after all, Willoughbys."

In another minute she would be blurting out Hester's name and disclaiming all responsibility. Hester swung around frantically, wondering if she could take a gown, cloak and shoes from the big oak wardrobe in her room and escape before her jailer came after her.

Just as she was about to run for her room, she heard another voice in the hall below, a blessed voice at such a moment, and Sir Charles strolled to meet the intruder. He was fully dressed, and had probably come from his bookroom.

"What is this about criminals in my house? Mother, you may retire now. This fellow – pardon me, sir – but you may accept Lady Willoughby's word if you do not accept mine. We do not harbour criminals who deliberately flout the law . . . Mother, you need your rest."

"My dear boy, of course. I was confused for an instant. After all is said, how often are the Willougbys accused of harbouring criminals? One is inclined to laugh at such insolence. Let me show you out, sir."

Hester wondered why she was so persistent. Her son

had made it clear that she was not wanted in this matter. He spoke up again.

"Mother, that is hardly necessary. Jorris will do that. Sir, do you insist on searching our house? If so, come along. Let me be your guide. But if you do not find Miss Leland, as your warrant indicates, let me warn you, His Highness the Prince Regent, and Mr Justice Percival shall hear of your intrusion."

During a long and terrible pause, Hester held her breath. She noticed one curious thing: the Russian was staring at Lady Willoughby. Hester could not see the woman's face. Perhaps he read haughty assurance in her eyes, at any rate he appeared to be satisfied, or probably alarmed by Sir Charles' threat. It surprised Hester, who did not think he would give up so easily.

With enormous relief she watched him shrug and step back.

"Jorris," Sir Charles ordered, "Show the – the gentleman out. Mother, I advise you to return to your apartments."

"Yes, dear boy, I shall." But for some reason, she made a little gesture and ushered the Russian out through the reception hall to the front doorstep, before returning. Here she stopped to say "Good-night, dear boy."

Hester heard footsteps on the stairs. Either Lady Sophia or her maid was coming. Hester hurried to her room and scrambled into the first gown she had unpacked from the bag sent by Lady Jerusha. She was ready to travel when Sir Charles called to her from the hall in a smothered voice.

"Miss Leland? Hester? Are you awake?"

She opened the door. "I am ready."

The strain he was under seemed written upon his

68

usually serene and confident features. He looked harried. His lack of confidence terrified her.

"I will go, Sir Charles. At once. I cannot remain and put you all in danger."

"Nonsense. You will do nothing of the sort. My mother wishes to become better acquainted with you, and she insists that you stay."

Hester could not help saying, "I believe Lady Sophia is trying to prevent your worrying, sir. I heard her speaking to her maid. She was anything but pleased at my presence. I have invaded—"

"No such thing. She knows quite well how I feel. After the visit – the intrusion, I may say – of that impossible foreigner, she tells me it is her special wish that you remain, at least through my birthday." He reached for her cold hand, tried to warm it between his. "Dear Hester, once you have considered the case – or do I mean to say *we* have considered it, we shall find it far easier to deal with those crass and greedy jewellers. If you run away now, you will only confirm their suspicions."

Hester was touched by what seemed to be his complete faith in her, and said uncertainly, "If you are convinced that your mother will agree."

Though why Lady Sophia should agree after her cutting remarks on the staircase earlier this evening was a mystery to Hester. The only answer seemed to be that the woman did not want to alienate her son. Well, tomorrow was his birthday, and tonight she was so tired she felt that she couldn't walk a mile to save her life.

Impulsively, she kissed him on the cheek. "Thank you, dear Charles."

He brightened noticeably. "My own Hester, yours is

the first kiss I have received on my birthday. It is just past twelve."

She was greatly touched. He would not give her up, surely. He would help her, keep her safe until proof of her innocence was found. When he drew her to him in his gentle way she thought: so this is what love is like, a warm, safe embrace which seems to give another so much pleasure. She was relieved to find, when his lips softly covered hers, that there was none of the terrible all-consuming heat of passion she had felt between her parents and that had shut out the world. There was no security in that, and one day it would burn itself out, leaving others to sense their own insurmountable loneliness.

She returned his caresses, careful not to respond with the passionate answer which the Russian had drawn from her against her own wishes. She raised an arm, winding around his neck. Her bared arm caught the candlelight, giving her flesh a special glow, and she felt the rising warmth of his body, all the more surprising in a man who so carefully controlled his emotions.

His lips brushed her eyelids and then her forehead. But the touch was so tentative she had barely begun to respond when he sensed his own uncharacteristic lack of control. He released her, murmuring hoarsely, "Forgive me, my dear. It was shameful to take advantage of a guest under my roof." He smiled quickly, patted her hand, and backed away to the door again.

Slightly flustered, Hester replied, "I understand, sir. You have been an angel of goodness to me."

She watched him close the door and told herself nothing could happen to her while Sir Charles was her protector. His embrace should have reassured her, but she couldn't

70

believe as he did, that if she gave herself up, her friends would win her freedom at her trial. Anyway, even if that was the case, there would be months in prison, with no knowledge of what was being done to prove her innocence.

And there was Colonel Kirov. She didn't think for a minute that he had given up, nor did she trust Sir Charles' mother.

When she was dressing for bed again she asked herself why the Russian had retreated so willingly. It was not like him. She had the awful sensation that he was still somewhere close by, waiting for her to betray herself in some way.

Chapter Six

Hester took pride in the fact that she was finally able to sleep, once she stopped shivering in the big, cold Willoughby guest bed. Her last waking thoughts were concerned with her relationship to Sir Charles.

No man had ever been kinder, gentler, more loving to her. Certainly not her father, a rough soldier who, as one might expect, did not take well to invalidism. When Hester blamed the government for abandoning this man wounded in the King's cause, her father had thrown a vase at her, yelling that he would have no traitors or Boney-lovers in his house.

When he died the loss was not so great a shock to her as her mother's death many years before – and yet, she had felt only an incomplete affection from both her parents. But her father had taught Hester one great lesson: never let anyone know the depth of your feelings for them. Perhaps Lady Jerusha would never know how dearly Hester cared for her.

And now, another aristocrat, Charles Willoughby, had befriended, protected, and best of all, not been afraid to profess his love for her. His greatest gift was his belief in her innocence. Nothing was as important. It was not the heated passion of the flesh that she had dreamed of some nights in her girlhood, but she knew better than to seek in real life such impossible love. The obsession that held her mother and father until her mother's death, had been punctuated by fiery quarrels and the throwing of things. Yet, they loved each other to the exclusion of everyone ouside their tiny world – everyone including their only child.

Hester was awakened by a Willoughby maid bringing the morning tea tray. Such luxuries were a bit haphazard in the Pomfret household, since one never knew whether Lady Jerusha would be sweeping through the house before dawn or sleep until noon.

Still, despite enjoying the rigidly perfect Willoughby service, Hester missed the house in Queen's Square.

She was cheered when Lady Sophia Willoughby came to see her and was excessively kind. Something, perhaps the frightening visit of Colonel Kirov, had seemed to alter her opinion of Hester's guilt. A woman of fading loveliness, her Ladyship moved gracefully, with a gentle smile that did not fit the cutting things she had said to her maid the night before.

Hester remained pleasant and grateful but privately suspicious for the first few minutes of her Ladyship's visit. Then, as if the woman guessed Hester's suspicions, she added quietly.

"You must forgive an old lady for not greeting you last night. I am not as strong as I could wish to be, and perhaps a bit envious of your youth. My son is very taken by your beauty. But you must be abundantly aware of that."

"He talks to me constantly of your Ladyship. You are always in his thoughts. He worries about your wellbeing."

"Does he, indeed? Dear boy." Her Ladyship was pleased. It had been the correct approach.

Hester could not resist referring to the subject that touched her most closely at this time. "I give you my most solemn oath, ma'am, that I am not guilty of smuggling that jewel out of the shop."

"I believe I understand, my dear. An incredible thing happened to my maid, Pankridge, some time ago. I was purchasing a series of linked gold chains, as I recall, and one of the clerks showed Pankridge a costly diamond parure; rings, armlets, tiara and all. The intention was that my maid induce me to purchase the set."

"Exactly my case," Hester put in.

Lady Sophia smiled vaguely. "Was it, really? I called Pankridge to me and we left the shop. In the doorway we were stopped. It seems that Pankridge still had one of the diamond earrings in her hand. Quite by accident."

Hester hoped this was true. It occurred to her that she was being as suspicious of Pankridge as the rest of the world was about Hester Leland. She was ashamed of this, but the question remained. No doubt the world said the same of her.

"As Sir Charles must have explained, ma'am, my friends intend to discover the truth and win a confession from the jewellers."

"So I have heard." Her Ladyship turned away, then, recalled to the rules of politeness, she said, "You have my good wishes on the matter." After an awkward pause and without looking at Hester, she added, "My son speaks of a betrothal if — when this matter is satisfactorily resolved."

Hester could scarcely blame her for her obvious disapproval. "We haven't discussed such a subject, your Ladyship. In any case, it would be inappropriate to speak of it now."

"Quite right, I am sure. I trust we may all continue to use such admirable common sense, Miss Leland."

"For my part, certainly. I hope to be out of your house at the earliest moment, if I can be certain the man pursuing me is gone from the area."

Lady Sophia was surprisingly generous on this score. "Now then, we must not be hasty. Though—" She considered. "Tonight, for example, the house will be filled with guests. They may recognize you. Some may even know you. They do wander about the house so freely."

Hester got up from the little table where she had drunk her tea. "I must go."

"No, No. It is too dangerous. My son would never forgive me if any harm came to you." She stopped, clapped her fragile hands together at a sudden memory. "But this is splendid, Miss Leland. The Willoughby family usually holds masque parties on our respective birthdays. There will be such an entertainment tonight. You will simply appear as one more masquerading guest."

"And when we unmask?"

"By that hour you will have discreetly withdrawn."

She seemed very pleased by her suggestion, with reason. Hester watched her Ladyship leave the room, carefully closing the door. It was good to know that she had at least one day to remain free. Hester knew it was necessary to be on her way as soon as possible, far from here. Then, too, Lady Sophia might be satisfied that nothing as yet had come of Hester's relationship with Sir Charles. But she would hardly approve of a hunted criminal as her future daughter-in-law.

Hester postponed all her thoughts about a future with Sir Charles. The person who must concern her now was

Colonel Kirov with his obsession to bring her to what he must suppose was justice. He might very well return here. Or worse, he might capture her as she escaped.

But what if she pursued the notion of a disguise, not just tonight but in order to escape from the manor and even from the shire?

The more she thought about it, the more this idea seemed the only way out of her dreadful difficulties. She would utilize the costume furnished her and escape tonight when the excitement at the unmasking was at its height.

Sir Charles came to see her a little later, guessing that she would be afraid to be seen in the large house. He was in excellent spirits, kissed her cheek, and insisted that she should go with him on an extended tour of the household.

"You know, of course, that Mother approves of you whole-heartedly, dear Hester,"

It was not quite the description Hester would have used. She saw it as more the acceptance of an accomplished fact, but for his sake she pretended to be delighted, and properly awed.

"Her Ladyship is too kind."

She accompanied him on the tour of the big, rectangular building so heavily and darkly furnished in the Jacobean manner. He spoke of the various rooms, salons, nooks and crannies, even the still rooms and kitchen garden, as though they might be in her charge one day. To Hester, however, the idea was oppressive. She had been used to closer quarters, a small set of rooms, one servant when she and her father or her mother were beforehand with the world. If this were possible, it was all predicated on the idea of Lady Sophia's eventual death. Hester did not wish anyone dead and, in any case, she was certain the supposedly fragile Lady Sophia was a far more competent mistress of Willoughby Manor than Hester would be.

Yet this was the busy but serene life she had always dreamed of.

Hester was deeply touched by Sir Charles' faith in her and his professed love. Who could tell? If she ever freed herself of the charge against her she and Sir Charles might work together for the relief of others falsely charged, or committing crimes due to their wretched condition in life.

Like many honest people who have no experience in crime, Sir Charles seemed to be enthralled by the subject. He pursued it that morning.

"As a female, and a beautiful one, dearest Hester, you have every right to admire lovely ornaments. I hope one day to adorn you with my grandmother's emerald set. Then such jewellers' objects will be of no interest to you."

"They are of no interest to me now, Sir Charles." Had he forgotten entirely her aversion to emeralds?

"Charles."

"Yes. I have no reason to take up an emerald, in any case, I loathe green. It makes me quite ill."

"You've forgotten, dearest. I can understand how that may be. But the jewellers distinctly testify that you held it in your hand, caressing it."

"They lied. I thought you knew all that."

"Naturally. As I say, I understand. A word was spoken. Your attention was distracted, you left the shop. These oversights occur constantly. My mother told me about her maid Pankridge, who—"

She began to lose patience. "I am aware of Pankridge

and her diamond ear-bobs. But I did not put the emerald in my reticule. It fell to the floor with several other stones and either I or Mr Girard picked it up." She added sharply, "I did not keep it."

"Of course, you did not. You would never consciously—"

"Or unconsciously."

"Quite so. Consciously or unconsciously perform an act of theft. I know that, Hester. I merely wanted to have you examine every facet of the matter so that, perhaps, an accommodation would be reached with the jewellers. It is my personal belief that they would prefer a settlement to a trial."

It was useless to pursue the idea that she had absent-mindedly taken the stone, since it would be a lie and still lay her open to a long prison term for a crime she hadn't committed.

Charles apparently wanted her to face trial, with only the defence of her word. It was not enough, and Lady Pomfret was right. Until that defence was forthcoming she dared not turn herself over to the court and jury.

Lady Willoughby came to her room shortly afterward, followed by Pankridge with several costumes over her arms. Hester was not anxious to deal with Charles' mother or Pankridge now. Pankridge's attitude in particular struck her as false.

The woman borrowed her manner from Lady Sophia who professed to be charmed by the excitement of transforming her guest. She explained that she herself usually appeared as a Roman Matron. This did not quite suit her fragile-looking exterior, Hester thought.

"And your son, ma'am? Is he to be a Roman as well?"

"Oh, heavens, no. Charles goes as his namesake, Charles The Second. So appropriate. My Charles too has possessed his little Cyprians, his *filles de joie*, as they say." Her expression became apologetic in a regret Hester did not find sincere. "But there, I do not mean to offend you."

"Nor do you, ma'am. A gentleman as popular and attractive as your son is sure to have many admirers."

Lady Sophia bit her lip and then tapped Hester's wrist with her painted fan. "How well you understand these things! So experienced in life . . . tea will be late today to fortify us for a busy night."

Hester did not feel any pleasure at the prospect of a long and busy night. Much longer than either Sir Charles or his mother might guess. Nevertheless, she felt it imperative to escape while the chance provided itself through the birthday masquerade and the costume that would disguise her once she put the little black vizard over her eyes. How much easier if she could wear the mask during her flight, but this was not Venice, where the custom prevailed.

After she left the house she must cover her face as nearly as possible with the hood of her cloak.

She had enough money to see her through the next month or more, and meanwhile, if she could escape from this shire, she might take the packet boat for Ireland or a coach to the Northern Counties or Scotland. In some fairly large city far from London she was likely to find a post she could fill, a seamstress, a cook, a laundress.

Lady Pomfret must be her only contact with England, despite her trust in Sir Charles. He might betray her in some ill-advised attempt to 'make an accommodation' with the jewellers. No, she must rely only upon Lady Pomfret to uncover the truth of the plot against her.

The gowns Pankridge laid on the bed were a curious assortment. There was an ugly fishmonger's outfit, every item too large, especially the boots. She pictured herself trying to escape in such a cumbersome costume. The same might be said of the panniered gown belonging to the past century. It was made for a very short woman, besides all else.

Only two costumes fitted her. One was that of a lady's maid, an abigail, in dove gray, full-skirted with a petite white muslin apron and a frilled cap. The other was a richly theatrical gypsy costume of many bright colours that would be flattering and sure to attract far too much attention.

When Sir Charles came to the door asking if he was permitted to view the 'disguise' his mother seemed to be discomfited.

"In a moment, dear boy." She did not wait for Pankridge but began to gather up the gypsy costume. She still had the skirt and bodice in her hands when Sir Charles entered.

He went at once to Hester, taking her hands and standing off to examine her from head to foot.

"Lovely, lovely," he pronounced her at last. "Mother, you've done well by our guest. No one will recognize—"

He broke off. He had looked over his shoulders at Lady Sophia and now frowned at the colourful burden draped over her arms.

"What, may I ask, is that?"

Lady Willoughby murmured haughtily, "My dear boy, I beg you will not take that tone with me. These are garments refused by Miss Leland. I am about to have Pankridge return them to the chest in the Blue Chamber."

"I trust so. It is totally unsuitable to the future Lady Willoughby to conceal her natural purity with garments of a thieving gypsy." He explained to the surprised Hester, "Gypsies are not Christians, you know."

She protested, "At least the costume would have disguised me. But it didn't fit."

"Fortunately." His features softened as he read shock and dismay in her eyes. "But there, let us say no more about it."

He kissed her hands, motioned to his mother and took the rejected costume from her, though he handled it with disdain.

It mattered little to Hester what she wore. She had been surprised by the near-quarrel between Sir Charles and his mother. Obviously, despite his many charities, his generosity and understanding, he had his little imperfections, his typical landowner's dislike of 'thieving gypsies', for example. His prejudice had served Hester well the previous night when Colonel Kirov, who looked rather like a gypsy, had come to collect her. Sir Charles might have been more reluctant to flout the King's Justice if the Russian had appeared to be an upstanding Anglo Saxon.

It was almost a relief to find that he was not the perfect giant she had begun to believe he was, as it made her coming flight a trifle easier.

Despite the prickling sense of danger she felt all day, she saw no signs of Colonel Kirov. It looked as if he had taken the word of the Willoughbys and gone his way. It was an enormous relief, as she had expected almost every minute to see him pop out and terrify her as he had at the inn when she tried to escape on the previous afternoon.

As the Willoughby guests were announced that evening, they were greeted by Sir Charles and Lady Sophia at the head of the Jacobean staircase. Meanwhile, Hester waited cautiously in her room. Charles had told her he would come and fetch her down after a number of guests had arrived, in order that she might mingle with those who were already masked.

Conscious of her approaching flight, she hesitated in her room as Pankridge saw to her last touches, the kohl outlining her eyes, the brightness on her lips. The woman was again surprisingly amiable, giving her a description of the costumes and personalities of the guests, reminding her several times, "It is quite safe, mum. None of them horrid Bow Street Runners and the like."

Trying not to call anyone's attention to Hester as a stranger, Sir Charles waited until most of the guests had arrived and fastened on their masks. Then he came for Hester. This time he was in excellent spirits and embarrassingly complimentary. He hesitated, then gently drew her toward him.

"Dearest, you are lovely. Yes, completely adorable. I must ask for your promise, I am determined on it."

"Anything. You have been so kind."

She looked into his clear eyes, startled, hardly believing he paid her the enormous compliment of asking her to marry him even before her name could be cleared. It only gave tender proof of his belief in her innocence, and nothing else mattered so deeply to her.

He mistook her hesitation and surprise, obviously imagining the great honour he showed her had taken her breath away. "Sir," she began finally, "Can you mean you are asking me to be your wife?"

Her simplicity made him smile. "Just so. As soon as we have settled your present difficulties."

"How kind you are, sir!"

"Charles. Say 'Yes, I will be your wife, Charles'."

Dazed, Hester replied "Yes, when it is over, I will be your wife, Charles." His belief in her was everything to her right now.

He held her close, touching her lips with his soft flesh. She thought for a few seconds that she had aroused his passion and waited for the hot violence she had experienced with Taidje Kirov but he was far too much the gentleman for that.

It would have been the sort of passion her mother would expect, but certainly not Hester Leland who knew the selfish and perhaps temporary passion such emotions that must entail.

Hester reminded herself, I am quite, quite different. This is what I want of life.

But when she had returned his kiss with even more emotion than she had intended, she retreated with shame. In a few hours she would be running away from the man who gave her shelter and had just professed his love. It seemed to her that she was deliberately using his love and his mother's kind condescension in order to escape the law.

But she could never entirely believe in Lady Sophia's own goodness or her motives. The lady might well have sinister reasons behind all that condescension. She would probably like nothing better than to see Hester safely away from Charles, in the hands of the King's Justice.

Hester tried to warn Sir Charles without betraying her plan. "Sir – that is, Charles, you have been everything that is good and generous and kind. I will never forget you."

"Nonsense." He coloured a little. "You will never forget me because you will be my wife. Let me look at you again. You will make a perfect Lady Willoughby.

Come along, I trust you do not object to the servants' stairs. Otherwise, you will attract too much attention. You are far too beautiful."

It was cruel to deceive him. "How good you are, Sir!" she told him as she took the arm he offered, "A true Sir Galahad."

He was pleased, and with every justification, preened a little. In his King Charles II silk, lace and leather, she thought him the handsomest man she had ever seen, and far too good for her. Though his complexion was wrong for the swarthy Stuart King, any woman of respectable tastes might conceivably fall in love with him. Was she really to share her life with him?

They mingled with the chattering, masked crowd in the ballroom under three dazzling chandeliers of crystal lustres. Double doors were open at the end of the room connecting it to a green salon. Hester drew back instinctively before entering the latter room with its emerald velvet drapes and carpet.

"Please," she began nervously, "I had rather not. May we go into the ballroom?" It was obvious he had never taken seriously her abhorence of emerald green.

"I have promised you, dear Hes—" He remembered the masquerade and amended to, "Dear Abigail, I have promised you the house is yours. Ballroom or Green Salon."

No green in the ballroom. It was a long room with gold damask drapes and gold-edged wall panels, as well as gold leaf *trompe-l'oeil* figures around the ceiling. All this provincial splendour caught the many lights reflected from the crystal lustres overhead. It looked very like a frame for Lady Sophia but not in the least

85

for the soldier's daughter who had never belonged to the Regent's aristocracy. She must learn. She must be a good wife to this dear and kind man. She must be proven innocent, for his sake as for her own.

She looked around, pretending an ease she was far from feeling, and was presented to a half-dozen laughing, grinning guests wearing everything from a toga to a *sans-culotte* costume associated with the recent Reign of Terror across the Channel.

Sir Charles apologized because etiquette forbade him to partner Hester in the minuet which would open the dancing. He grumbled a little when explaining that the ancient Duchess of Pentland must be honoured, but she was too nervous to hear all that he said.

Hester found no lack of partners herself for the dances and was fond of dancing, but she kept wondering what would happen if any of these eager young sprigs realized they were going down the dance with an accused thief.

As the evening wore away, Hester's anxiety deepened. The moment of her flight was nearing. She was afraid to stay here, but she dreaded the flight itself, which would lead her nowhere and might so terribly disappoint Charles.

Hester was content to remain in the background at the supper. Charles was surrounded by all the young (and not so young) beauties of the neighbourhood, wishing him well and hoping to win a place in his affections. Hester felt herself to be like a creature under enchantment. She dared not enjoy herself tonight for she knew that at midnight she must be on her way.

She avoided the ancient but highly regarded peer whom Sir Charles sent to escort her into supper, and kept thinking, shall I try for an escape now, when their hands and faces are filled?

She was still hiding from the aged peer when she was discovered by a jolly pirate and a short gypsy, both young, eager and a trifle bosky. They found her half-hidden by the heavy gold portières and both insisted on taking her to supper. They were just drunk enough to be annoying, to insist on her unmasking as many others were doing, and she didn't want to provoke a scene by her refusal. She agreed that when they returned with her plate and glass she would unmask.

Each of them took one of her arms. They outdid each other in praising her 'beauty', her 'charm' and 'wit', all of which they apparently discovered through her silence and in spite of her mask. She could think of nothing to say to them. Her mind was occupied with her escape and she solved the situation by simply smiling and agreeing with their absurdities.

The pirate with wisps of red hair sprouting from beneath his head rag, insisted that he had discovered the lady first. The blond male gypsy then went to bring back a plateful of the excellent Willoughby patés, pasties, and creamed oysters.

Hester decided now was the time to make her escape upstairs to get her cloak and reticule which would hold more than a purse.

"I have a dreadful thirst," she complained, giving the red-haired pirate the most soulful look she could manage through her mask.

He loped away to find a footman with a champagne tray while Hester ran up the servants' stairs to her room. She had laid out her cloak but meanwhile one of the servants had obligingly hung it up in the clothes-press and it took a few minutes to locate it. Luckily, the reticule was in the upper drawer of the clothes-press where she had left it. She wrapped herself in the cloak, took up the reticule, and started out.

Having come down the servants' stairs she saw no one in the hall below but a red-robed Cardinal Richelieu, unexpectedly vigorous-looking in his movements, appear in the doorway at the far end of the hall. The butler had just admitted him and his mask was already in place, though most of the guests were unmasked by this time. He exchanged a few words with the butler while Hester waited in the dark at the foot of the stairs for him to move into one of the salons.

The music from the string orchestra in the tiny balcony over the ballroom wafted its way upward and she felt the pain of knowing she could not stay with Charles, love and join him in his good works as he planned. In other circumstances, his useful life might have given her perfect satisfaction.

The Cardinal strolled to the dining salon and entered. He went across the room to stand beside the double doors opening onto the terrace while he watched the chattering guests.

Having seen the Cardinal leave the hall, Hester made her way toward Sir Charles' bookroom to escape across the terrace.

A piercing shriek brought her to a halt just as she pushed open the bookroom door. She looked around, and servants were running in all directions. The little housekeeper swept down the hall toward Hester, looking determined, her round jaw set, her eyes hard. She stopped before Hester, asking flatly,

"Have you taken a chill, miss?"

There was no explaining the cloak. Hester said haughtily, "I could not remain with those light-hearted creatures. My own future is dour enough."

Lady Sophia's maid, Pankridge, came running along, the ribbons of her cap flying.

"Mrs Jenkins, hold that female," she cried. "Her Ladyship's coral locket is missing. She was wearing it this afternoon in that female's room."

The housekeeper needed no second invitation. She reached for Hester's arm.

"Not so fast, miss. You was running mighty quick when I saw you."

In one terrible moment Hester knew why her Ladyship had kindly visited her today. It had all been arranged so beautifully, like an oriental puzzle box.

Guests poured out of the ballroom, the green salon and the dining salon. It seemed to Hester that all their eyes accused her.

"Good Gad! It's the beauty who stole Old Girard's emerald," one dashing cavalier exclaimed.

Hester's own escorts, the little gypsy and the red-haired pirate gaped at her. The pirate stammered, "Oh, I say now! Does anyone know for a certainty?"

"I do, sir," Charles told him sternly, pushing his way between the pirate and the gypsy. "The charge is an outrage, Jenkins, let her go. Pankridge, you will answer to me for your impertinence."

He moved to Hester's side and put his arm around her, a protective gesture that warmed her heart.

Lady Sophia moved out of the crowd as well. She was gently apologetic to her son and to Hester.

"My dear, it is all nonsense. I should never have cried out when Pankridge came to tell me. Of course, it was

89

not you. Why should it be? A simple coral locket. But it had a sentimental value. My dear Charles, what are we to do?"

"Nothing easier." Charles squeezed Hester's shoulder. "Dearest, will you prove to them how wrong they are and submit to a search by – by Mother, perhaps?"

Hester hesitated. She sensed a trap, she had no faith whatever in Lady Sophia's protestations.

"Surely, every guest in your house will not submit to such a shameful business?"

Sir Charles was placed in an awkward position. Not so, his mother.

"Certainly not, my dear. But you are leaving, and without the slightest word to us. It is only that you – I beg pardon – your past makes my servants leap to unfounded suspicions."

"I was innocent before, and I am innocent now," Hester said, rather too loudly.

There were murmurs among the guests, broken by Pankridge's cry, "Will you look at her cloak now? Threads about the hem. Like someone sewed up the hem mighty careless." She reached for Hester's cloak, yanking it so hard she pulled it off Hester's shoulders.

Sir Charles' arm had slipped away from her. He was puzzled and confused, doubtless wondering why she did not submit instantly to a search. But she saw the trap coming and there seemed to be no way out of it. With the cloak in Pankridge's hands, she knew the answer.

So that is where they hid it, she thought, edging back into the open doorway of the bookroom. Her hands were clammy and cold, but fury at the treachery of Lady Sophia and her hirelings gave her the needed courage.

Pankridge tore at the hem of the cloak, her beady

90

little eyes dancing, and waved on high a coral locket set in gold.

"I don't believe it," Charles said staunchly. "Let me see it."

"Dear boy," his mother murmured, "The facts are so evident."

He was shocked. "I beg pardon, Mother, but you were mistaken. Question your maids."

"My dear boy!"

"I must insist. Pankridge, please do so at once. One of the maids is responsible."

Hester gritted her teeth. Sending Pankridge to question them was like setting the fox to guard the hen house. She knew there would be no help from Sophia Willoughby or her maids.

She seized her chance as a dozen people crowded around to examine the locket. She stepped back further, slammed and bolted the library door in the dark. Another few steps and she would be out on the terrace, in the wind and the night, momentarily free.

Suddenly, to her stupefaction, the oil lamp on the desk blazed up, lighting the room. She swung around, almost blinded by the scarlet apparition across the room, a barrier between Hester and the terrace doors.

He had removed his mask. The blood-red cardinal's robes only added to the terror Colonel Kirov aroused in her. His oblique almond eyes caught the lamp's glow and made him look as if he were amused by his effect on her.

"Come, we've already lost a day."

She braced herself to restore her courage.

"I didn't do it, you know. His mother wants to be rid of me."

She heard the rattling of the door latch and Sir Charles' voice. "Hester! My dear! Let me talk to you. I understand about the blasted thing. You cannot help your irresistible impulses. We must talk." He rattled the latch again. His voice, more distant now, called to his guests, "She is my intended wife. I will not betray her now."

He was still loyal to her. He still expected to marry her when her innocence was proven. How honourable he was! She must never forget.

With hands that trembled, she reached for the door bolt. Behind her the Russian said in the crisp voice of authority.

"All this has nothing whatever to do with the man Girard and his emerald." He took her wrist in his hard, lean fingers, "Come along."

Chapter Seven

"The stars are out. A good omen," Kirov said when he had nudged her all the way to the stile beyond the garden. He bundled up the cardinal's robe and biretta, stuffing them beneath the stile. Under the robe he was wearing black breeches and one of his peculiar, tight-collared, tightly belted Russian shirts, this one in a sombre, depressing green. From this cache beneath the stile he drew out a wrinkled black travel cloak. She stared at him, unaware that she was shivering. He shook out the cloak and looked her over.

"Where did you get that servant's cap?"

"Lady Willoughby must have thought that it disguised my hair."

"It doesn't. I suspect she knew that. Take it off."

"Off?" She was more puzzled than alarmed when he reached for her. She hardly knew what to think. If he meant to assault her, he had chosen a ridiculous spot for it.

Before she could back out of his reach, he untied the silly little muslin cap with its lacy trim.

"Hold this."

She did so and found herself shrouded in his black cloak that smelled not unpleasantly of grass and wood smoke.

While she stared at him he pulled the collar of the old

cloak so high around her face she was almost lifted out of her morocco slippers. She couldn't help smiling.

"Thank you, Father."

He was taken aback until she explained. "My father used to do that. He claimed a lady never revealed her throat except at a ball. And we had precious few of them."

He pretended to pay no attention to this and pulled the cloak's hood down over her head. She felt like a monk on a furtive mission. He said brusquely, "All that's as may be. Over the stile with you now, and mind, no tricks."

He was still limping. He prodded her again. She climbed the stile, stepped on the many hems of her petticoats and the dragging black cloak. She had the dubious pleasure of looking to him to rescue her. He boosted her over the stile, into the ploughed field beyond.

She had been too shocked by the appalling extent of Lady Willoughby's hatred to complain over Kirov's rough treatment. But at least he didn't believe she was guilty of taking the cameo. That was something.

After several minutes of slogging through the field, she could not forbear asking, despite his dour mood, "Do we walk to my hanging?"

He looked at her with a glimmer of a smile. "Not quite. I've tethered a horse and cart in that copse yonder, and that may get us to Taunton."

This did not give her any incentive to reach the horse and cart. After a while she asked, "As a matter of curiosity, how did you come upon your cardinal's robes? Are they furnished by my judges for the purpose of your disguises?"

"Far from it. Your prospective mother-in-law furnished the robes."

She felt the chill of this fresh blow. "How she must hate me!"

His voice had an edge to it. "She fears you. Her kind will always fear a woman like you."

She did not know what to think. "I wish I might take that for a compliment."

"You may, if your object is that pretty fellow, her son." That silenced her.

A few minutes later, having reached a horse and wagon beside a trickling brook, she stopped. She was abruptly flung up to her place on the box. Her captor swung up beside her, took the reins, and the patient mare made her way out toward the High Road.

Hester was at least warm, seated close beside Colonel Kirov. She tried to banish the future, concentrate on the next hour, even the next minute of her life. She was not condemned yet. Nor yet delivered to the filthy, vermin-infested prison where she would await her judges and the verdict. Under a black sky still dotted with stars, she tried to be hopeful.

Out of nowhere and without looking around at her, Kirov said, "I am not one of your judges. It can't matter what you say to me. But why did you take the stone?"

She had been sitting in a kind of daze, with her eyes closed, but they snapped open now. "For the hundredth time, I did not take it. I detest emeralds."

"Why emeralds?"

"I loved my mother very much, and she was Papa's whole life. She and the army. She was run down in a London street by a panic-stricken horse dragging a carriage. She pushed me out of the way as she fell. And I lay there trying to scramble up and help her, while Mama's emerald green skirts spread out like a

95

flower around her." She cleared her throat. "Her blood trailed toward me across those pretty skirts."

"I see." He didn't try to convince her that she must banish the memory, as so many had done.

He was silent for a long minute or two. He asked after some thought, "How do you think the emerald theft happened then?"

"I know how it happened. Mr Girard wished me to persuade my employer that she must give her custom to Girard And Hailsham. Mr Girard slipped the emerald into my reticule and then drew it out when there where suitable witnesses. He—" She hesitated, then blurted out, "He liked to touch females. If I was 'kind' to him, he said, he would be lenient. But you know all that."

He turned his head. She saw him looking her way, though he must have found it too dark to see her very clearly.

"And you would not yield?"

"Certainly not. My person is my own, to bestow as I please, and when I shall choose to do so." She recollected herself. "That is to say, unless I am found guilty, when I shall have no choice in the matter."

"And is this true of Mother Willoughby's lad?"

Offended at his impertinence, she reminded him, "That is no concern of anyone but Sir Charles and myself."

"And the Lady Sophia."

She raised her chin, trying not to let him tease her, but she caught the flash of his teeth. He must have found her answer amusing. She couldn't imagine why.

His curiosity seemed to be satisfied for the time being. She was relieved. At the same time it gave her more time to think about their destination and she found, surprisingly enough, that she missed their duel of words. By the time they pulled up at an inn in the dead of night and he got down to look after the mare, she was half asleep.

He woke her to ask, "Would you care to refresh yourself at the inn? It appears reasonably clean."

"And highly respectable?" she asked, teasing him for his concern. At first glance he did not look like a man who noticed such matters.

"That I would not know."

Without waiting for arguments, he lifted her down and escorted her across the inn yard which was empty of all save a cart and a richly caparisoned coach whose team was being changed. Inside the taproom the probable owner of the coach outside was bent over a glass of something that appeared to be gin. From his slovenly posture he must have drunk more than one.

There were three men at the tapster's bar, sheepmen probably, exchanging the latest tales about King George's madness.

When Hester heard this gossip in London or Bath the wit and sly humour disgusted her, but the old-fashioned yeomen of the countryside were neither as cruel nor as witty. On the contrary. From the little she heard they seemed shocked by the old King's helpless state.

"Wait", Colonel Kirov ordered her, "Do not let them see you, while I have a look around."

She wondered if he wanted to protect her from their attentions or, much more likely, to protect the men from her wiles. It was a sensible order and she obeyed, careful to remain out of sight in the drafty passage until he came out.

"There is no private parlour. Do you wish to go on to the next village?"

Annoyed that he persisted in thinking she demanded

the best, she said sharply, "I see no harm in this place. I'll stop by the kitchen."

His black eyebrows were raised. "Very sensible. I'll hurry the change in horses, but I want to be sure our old mare is well-treated."

She watched him as he returned to the inn yard. He pleased her by his apparent care for animals.

When she went into the aged, smoke-stained kitchen to see if there was a water closet in the building, it was awkward to find that the cook was a male. She interrupted a short, stout man busy stirring the porridge in a blackened kettle. The kettle swung from an equally blackened hook, ready for early travellers who didn't fancy a slice of the handsome mutton leg still warm above the low-burning coals.

The skullery girl, if any, was gone, probably asleep so she could get back to the kitchen before dawn, but the cook proved jolly and obliging. He stopped stirring in order to grin as he pointed his big, dripping spoon toward the rear door.

"Right yon, ma'am. Out that door and to your left."

Hester followed his directions, more than ever amused at Colonel Kirov's notion that she was a helpless aristocrat. Having removed her gloves and washed in the rain barrel, she came back through the kitchen. The cook went on stirring but he pointed toward some bread on the old, scarred deal table, saying "Take it, Ma'am. Baked it myself not an hour gone by."

She thanked him gratefully and cut a chunk off the loaf with his butcher knife. It was good, delicious, and in fact she broke the still warm piece in two, deciding she could be generous to Kirov as well. Before leaving the kitchen she put down the first coin she found in her reticule. It was silver and very likely she would need it, but the bread was worth it.

The cook nodded his thanks and she went out of the inn through the narrow central passage. It wasn't until she had reached the pebbled inn yard that it suddenly occurred to her she had completely forgotten to escape when she had her chance.

Hesitating while she made up her mind, she saw the shadow of a man in the passage and realized she was too late. She started toward Kirov's old but sturdy wagon. Surely, there would be another chance.

She heard the loping, booted footsteps on the pebbles behind her. Not the sounds she expected. This panting fellow in a hurry was certainly not Colonel Kirov, but when she stepped out of the man's way, he followed her more rapidly.

She realized he must be the owner of the coach across the inn yard, undoubtedly the man she had seen earlier, huddled over his gin in the taproom.

She turned just as a fog of spirits nauseated her and two thick arms locked around her body, one across her bosom and the other around her waist.

"Ay, it's our lovely thief, so it is."

Half-stifled, she tried to wrest herself free of his clutches. She knew Sylvester Girard, the jeweller, whose lies had brought her to this pass.

She cried out in fury and a good deal of fear as she realized that she was no match for the detestable creature. Her cry was silenced by the fleshy, moist wanderings of his mouth over hers.

Chapter Eight

In her wild loathing of his touch Hester heard no sound beyond the scuffle of their feet on the rough ground, and above all, the jeweller's deep breathing. When she bit his flabby lip and freed her mouth momentarily he chided her.

"There'll be worse waiting for you in prison, my dear. I'm on my way to testify to your vixenish ways. But I can be generous, even speak for you. Best resign yourself. Your fate must lie solely with me."

He broke from her with such force she swayed and fell against the flank of the now skittish young mare. Her attacker had been whirled around by his high cravat, and he landed hard on his backsides, staring up at Colonel Kirov.

Hester stammered, "He – I – he is foxed. He swears he will be generous in his testimony if I—" Kirov motioned her to silence.

The jeweller was still spluttering, promising Kirov a dire fate when the Colonel cut him short, accusing Girard in the official, unemotional voice that had terrified Hester at their first meeting.

"Attempted bribery of a prisoner under the King's Justice? Things will go hard with you at the Assizes. I suggest you stagger back inside and douse your head in water."

Hester heard her own hysterical laughter and for an instant didn't recognize it. She might have expected Kirov's violent interruption but not the actual form of his threat. Righteousness in the King's name was not a quality she associated with him.

He closed his hands around her waist and boosted her up on the box, then went to calm the horse. Meanwhile, Sylvester Girard got to his feet with much huffing and puffing and stumbled back to the inn where he stopped to bellow at Kirov, "I won't forget this. Mark me, you'll answer for it, you heathen."

Kirov ignored him, looking up at Hester.

"I had some food for you but thanks to your friend, it's gone now."

She was touched by his solicitude. "We are quits then. I had some new-baked bread I thought you might enjoy. But I dropped it."

He looked around under the smoking lantern of the inn while she pointed to her abandoned chunk of bread, now hopelessly trodden under foot. He shrugged and swung up beside her with his muscular ease.

By the time they were on their way dawn was beginning to brighten the east behind them. They were closer to her destination. The suspense of not knowing her fate was so great that Hester was almost relieved to be approaching the end of this tense and sinister ride. However, the events at the inn had given her a tiny seed of hope.

Perhaps, for all his official stance, he had begun to believe in her innocence. As the cart rattled out onto the High Road she decided to approach him on a note of friendly curiosity.

"Colonel Kirov, I should not wish you to think I am inquisitive, but how do you happen to find yourself a

102

British prison guard? Or a warder, if you like. Are you a subject of King George?"

She could scarcely call his smile a pleasant one.

"I am a subject of the Emperor Alexander, Tsar of all the Russias."

"Then why—?"

He gave the mare a signal, and it was as if the ride and the road ahead occupied all his attention.

"The Emperor put it to your Prince Regent last year at the great Waterloo celebrations that he wished a trusted Russian officer to investigate the ways of British law, including treatment of prisoners, pre-trial questioning, use of witnesses, and conditions of holding cells and prisoners themselves." He paused, then added, "There was to be special attention paid to the West Country."

Puzzled, she looked at him. "Why the West Country?"

"Because I wished it so. You are my third task in the West Country. I was sent to the Northern Counties on one task, and once to Royal Rye."

"Task," she repeated. He hadn't the least satisfied her curiosity, but she managed to say, "It is a great compliment to British law."

"Not at all. I had my reasons."

Her attempts at friendship were rebuffed. She still had the burgeoning hope that he would testify on her behalf about Girard's attempted assault. But perhaps he considered that no worse than his forceful embrace at the time of her escape at the inn.

After stops to change horses through the day and to see that Hester was properly served, they moved on toward Taunton. The air darkened rapidly at dusk but every distant church spire or manor house that loomed up on the horizon gave Hester a sense of dread. Was this Taunton? Had they arrived at last?

Her companion had been silent the last half-hour and she suspected he too was remembering what lay ahead. He was unlikely to have his good will purchased by all her efforts at charm and warmth.

She did not feel charming, and the closer they came to Taunton, the less warmth or confidence she felt in her fate. She tried to bring the matter up lightly with an ironic twist to her words

"My mother once told me that many a good Somerset lad taken in the Monmouth Rebellion was tortured up there at Taunton Castle. Is that to be my fate?"

"I doubt it. That was a trifle before my day. My orders are to deliver the prisoner to one of the magistrates, Sir Giles Cartaret, for interrogation at his chambers."

"Quite cozy, in fact."

He ignored that. "I am told repairs have begun and prisoners are now remanded to temporary holding cells below the chambers as they were a score of years ago during similar work. But not, I assure you, at Taunton Castle."

She bit her lip, not wanting him to guess the terror he conjured up for her. He looked at her. His hard, strange features did not soften but she thought she detected a little feeling, masked by outward indifference, as he reminded her, "You are not hanged yet, you know. With any luck you may find you have had all these qualms to no purpose."

She tried gentleness. "I want you to know how sorry I am for the trouble I have given you. I should like us to part as friends."

He looked at the hand she offered him. "I wish I might believe that."

"You may, I assure you." She laid her hand on his arm.

He did not look as though he trusted her, but when she remained motionless he picked up the gloved hand in his palm and seemed to find it interesting. Her warm expression did not change. She hadn't the slightest idea what he would do but she hoped that he would be encouraged to speak up for her, describing the jeweller's attack upon her at the inn yard.

He still had her hand in his palm, his fingers closing tightly around it, when he leaned toward her. She felt her heart beating faster, partly with anticipation and partly too with alarm.

What would he do when he realized she had her own motive for pretending to yield?

His lips brushed hers, feather touches that disturbed her by the sensations they aroused in her.

Then she saw his strange eyes that shone like dagger blades. He thrust her hand aside rudely and turned his attention to the reins, remarking with the utmost indifference, "You must practice more. You are not very adept at the Delilah role."

She felt her flesh go hot at the insult. His easy dismissal shamed and silenced her.

They reached their destination well into the evening. There was little of the busy Somerset town to be seen at this hour. It was said to be medieval in its beginnings, at various times a market town, and now the seat of capital trials in this area of the West Country.

Obviously, Colonel Kirov had been here before. One of those three 'tasks' he had mentioned, no doubt. At all events he knew his way about the town, even under the flickering lights that provided a fitful illumination. They passed a market square, now empty and eerily silent, and drew up before an imposing mansion whose frigid stone exterior was cold enough to frighten the worst offender. Though not as large as many a great mansion, in its own green parkland between London and the West Country it was every bit as forbidding. Hester would not have been surprised to learn that cells for holding prisoners before trial were in the cellars of such a stern, narrow-windowed building.

Kirov remarked briskly, "These are the temporary chambers of several Crown Officers. If it can be arranged, you may be given a cell – a room," he corrected himself. "Until you come before the Assizes."

"You are too kind." She said it flatly, without expression. She could not bring herself to speak gratefully.

He roused a footman in the silent building and turned the horse and cart over to him. By the time he led her up a gloomy central staircase they had passed several unsavory-looking men, each in the custody of a warder looking quite as ferocious. Every prisoner was manacled. The prisoners evidently awaited either a first hearing or an appeal from their sentences.

An even more alarming portent was a wild-eyed woman whose white hair seemed to fly out from her head in all directions. She too was manacled, despite her age and frailty. A murmur started up as Hester and the Colonel passed with Kirov's palm under her elbow. She knew better than to be flattered by the interest of their audience.

She could hear voices somewhere beyond the audience chamber in which she and Kirov were ordered by the usher to wait.

When a nervous townsman in clean linen and polished boots was called and then vanished through the door at the far end of the chamber, Kirov settled her in the chair the man had left. It was the room's only armchair. Its leather cushions had been badly sliced by some sharp instrument.

Kirov surprised Hester by telling her in an under-voice, "I will accompany you when you come before Justice Cartaret."

She nodded. She could not speak. The powerful stench of bodies threatened to make her retch. They must have been long unwashed and left to lie for weeks in their own filth before their hearing.

Kirov stood more or less casually before her, evidently to protect her from the blank, expressionless gaze of half a dozen prisoners. Three of the males, plus a dark-skinned, scrawny, boy of twelve or thirteen, were manacled. The boy was crying and occasionally tried to wipe his dark eyes with the knuckles of his hands. He wore a torn red shirt and a filthy leather jerkin. Every time he raised his hands the room echoed with the grating of metal.

Hester felt for a lawn handkerchief, lace-trimmed, in her reticule and gave it to Kirov with a nod toward the boy. For a second or two he didn't understand. Then he left her and crossed the room. The boy looked from the bit of lawn to the strange, barbaric fellow who had offered it, and suddenly he bore a slight resemblance to Kirov. The Colonel ruffled the boy's spiky hair in a friendly fashion.

The boy grinned. Then, with his manacled hands, he smoothed the handkerchief out carefully and instead of using it, tucked it into his jerkin. To Hester's sympathetic eyes he seemed to sit up straighter with a kind of pride.

The heavy oaken door of the inner chamber opened and an old man in the breeches, stockings and buckled shoes of the previous century came out. His shoulders slumped under an ill-fitting coat with stiffened skirts. He removed his spectacles and polished them against his sleeve.

The waiting prisoners all watched his movements tensely, though it was clear the old man represented only one of them. Perhaps they felt his report would be an omen. He crossed the room. Hester held her breath, hoping against hope that his news was not as bad as his expression indicated; for he had stopped in front of the boy.

Colonel Kirov's attention was fixed upon the door to the inner chamber which was ajar. He said, "I had better see him now, while he is free."

Hester scarcely heard him. Like everyone else in the audience chamber she was watching the old man and the boy. The old man squeezed the boy's shoulder.

"No use, my lad. Dealing in bad coins was a hanging offence. You were warned the first time."

The boy stared at his manacles. He had stopped crying. He mumbled, "Me Pa said it was a'right, so long as it was 'im that gi'me the word. He said the *Gaje* wa'n't know."

Hester caught her breath. Kirov touched her hand and she looked up. He took her arm, escorting her toward the door of the inner chamber. So now it was her turn. As they went inside the austere quarters of Sir Giles Cartaret, she was painfully aware that the eyes of all the waiting prisoners were upon her. She shivered, and could not look back at the boy.

Sir Giles was nothing like Hester's mental picture of the man who would decide whether she should face prison and ultimately a life or death trial. A tall, splendid specimen of the Anglo-Saxon landowner, he gave an impression of kindliness and benevolence. He arose from his chair at sight of Hester, though he greeted only Kirov.

"Ah, Colonel, back again? This should be your third wrongdoer. Let me see. The old woman who expired as she was taken to the holding cells. And the coiner who was shot during that ill-advised escape attempt. . . . But you prefer our winter climate, no doubt."

"No doubt."

"Still, I found St Petersburg a city of marvels," the magistrate went on in his jovial way. "Must be all of thirty-five years since my father first presented me to Empress Catharine and her court. A great lady. Truly great." Seeing Kirov's eyebrows go up, he added diplomatically, "Not that your present Emperor isn't a fine fellow. Popular with the ladies. Even Boney's wife is said to have favoured him."

"So they say." Kirov took a thin sheaf of papers from his coat. "The case against one Hester Leland. Accused of High Theft. Your case now, Sir Giles." His respectful bow was hardly more than a nod.

His manner did not trouble Sir Giles, though he glanced again at Hester and then sat down slowly and began to peruse the papers, looking up every now and then, making Hester more nervous than ever.

He set the pages aside at last but kept them under his right palm. Still speaking in that deceptively jovial way, he remarked, "So this little lady has a fancy for emeralds."

He was not looking at her but she said, "No, Your Excellency."

109

Sir Giles gave Kirov the significant smile of one knowing gentleman to another. "Naturally. One understands these things. In fact, the young—" His glance encompassed her. "— young person despises emeralds and all such flummery."

She knew it was disastrous to be insolent but she could not help clipping off a cold reply.

"I do despise emeralds, Excellency."

He gave an elaborate and theatrical sigh. "Colonel, you have seen how my time is filled. Good Gad, Man! Those cases out in the antechamber have appeared at the last Assizes, before other judges. It is not necessary but it is my custom to hear a review of those in which there may be a shade of doubt. Clemency, my boy. Clemency. But the King's Justice must be carried out. Now, what is the case in this person's favour? It is not presented in these pages. In fact I congratulate this Wiltshire magistrate, as there seems to be no question of the Leland female's guilt."

He did not look at her. Hester felt as if she were invisible. Once Sir Giles had satisfied himself of her guilt she ceased to exist for him. He raised his hand, returning to the various points made in the neat script of the accusation against her.

"Perhaps you haven't read it. The jeweller Girard, his partner, Hailsham, Enderby, respectable spinster, and a child named – what? Oh, yes, Fambles."

"There seems to be some question of Girard's motives," Kirov remarked.

Hester stared at the Russian, surprised and deeply gratified. She began to believe he would defend her in some way.

"Motives? Motives? My dear fellow, what have motives to do with the female's guilt? Either she took the emerald, or she did not. Four witnesses say that she is guilty. They, in effect, witnessed the crime. What's this about motives?"

"Nothing, obviously." Kirov's apparent indifference to the matter almost destroyed Hester's newly reborn hopes but then he added, "This fine fellow, Girard, attempted an attack upon my prisoner at an inn some hours ago. I heard him offer to amend his testimony if the prisoner agreed to become his mistress."

Sir Giles was shocked. "My dear Colonel, this is not barbaric Russia. A gentleman simply does not make such demands of a female who has made off with a trinket worth twelve hundred guineas."

"It was worth a thousand the day before Miss Leland came into his shop," Kirov said drily.

"Eh?" The magistrate looked up, glanced from Kirov to Hester and then, clearly remembering his authority, he shrugged. "Very likely. However, there is no law broken by a merchant who sees to a rise in the worth of his merchandise. Emeralds and the like are forever moving up or down in value."

"Sir, please hear me out." Hester could keep silent no longer. She took a quick step to his desk, a surprisingly dainty lacquered piece that already showed ugly scars. Perhaps they were left by prisoners as desperate as Hester.

The swiftness of her movement alarmed Sir Giles who shrank back in anything but the heroic mould.

"See here – Colonel, what is this female about?"

Hester wanted to laugh at the spectacle of a King's Magistrate cowering in fear of her. Kirov took his time, simply closing those hard fingers around her upper arm. She ignored him.

"Sir Giles, I swear to you on my mother's grave that I did not take Mr Girard's jewel. I have a fear of emeralds, as to me, they mean death. Mr Girard showed me three stones, a ruby, a sapphire and an emerald. He wished me to bring my employer into the shop to purchase them. He offered me a 'pretty bauble' if I consented. When I refused and left the shop, he followed me, reached into my reticule and brought out the emerald. After accusing me, he said he would show clemency if I agreed to become his mistress." She leaned toward him over the desk, "He put it there himself."

Sir Giles drew back and Hester saw Kirov grin contemptuously. She knew that however amused the Colonel might be, her excitement and desperation had lost her case with the Judge.

She managed to say, "Forgive me, sir, but I can only plead the truth." She tried to shake off Kirov's immovable hand, finally addressing him in her angry despair, "What can I say but the truth?"

Kirov remained calm. "Sir Giles, you will allow that I am an impartial witness. You have my word that this Girard attempted to assault the prisoner on the Bristol High Road. I will give evidence that he promised to reduce his charge if the prisoner yielded to his advances."

"Yielded," Sir Giles repeated, his pale blue eyes studying Hester.

"Sexually."

The magistrate stiffened as though he had never heard the word spoken aloud. His cheeks reddened.

"We need not discuss those subjects here, Colonel, no matter how freely they are regarded in the Russian Court. The charge is before me. I see no changes, no pleas for leniency. No refutation of the basic crime, observed by three other witnesses. Miss – er – Leland – you do not claim that they also made shocking advances to you in return for your favours?"

"No, sir. Only Sylvester Girard."

His Excellency glanced skyward with impatience at her obstinacy.

"I see nothing here that warrants my interference. Colonel, will you summon a guard? A few weeks in detention will give the prisoner ample time to prepare her defence for her trial. Please make note of our methods to your Emperor. We are nothing if not just."

"How well you put it, Sir Giles!" Even to Hester Kirov sounded ironic but the magistrate accepted the praise complacently.

"Well, well, so you are now off to study another felon and our system for your Tsar."

"Briefly. A malefactor to Bristol and then home to St Petersburg."

Hester heard this bitterly. She had hoped he would make a stronger plea on her behalf. But she had no more time to think about this betrayer. A big, heavy-set man who limped a little came in at Sir Giles' order.

Hester thought she was prepared for everything, but the sight of the manacles in the burly guard's hands, and their hideous, metallic screech as they rubbed together, made her limbs feel weak.

She was too humiliated to look at Kirov, which was just as well. He seemed to have lost all interest in her. She stared down at her slender wrists locked in this horrible way. The manacles were huge, and rubbed against her flesh constantly.

"Come along, ma'am," the guard ordered her. His voice was rough but he was not brutal, as she had expected.

113

Rather ostentatiously, Sir Giles Cartaret turned back to the papers on his desk while Kirov, before Hester's shocked eyes, held the door open to make their passage easier for the guard and his prisoner.

She tried to flash a haughty, confident smile for the benefit of all those eyes watching her in the antechamber. She kept thinking of the late Queen of France who had gone to the guillotine head high and haughty as ever. Nevertheless, her innermost thoughts told her that the Queen of France was made of sterner stuff.

When the guard ushered her through the antechamber, to run the gauntlet of all those other unfortunates, she raised her chin and kept her gaze straight ahead.

She heard one of the waiting prisoners cackle knowingly, "There's a proud 'un. Gallows' bait, ye can allus tell."

Chapter Nine

These rough stone steps were narrower than the front staircase by which Hester and Colonel Kirov had reached the Magistrate's antechamber. The walls held the odour of decay, of moisture never exposed to the light, and of whatever dead creatures remained in their former life habitat.

It seemed to Hester as though the steps plunged down to the bowels of the earth, or to hell. When she tripped on a broken step the guard seized her by one shoulder, which almost wrenched her arm off but at least kept her from breaking a few bones.

He apologized roughly, as though the hellish place might be his responsibility.

"Wa'n't meant to do ye harm, ma'am. But the Holdin' Cells, they're under repairs and the judges, like Sir Giles, they're makin' do whilst their chambers are clewed up shipshape."

The lantern in a niche at the head of the stairs had been passed long ago and only now she began to glimpse another lamp, far below at what seemed to be the ground floor of the building. In her bitterness Hester had been determined not to speak to anyone but her guard seemed to mean well and she asked, "Are you a seaman?"

"Was, ma'am, that I was. Saw action off Trafalgar

but that was long gone by. Took a near-miss from a Frenchie cannon ball. Splintered my innards, in a manner of speakin'. No room for a splintered old growler in the King's Navy, so it was a bit of luck findin' this berth. Near on to starvin' afore I was took in here."

She said nothing and he went on cheerfully, "World an't all made up of bad-uns, ma'am. They're good now and agin."

Trying to grope her way around a turn in the steps with both hands manacled, she muttered, "I wonder."

The grating of the metal never ceased to remind her of her degradation, and she fancied she could still hear the croaking of the old woman in the antechamber: "Gallows Bait!"

She had not thought it possible there was another flight of steps below the ground floor lantern that flickered with a dying light. She was just turning toward a heavy, splintered door leading to what she assumed was the ground floor passage when the guard nudged her on, around a stone wall, and she found herself on the top step of another flight.

The sea-going guard seemed to feel a sympathetic interest in her. He took her arm and when the movement made her manacles clash in that sickening screech and stopping her on the turn of the step, got out a filthy kerchief such as seamen wear around their necks. He then stuffed its corners into each manacle.

"There now, ma'am, ought to ease the rubbin' some'ut."

She thanked him gratefully, reflecting that he was the only stranger to show her unmotivated kindness since the morning Lady Pomfret sent her to Girard And Hailsham's. Her wrists were raw and they burned at the touch of the kerchief, but his action itself had touched her.

"I should like to thank you by name, sir," she said, as they passed the smoking lamp in a niche where several bricks had been removed.

His heavy face and small blue eyes looked unexpectedly touched. "Well now, ma'am, that'll be Peter Patterson, if you're so minded."

But Seaman Patterson was very much aware of his duties. "Beggin' your pardon, but I have to search you now. I'll make it as easy as I may." He patted her from head to shoes but did so in a timid way as if it were a shameful business. He looked into her reticule hurriedly, then let it dangle from her arm. "That'll be all, ma'am."

Wondering at a curious, distant sound like the drone of voices and assuming that was very likely her destination, she murmured, "Thank you, Peter Patterson."

Below them the steps ended in a stone-floored little room with a high ceiling crossed by time-warped wooden beams. The room opened into a deep alcove on the right.

Patterson, seeing her apprehension, explained, "This'll be what they call, in fancy, the audience chamber. On your right is a little room like. We can see you and your visitor, but we can't hear you. That's so he can't pass nothin' to you. On t'other side, they're the Holdin' Cells you hear, the ladies bein' a mite talkative as ye'd say. They're just yonder, beyond that door."

The door was on the left of this stark, so-called Audience Chamber. The door was not steel but stout wood, with a barred window through which she could see dim light, probably rush-lights or smoking lanterns. Each side of those little darts of light faces stared out between the bars. Hester assumed they were women, but she could only make out the eyes glistening in the light of the audience chamber.

While Patterson unlocked her manacles, to her intense relief, he reminded her, "There's some as leaves here free as birds. One was gone this very day, her time served afore her trial. She was found not guilty two days gone by. So keep to that notion."

Time served before her trial, and then she was found innocent! Hester forgot her dread – bitterness was too deep.

One of the faces at the barred window guffawed and Hester, startled, found herself looking up into a pair of colourless eyes surrounded by uncombed and vaguely graying yellow hair.

"Come along in, dearie," the creature said, raising a hand apparently with difficulty, and beckoning to her. "Don't you be shy, we're all friends here. Like Patterson says, 'we're in the same boat,' so to speak." Hester smiled and waved two fingers at the blonde in a kind of salute. Her smile must have been a travesty of itself but instinctively, she knew that equality would be the only principle they accepted. This was not a place for ladylike airs.

Several women had been clinging to the barred window in the door. Apparently, the window was too high for them to see the so-called Audience Chamber without standing on something. Patterson called out a warning, "All down, me ladies. We've another lucky lady to join us."

Grumbling, they dropped down from whatever they were standing on. One of the women shrieked: "Ye're steppin' on me 'and, Meg. Off wi' ye!" She followed this with some gutter profanity so colourful Hester had difficulty understanding the words, though the meaning seemed clear.

Hester had pictured these wretched creatures trying to tear her to pieces and had steeled herself for a fight. Her mother may have been a lady, but the alleys of London had taught Hester at least the rudiments of dealing with street urchins. Until this minute she assumed that women awaiting trial for theft, prostitution and murder were merely the urchins of London grown large.

After several of the women crowded around her asking impudent but friendly questions, it occurred to her now with horrid clarity that to the world these women were her equals. Whether they were innocent of crime, or even whether some of them had been driven to crime, she was no better than they.

It was almost a relief to recall what she remembered of her childhood acquaintances and use it now.

"Ay, ladies, they've sent me to join you here at Carlton House. The Prince Regent, he's right behind me."

That brought laughter and jeers, though a thin-faced, angelic-looking creature with black curls cut into this levity about the Prince Regent's notoriously elegant London residence.

"None of that against Prinny. I had him once. Sweet as honey. When I played at Drury Lane they brought me to him naked like Cleopatra all wrapped up in a stinking dusty rug. He gave me five guineas. More than I've seen on the High Road, even with Gentleman Jamie."

A highwayman's girl? Interesting, if a trifle alarming. Curiously enough, no one seemed inclined to jeer at the little brunette. They never doubted her claims. It was almost as though they were in awe of the small creature, and Hester wondered why.

The room itself was a long cellar of some kind, obviously temporary quarters for the women awaiting trial. The stone floor was bitterly cold. Hester could feel it through her low-heeled, thin-soled slippers. These may have been fashionable on the parquet floors of the ballrooms in Bath, but Hester began to wish she had worn bad-weather pateens.

Seaman Patterson brought in Hester's portmanteau and set it in what looked like a horse stall. There were a number of these partitions in the long room, dividing the women into twos and threes.

"Mark'ee now, ladies," he reminded the women as they crowded around Hester with their questions. "No thievin' of each other."

One of the women from the other side of the long room called, "What'll ye do to us, Patterson, you old sea dog? Send us to the hulks?"

"Ay. We'll mind our own affairs," Hester told him loudly and everybody laughed. They seemed pleased that she made herself one of them. When he was about to slam and lock the door Hester touched his hand lightly.

"Thank you."

He appeared to understand, murmuring, "A pleasure to make yer acquaintance, ma'am. They'll have you out of here in a trice, you'll see."

Nevertheless, when he was out in the Audience Chamber, and Hester heard the heavy grind of the key in the lock, she felt a sudden, ghastly sensation that she had been buried in her tomb.

The graying blonde who had called to her from a

three-legged stool against the door now put a rough hand on her arm.

"It's a common bit a noise. After a fortnight you'll never hear it."

Hester forced a laugh that sounded as harsh as the key in the rusty lock. But her companions found nothing odd in it. Doubtless, they had felt the same when they first found themselves in this place.

There was a surprising amount of camaraderie here, despite some personal animosities. Most astonishing of all, Hester seemed to be wanted on several sides of the petulant feuds. Her 'wealth', as they called it, was one attraction. There were any number of corporate initiatives in action within this one long stone chamber. Straw mattresses and pillows were bought and sold, with considerable activity after anyone left the prison. Those who were found guilty and went on, some to Newgate in London, some to the hangman's noose, and others to lesser prisons, generally kept their few possessions along with small gifts from those inmates who were left behind.

The grey-blonde, Bess Camber, chuckled at one gift.

"'Twas Binty Sal. Goin' to the Nubbin' Cheat for slittin' her man's throat."

"Slitting his—"

"He'd it comin' to 'im. Burnt her with hot coals, he did. So I give her my own lad. He took that good care of 'er you wouldn't believe. Right up to the mornin' they carted her off to be hung. They do say she had a smile on 'er lips. That's my lad for you."

After several of these tales Hester no longer shuddered, but her first night's sleep was fitful. Despite the general willingness of the women to accept her, she curled up at night with her reticule beneath her skirt and her purse of coins under her shift.

The financial aspects of the Ladies' temporary Holding Cells had been explained to her at once. The lucky ones found not guilty were expected to leave behind what the better educated called 'remembrances', which included a straw pallet and pillow (if one owned such luxuries), eating implements of pewterware, far superior to wooden spoons passed around, and bits of money that could always be used to purchase small luxuries from the guards.

Hester shared a 'stall' with an aged woman universally called 'Sarey' and with Bess Camber, her first acquaintance, who had clung to the window bars and called to her as she entered the audience chamber. Snag-toothed Sarey had stolen sixpence from the Poor Box and when anything in the cells disappeared it was Sarey whose tiny horde of treasures was first examined.

The morning after Hester's first night in the Holding Cells, the women began asking flat out what Hester had been accused of. She knew that question and one other would be all-important.

"Y'er carryin' some coins with you, surely." And with less hope, "Not likely they let you keep any gold ones."

Hester obliged them by saying she had a few coins and they all would decide what was needed first. As for the information about her 'crime' she suspected that this might have preceded her arrival among them, so she told them succinctly.

"Theft."

"High or Low?"

"High."

That impressed them. The pretty girl with black curls

had begun the inquisition. Her voice, unexpectedly deep, scratched out her words and Hester got a clearer view of her in the light that poured in through the bars of a window at the opposite end of the long room.

"Angele," the women called her. She was all skin and bones, her condition made more obvious by the faded and stained gown she wore, hardly better than a long shift. One sleeve was gone, the other torn off at the elbow. She coughed half the night and Hester was sorry for her but wondered why none of the more quick-tempered women did not shout at her the useless command, "Be quiet!" In an undervoice Bess Camber had explained to Hester without being asked. "We an't the ones to ruffle Angele. She's a highwayman's doxy. She'd as soon cut y'er heart out as look at you. Ay, sooner. We let Angele queen it where she likes."

"Do they allow knives in here?"

Bess looked at her with good-natured contempt. "They ain't crazed, you know. But Angele has ways."

Strange world, Hester thought, knowing she would never forget it, if she lived to return to that other world above this cellar with its stalls. All the same, she took care to remain on good terms with Angele. In spite of it all, she felt sorry for the girl. It appeared to be a race between a coughing death and the hangman for the luckless young highwayman's doxy.

Angele demanded hoarsely, "What did you nip that made you High Theft?"

"I didn't steal anything."

A chorus of laughter and jeering answered that and she added quickly, "But I was accused of taking an uncut emerald."

Somebody whistled. Even Angele's big dark eyes

stared at her with new respect. Hester sensed danger and decided to give them a reason for protecting her.

"The emerald was found. But I do have friends. Now and again there are a few coins. Nothing large, but sixpence here, thrupence there. Never know. They can buy us a few little pleasures."

They exchanged glances. They obviously liked her mention of 'us'.

"No offence, Leel," a heavy, middle-aged woman told her, "but ye're the sort we hope has a long wait afore they call ye up."

Bess patted her on the back.

"If ye're bound for the noose anyway, Leel, it's best they take their time afore you go up to the Assizes."

Hester was chilled but she was rapidly learning not to react.

From this conversation onward she answered to the name of 'Leel'. Even the name Leland had been taken from her, she told herself grimly, wondering if she had also lost Lady Pomfret, Sir Charles and any other friend she once possessed. She knew she would never forgive Colonel Kirov for his part in her disaster.

There seemed to be a code among them of laughing at their fate. When, that same day, one of the older women was called to the Audience Chamber and told to bring her possessions, practically all her recent companions expressed their regret and wished she might 'remain among friends'. They took turns balancing on the stool to watch her climb up the steps and out of their sight. She was on her way to what her companions, and even her young day guard, assured Hester was a Not Guilty verdict.

"I should think you would be happy for her," Hester protested.

The truth of the matter was carefully explained to her.

"Micheleen Quinn lost her man in the Spanish Wars and her grandson died of the typhus. She's nothing to go out of here for. In here at least, there's us, and when each of us leaves, there's another good 'un to take her place. Outside, there's nothin'."

"But these are temporary quarters. This isn't a prison. It seems to have been used for storage or a root cellar once."

Another of her new companions cut in. "They used it about a quarter-century ago, I hear tell, during repairs to the law courts. That was when the gypsy escaped."

"Then it is possible to escape."

Angele picked from her teeth a greasy string of what passed for food. "Gypsy was shot."

"Dead she was for all her trouble escaping," Old Sarey croaked. "One of 'em toffs seen 'er a hidin' in that garden over yon, past the alleys an' the new courts."

Angele put in, "Lord and Lady Stamsbury's Ball, it was. It's said the guards came along to the Stamsbury gardens and one of the fancy guests betrayed the gypsy. She made a run for it and they shot 'er."

"Ay. They do say she went down – bang! – like that. In 'is Ludship's own garden."

The talk of a gypsy brought Hester thoughts of Colonel Kirov. His Russian identity and background was vouched for by the odious Sir Giles Cartaret, but for the first few minutes after she heard the story Hester wondered if there could be some connection. Kirov had mentioned to Hester a purpose in bringing prisoners to Taunton, but he had only begun these dreadful 'tasks' a year ago. Such a long delay since the gypsy's death did not argue a deep interest in the gypsy.

125

Before her recent experiences Hester, like most law-abiding citizens, would have wasted few thoughts on the fate of a gypsy woman, who was doubtless guilty, awaiting trial. Now, she thought the betrayal in Lord Stamsbury's garden was repugnant, even if the gypsy woman had been guilty. And suppose she had been innocent! Judging by Hester's own experience, it was entirely possible.

But her imagination was overworking. After all, there were more than a few gypsy bands in England and Ireland.

By the time she had shared these women's discomforts for twenty-four hours and heard the humorous, seldom bitter tales of the life that brought them here to trial, she felt she had a greater understanding of human nature. She began to lose her judgmental attitude toward them, and a sense of comradeship replaced her first revulsion and pity.

They would not have understood pity in any case. They seemed to despise its outward manifestations.

In the warm autumn afternoon she borrowed the three-legged stool and looked out at the jungle of alleys called 'ways' or even 'streets'. Buildings so old they must be medieval lined the two noisome alleys she could see, though the stench of those alleys forced her to turn away and breathe the fetid but now familiar odour of the Holding Cells.

Those women who weren't walking in circles for exercise or to relieve the monotony, watched and laughed at her. She asked them, "How is it that this place doesn't smell as bad – not quite – as those alleys and buildings out there?"

"'Cause we takes out our slops," one of the younger

126

girls explained. "Takes our turn proper-like. We gets thrupence. It helps out. The guard goes with us, so we can't get away. But no matter, I go up for trial next week."

"And meanwhile, you throw our slops in the alley," Hester guessed.

When the girl said "Sure and where else?" she had to laugh. Even Angele, that dangerous little beauty, laughed with her. It was only later that Hester saw Angele making hand movements back and forth with something that sparkled in the light of the night lantern.

Angele was sharpening the broken point of a soldier's bayonet against an uneven stone in the wall. Her action sent off sparks and made her cough.

Bess Camber whispered to Hester, "When she's at that she's feelin' bad."

Hester stared at the shining steel point in the girl's hands with a kind of fascination. She thought, I'm gaining an education here that I never got at Mama's knee, and she remembered Charles Willoughby's ambition to help all such 'creatures'. How kind and dear he had been to her! If she ever was released from here, one way or another, she would devote her life to Sir Charles' work.

Charles Willoughby was a great man. She had felt warm and comfortable with him. How different from the dangerous excitement in Colonel Kirov that she had scarcely acknowledged to herself!

She shook her head at the memory. He was as much responsible for her incarceration as the loathsome Sylvester Girard. He had hunted her down after her first attempt at escape and deliberately seen to it that there was no second attempt; yet he knew what Girard had tried to do to her at the inn on the High Road. Surely that had shown him she was telling the truth.

He was a ruthless and treacherous man and she would very likely never see him again. She hoped she would not.

Chapter Ten

At first, she had counted the hours. She would not admit it to her companions but secretly she based her hopes on Lady Pomfret who must have bribed someone by this time. After the first twenty-four hours she counted by days, marking them off with splinters from the stall she shared with Bess Camber and Old Sarey.

On the second day, following the careful advice and assistance of her companions, Hester bargained with the young Day Guard for another straw pallet, two straw pillows and, most importantly, four spoons, one of which was a stained but serviceable pewter utensil. For the moment this ended the disagreeable habit of drawing straws to see who first used the available spoons for the meal.

By this time Hester would have given a good deal to sleep in a bed with a coverlet and a comfortable pillow, but she was able to bask briefly in her popularity with the women. It was well to make what she could out of it, since her popularity was soon exceeded by that of the not-quite-angelic Angele.

Although the covetous young guard, Matthew Griggs, always tried to squeeze every farthing out of the women, they received one benefit after he ordered Angele out into the audience chamber on the pretense of questioning her about the women's food. The interview took a surprisingly long time. Hester supposed some women would find the stick-thin, sharp-featured Griggs attractive, despite his greed. Clearly, Angele did. She winked at the women as the door screeched open and Hester suspected she had sold the only valuable thing she possessed: her starved, bony, ill-used little body.

When she returned, swinging a dusty bottle, all the eleven remaining females were treated to a swallow of rum. Its fire warmed Hester as it warmed the others and some of the younger women began to dance. It was a jig but not a dance that would have been recognized by London's *haut monde*. However, Seaman Patterson, coming on duty at that minute, peered in through the grilled door and clapped his hands in time to a sailor's dance he knew well.

Two of the women were Dissenters up on false charges, according to the rumour. For that or other reasons they were not popular. They remembered that this was the Sabbath and tried to stop the dancers who were full of high spirits. The ensuing mêlée brought Seaman Patterson directly into the cells to settle the matter, much to his own dismay. Having put an end to the frolicking for the night, he apologized to one and all and retired, turning the key in the lock with its usual grating protest.

The first few nights had not given Hester very much sleep. Bess kept her own place under an ancient night robe someone had given her on departing from the group. But Old Sarey, asleep or awake, persisted in dragging the straw pallet to herself, which left Hester cold and shivering, with straw twigs sticking into her hair like dozens of small darts.

She tried to prolong the hours before sleep and almost

130

looked forward to the time when it became her turn to carry out the slop bucket just before all the lights were snuffed except the lamps in the Audience Chamber.

She hoped her own trip to Slop Alley would occur on the watch of the good-hearted seaman, Patterson Pattridge. It was too much to expect. Matthew Griggs was on duty for the following three nights and called her out just as Old Sarey was creeping across the floor, intending to establish herself over the width of Hester's pallet.

Bess Camber had been tying rags around some strands of her hair in the hope of bringing back its once familiar curl. At sight of Sarey, she kicked her on her terribly skinny buttock, warning her,

"That an't your property. You know better. Leave it be or you'll get what you didn't bargain for."

Matthew Griggs made no attempt to stop this pretty little squabble and it was still going on when Hester started up the steps carrying in one hand the bucket with its foul stench and in the other arm the empty water jar.

Bess, her friend, defending her property. . . .

Strange, how close she felt to Bess and the others. Except for her mother, she had never felt this closeness to any human being, not even her father or Lady Pomfret.

It was the desperate necessity of sharing that brought her close to these women.

She could hear Matthew Griggs' booted footsteps grating on the steps behind her. He was closer now and she hurried on up to the wider corridor on the ground floor. She had seen it before, the night Colonel Kirov took her up to that dreadful antechamber with its wretched creatures waiting. Like Hester Leland: no better, no worse.

That child of twelve or so must have been hanged by

now. He had been so terribly frightened. She understood that boy all too well.

"You! To the left."

Griggs nudged her hard between her shoulder blades with his knotted fist.

For a minute she couldn't find the door. It was within an alcove which ended the main corridor. She set down the slop pail and tried to slide back the bolt of the inset door. Griggs reached over her head, pushed open the door and shoved her into the fetid darkness, a passage faintly lighted by a barred aperture above the alley door, at the far end of the snake-like tunnel.

The little passage smelled abominable and Griggs said, "Hurry! You'll not be stayin' the night through, surely."

She said nothing. It was all she could do to keep from retching. He made his way ahead of her, unlocking the alley door and standing aside. In the moonlight the alley was crisscrossed with shadows made by a church spire, distant trees and heavy, medieval buildings surrounding the alley.

Hester guessed at the outlines of the pistol under the guard's jacket before he tapped his jacket, warning her,

"Try for a run, mistress. This here pistol's got a ball to blow a nasty hole. Try me."

She ignored him, staggering a little as she gave the pail to the hunched old man who had limped across the rough stones to receive the pail and exchange it for an empty one.

Griggs bellowed, "Bring it with you. Are you daft?"

The old man stared at her through rheumy eyes, only half-seeing her, but he exchanged the pails for her. It seemed to be a temporary arrangement, used only while the old law courts and great trial chambers in another part of the city were under repair.

She wasn't sure where to find the all-important water to fill the big pitcher for the women of the Cells and swung around in confusion.

Griggs strode over to a dark corner where the building formed right angles with what appeared to be chambers for men of law working late. She could see the lights glow and flicker in several chambers above the alley.

She found the water tap finally, wondering if the water running continuously into a shallow basin of stone was fit to drink. Apparently, the water did no harm to a scruffy cat who lapped from the pool before padding silently away.

"Come along," Griggs ordered her before she had finished her work. She waited a minute longer until the jar was full and then carried it to the dim passage he called the Slop Tunnel.

Blinking, she made her way toward the door leading into the ground floor corridor. She heard Griggs behind her and moved faster, wishing she had not been hampered by the heavy jar and the empty slop pail the old man had given her.

She felt Griggs' breath, hot and revolting against her cheek before his hands prowled their way around her waist. His fingers began to explore her breasts and then moved downward over her abdomen.

He whispered, "We'll have a bit of fun-like, eh, Hester. They'll never miss us for an hour."

This tunnel-like passage was no place for her to attempt a struggle but she knew she would scream if he ran his hands over her groin again. She stopped so suddenly he ran into her.

"This is heavy, sir. I can't hold it. I don't want to drop it on your feet."

He grunted and reached around her to open the door. She hurried through and started down the steps. By the time she reached the lighted area called the audience chamber and he caught up with her, two women were looking out through the barred opening in the door.

"Look at the bastard, tryin' his tricks with our Leel," Bess called out.

Angele's unexpectedly deep voice added, "You're a fickle one, Matt. Thought you'd cross me. It'll cost you more next time."

He pretended to ignore them but Hester suspected he was a bit discomfited. When he unlocked the door she rushed in, spilling some of the water and dropping the empty slop bucket. She had never thought she would welcome the closing of that noisy cell door.

When the women crowded around her, wanting to know how far Griggs had gone with her, Hester was too ashamed to describe it or make a joke as she should have done.

Next time, she decided, if I have to, I'll throw the slops on him.

As she tried to rest on the pallet that night she remembered once more whom she had to thank for bringing her to this abject humiliation: Girard, Kirov, and Sir Giles.

Several mornings after Angele earned the rum for her companions. Hester awoke at dawn as usual, half-frozen and almost ready to do battle for a share of the pallet and her own travel cloak. Before she made an audible protest she was distracted by motions from one of the women at the far end of the room.

134

This area directly beneath the barred window above the alleys was much sought after by day for its sunlight. By night it was shunned as the coldest area in the Cells. The girl standing on the stool in her thin dress as plain as a shift, was Angele.

What she wanted Hester could not imagine. They had never been friends or confidantes the way she was beginning to regard Bess Camber, the first woman to welcome her from the barred opening in the door.

Hester removed herself as quietly as possible from her companions and, carefully stepping over the recumbent bodies, she finally reached Angele whose dark eyes burned feverishly with excitement.

When Hester started to question her Angele put a finger to her pale but still sensuous lips. The finger looked transparent in its fragility. She whispered, "My Jamie, he won't let me die in the cells. I'm to go up to trial."

Hester was alarmed. She understood the girl's haste. There were already tiny flecks of blood on her gown and her intermittent cough wracked her body. Violent exertion might kill Angele before she ever reached the outside.

"Can you succeed? You must take care."

Angele smiled. "Why d'ye think I give that bastard Matthew Griggs my time? He's in the plan. Thinks I'm to wait for 'im on the outside. Some hovel he owns. You know how many others he's had from this hellhole? He give 'em rum or Blue Ruin. They give 'im what 'e wants."

She read Hester's revulsion in her face and snapped, "Who else they gonna give it to? I've got Gentleman Jamie. Most of 'em got nobody."

"Why do you tell me?" Hester whispered. "Am I to help you? What do you wish done?"

Angele exhaled impatiently. "How stupid you are! You are to go with me. The money for the bribe to Griggs belongs to a great lady that knows you."

"But I have no—" Then Hester remembered. Of course. This wild and dangerous plan was the brain-child of Lady Pomfret. It sounded exactly like her. Hester wanted to laugh at the fantastic scheme but refrained out of compassion for the desperate Angele.

The girl must have guessed her thoughts. She leaned nearer. "My Jamie tells me it's settled about you. The bloody jeweller is in Taunton. He accused you of theft and an attack on him when he brought you back to 'is shop. You're for it, Leel." She pointed to Hester's throat with her cold finger.

Hester flinched. The horror of her fate flashed before her eyes.

Best to try for an escape. The brain of Gentleman Jamie the Highwayman and the golden guineas of Lady Pomfret were her only hope. Perhaps they would even save her life. A highwayman ought to be the equal of her Ladyship and restrain her wilder impulses. It wasn't as though this place was London's Newgate Prison from where it would be impossible to escape without spies reporting every step of the way.

"You're with us?" Angele's hoarse voice revealed nervousness for the first time.

Hester suspected that this personal interest in her as a flight companion was based on the money that would be furnished, undoubtedly by Lady Pomfret, but she admitted, "I think I must join you. When?"

Tilda Clavering, one of the women on a pad near them, sat up slowly. The morning light had not touched her yet and in the grey dawn she appeared to be a phantom.

"What're ye sayin' that takes whispers?"

She was a spiteful young woman, hardly twenty, very proud of her auburn hair and rather pretty in a petulant way. Her youth and good looks made Tilda a natural rival for the dark-eyed Angele whom she detested. The feeling was reciprocated, although Tilda had been warned not to antagonize the dangerous Angele.

Hester cut in hurriedly, seeing the violence begin to creep over Angele's sensitive features.

"We are going to deal for more mutton in the stew. Angele thinks I offer too much."

Tilda preened herself, fluffing up her hair which she combed with her fingers.

"Why not? What she gives ain't worth the difference."

Angele's hand was wandering behind her under the straw pallet and in desperation Hester drew Tilda Clavering away, as if to give themselves privacy. She had already decided to gamble upon the planned escape, and wanted nothing to interfere with it. She spoke to Tilda in an undervoice that was, nevertheless, audible to Angele.

"Say nothing. It's a secret."

"Ay. You may count on me."

Hester would certainly have doubted that, but she confided, "She's learned there is no help for it. She will die."

Tilda shrugged. She had hoped for more exciting news. "So will we all. One more pocket I slit and I'm for it as well. But I'll be out afore that time. I've a friend on the outside. He's bribed the dog that charged me."

She moved away, having lost interest in Hester.

Meanwhile, the highwayman's girl relaxed, as did several others who heard the volcanic rumble behind

Angele's paroxysm of coughing. After a few minutes however, Angele found her glittering piece of bayonet steel and stuck it back into a tear she had made at the waist of her gown.

Bess Camber, who was used to being in her new friend's confidence, wondered at Hester's silence that day.

"An't you joinin' us ladies on our little stroll? Warms up yer insides."

"I should, I know. But I feel so discouraged. There is a story circulating that the accursed jeweller has brought new evidence against me. It seems—", she pretended to laugh off her dread, "it seems my fate is already decided."

"Rubbish, nobody's fate is decided afore you go to the jury. You might plead your belly. That's worked afore. Just lay with Matthew Griggs once. There's females I know who've put off the hangman for years by that plea. I'm thinkin' of usin' it myself if things go ill with me."

Hester began to laugh in earnest.

"I don't know which is the worst. Matthew Griggs with all those little teeth, or the public hangman."

Bess was philosophical. "At the least, Young Matt's more private. It's all them eyes watchin' that I hate about hangin' Nothin' like that with Griggs. He's got a nice little mattress in the slop passage off the ground floor."

This brought on Hester's second fit of laughter but she got up and began to walk in a line of twos with most of the other women. The exercise at least stretched her muscles.

She still had no awareness of what the escape would entail or when it would occur, but she feared the worst when Angele went off obediently with Matthrew Briggs that afternoon and came back to wink at Hester.

Shortly afterward, Angele called her over to the barred window opening on the alleys. Her pretext was the necessity of pointing out a different point where the women would meet the old man with the slop wagon the next time they were sent out.

"It's for tonight."

"Oh, God!"

"You're not cowardin' out?"

"No. And don't keep handling that weapon. I know you won't use it. We're too close to escaping."

Angele grinned. "And Jamie needs your money."

Hester had no doubt this was true. She would not jeopardize their chances by arguing about it. Angele looked her worst and Hester could only hope she felt better than she looked.

Chapter Eleven

The afternoon turned cloudy with fog rolling in from the Bristol Channel and depressing the women of the Cells. The only hope for a cheerful mood in this area was the light from the barred window onto the alleys. When the sunlight failed, as it often did, there was a perpetual twilight in the Cells.

Worst of all, Angele began to cough, the deep, terrible noise that acted on the women's nerves and made some of them yell at her. She seemed to delight in disturbing them.

Hester said nothing. Over and over again she examined what remained of her own property in the portmanteau, taking out small items that she would want to keep.

Since she would undoubtedly be searched sometime during her presumed emptying of the slops and filling of the pitcher with fresh drinking water, she knew she could save very little of her treasures beyond miniatures of her father and mother, and what remained of her money. However, the rest, the clothing, the small bits of jewellery, the ribbons and other decorating objects seemed to be worth something to the women who remained behind. If nothing else, they would be bargaining objects that would give Bess, Old Sarey and the others a few small comforts.

The clothing, though attractive, was hardly practical in the Holding Cells. All the same, she was sure there would be quarrels over who was entitled to some of the delicate gowns, the shifts, hosiery and shoes.

A guinea and some silver remained after she had bargained recently for items and food upon the advice of her new-found friends. Heaven knew what the women would purchase from the guards out of the guinea-piece.

By the time the evening meal of soured fish and turnips was left for them and the women passed out their new spoons with which to eat, Hester devoutly hoped she was ready for whatever nerve-wracking dangers were to come. She certainly had no appetite for stinking fish and mouldy turnips, but even if the food had been equal to that prepared at Lady Pomfret's home, she was far too nervous to eat.

Patterson, the ex-seaman, had been on duty during the day and was replaced at darkness by the small, less athletic Matthew Griggs. Aside from the fact that Griggs had been bribed to take his part in the escape, Hester was glad Patterson had not become involved. His comments to Hester on the night he brought her to the Cells had given her a genuine sympathy for him and she didn't want him involved in anything dangerous. He would be sure to lose his post and that meant everything to him.

Late in the evening when the women were curling up on their pallets or mattresses, in whatever garments they owned to keep out the cold, Griggs came to the door and called for Angele. The women still up exchanged all-knowing glances and nods as Angele, coughing a little, made her way between the little groups of women after one quick look at Hester.

Tilda Clavering had been standing behind the door

142

hoping to eavesdrop on Griggs and Angele as they went up the steps. The door opened with a bang, hitting Tilda who shrieked, "Yer a bloody bastard, you and the bitch yer huddlin' with!"

The women trying to sleep told her to "keep her clapper shut!" Hester's own sympathy for her vanished when she saw that the woman rubbed the wrong arm during her complaint. Still, Hester knew the woman might make trouble and tried to show her the good side of Angele's summons.

"Perhaps there will be more rum for us all."

"Likely! I make no doubt the witch is up there now, beggin' Griggs to get her out of here."

Guiltily, and nervous because she was guilty, Hester tried to lead her away from the subject by asking questions about the water pitcher she was to take out tonight with the slops.

Almost too soon Griggs came running down the steps, much faster than he usually moved. Before reaching the barred door he bellowed, "You, Leland, get your pitcher and slops. I'll be needing your help on the way. The other one is took sick."

While the rest of the women stirred, grumbled and complained, Tilda Clavering gave a raucous laugh.

"I could've told you. Try me, Griggs. I'm a deal warmer, innards and out."

Griggs moved her out of his way with one sharp elbow and motioned for Hester to go out into the Audience Chamber before him. He clanged the door shut behind her, locked it and hung the ring of keys on a peg in the alcove beyond the chamber.

The load Hester carried in her two hands was as clumsy as it had been the first time. The slops smelled dreadful as

143

usual. She was glad to be busy at this work, all the same. It kept her from worrying about just how their flight would be handled.

Matthew Griggs bounded up the stone steps so rapidly she could scarcely keep in front of him.

"Where is Angele?"

He did not answer.

At the point where the steps ended at the ground floor corridor Hester remembered the flight of steps she and Kirov had taken up to the Magistrate's antechamber. Across the main corridor on this floor was a room no larger than a powdering closet.

Griggs muttered, "Take care, someone coming. I'll stop 'em. This'll cost her precious highwayman extra."

"Yes, yes, hurry!"

She dropped the slop pail in a corner beyond the door of the little room. She had barely reached the room and closed the door when she recognized one of the voices as two men approached the ground floor corridor: it was Sir Charles Willoughby.

Was he here on her account? How good of him! Far kinder than she deserved, running away from his house without even a word of explanation.

"I cannot believe a respectable young female will be found guilty when the theft was not consciously committed. I'd stake my life she pocketed the emerald by accident, anxious to escape that wretched jeweller's attentions."

"My dear fellow, we can make no allowances for High Theft committed in such circumstances. Every thief in the country would rely upon the excuse." That would be Sir Giles Cartaret. Hester gritted her teeth.

He persisted with a pleasant, theatrical sigh. "Hanging

young females is always a carnival for the bloodthirsty. I should prefer that such matters be conducted in private . . . Griggs! What the devil are you about? You should be below, watching over your charges."

"One of 'em's ill, sir. I was looking to find a syrup of some sort. Her coughing disturbs the women."

"Good God! Not Miss Leland!"

It warmed Hester to hear the concern in Charles Willoughby's voice.

"No, sir. The highwayman's doxy."

"A pity," Sir Giles Cartaret remarked. "She was formerely an actress before Gentleman Jamie took a fancy to her. Another bound for the executioner's cart. Not tried yet, but murder is involved, on the Bristol Mail. Well, Sir Charles, I'll bid you a goodnight. I wish you well in your efforts to help these women, and I know you will pursue the case of this Leland female. Nevertheless, I am afraid the evidence is against her."

Near the door Hester could hear Charles take a deep breath. He said unhappily, "I fear so. But I shall not give up my efforts, you may be sure, Your Excellency. I will not permit Miss Leland to be hanged, even if I must plead for her in London. Or before Prinny himself."

"Admirable sentiments." The Magistrate directed him then, "You will find your way to the front of the building straight ahead. Best bundle up, it's brisk outside."

Their voices faded, and Griggs opened the door to Hester.

"Come along. The woman is across this corridor. In the passage to Slop Alley. She may be dying."

So it had not been a ruse. Angele really was more ill than usual.

"You should never have left her."

145

He shook his head at her stupidity. Then, with an effort he forced open the heavy oaken door. Hester picked up the slop pail and hurried into the passage before him. An outpouring of icy air met her and she gasped for breath. How could Angele exist ten minutes in such a place? It was colder than it had been last week.

Hester could hear her companion now. Each racking breath Angele took was loud and painful. Hester hurried through the stone passage, following Angele's sounds. The sick woman was huddled forward, clutching her bare knees, no longer coughing but trying to pull each breath out to sustain her.

"Can you carry her?" Hester asked Matthew Griggs, who pushed ahead of her and took a stance with his back to a narrow door. This must open onto the alley and freedom. Dim and ghostly starlight managed to illuminate the passage to a certain extent. Above the alley door was an opening to the outside, perhaps for ventilation. As usual, the passage smelled of excrement. Either the guards used this place for a water closet or the women who carried the slop pails sometimes emptied them here to avoid the even colder regions of the alley.

Angele's skeletal fingers picked at Hester's sleeve.

"Don't let me die here. Promise? Get me out to my Jamie. Promise?"

"Don't worry, we'll get you to him." Hester felt that she would do it or die in the attempt. All she had seen in the last few days made her determined to outwit the callous, archaic laws of this place. One way was to free Angele so she could die in her lover's arms.

Hester looked up at the guard. For some reason he had folded his arms and seemed to regard the two women with something like amusement. This was a new complication – he intended to demand the extra payment he had mentioned.

"It's worth a deal more than five hundred guineas, this business. I'll have a knock on the head and no job beside all else."

"You can live a lifetime on five hundred guineas," she reminded him, raising her voice. "Open the door!"

With Hester's aid and breathing painfully, Angele got to her feet, giddy with the effort. Frail as she was, Hester found her a dead weight and difficult to move, but the two women stumbled toward the door and its sly guardian.

He put out one hand to stop them and suddenly Hester saw the bayonet steel in Angele's palm. Where she got the strength for that threatening hand Hester could not imagine. There would never be any hope for them if it came to murder.

She cried, "No! Not that way."

With her left hand still clutching Hester's arm Angele kept staring hard up into Matthew Griggs' eyes.

"Open the door." She raised her voice. "Jamie!"

Griggs expected violence but he obviously did not expect the two men who thrust their bodies against the door. The door broke away from one hinge. They pushed it aside, knocking down Griggs who fell on one buttock, momentarily breathless.

Hester saw that their rescuers were both dressed like sheepmen, in rough lambs' wool jerkins. Judging by Angele's reaction the huge fellow with the friendly, almost boyish face and flat nose was the celebrated Gentleman Jamie. Their other rescuer had a full head of the grey-white hair of an older man. He moved toward Hester with a catlike tread and while she tried to make out his features in the shadows beyond the starlight, action was occurring beside her.

The guard recovered his senses and began to pursue the old argument.

"It's worth a thousand guineas. I already broke my bloody back."

"Another time," Gentleman Jamie said.

Angele was choking over a cough and he started to lift her. At the same time Matthew Griggs said steadily, "Now". He had one hand in his jacket, and Angele broke from her lover, the bayonet end in her palm, her arm raised to strike at Griggs. At the same moment the explosion of his big pistol shook them all.

The older man behind Hester leaped for Griggs, the heel of his hand catching Griggs in a chopping motion across the side of his neck. Griggs collapsed unconscious, his pistol falling.

Angele was slumped against her lover. The bayonet dropped from her palm which was bloodstained where she had gripped the sharp edges of the blade. Hester knelt beside the girl and her highwayman lover. The pistol ball had evidently struck Angele's breastbone. Hester cried, "Give me a kerchief, anything, to stop the bleeding."

Gentleman Jamie raised the girl's lolling head to his shoulder.

"No use, I know them wounds. Come, Sweeting, you're not dying in this hellhole."

Angele could not hold her head up. The blood welled from her breast in dark spurts. Her huge, black eyes appeared to see nothing, but she heard him. Her unstained hand tried to reach for his face.

"Get her into the cart," the white-haired man ordered Jamie. Meanwhile, he scooped up the protesting Hester.

148

"We've no time to lose, they must have heard the shot."

There were sounds somewhere, running feet. Hester became silent, staring up at her rescuer. Nothing familiar in that white-haired old man, but she could not mistake the voice. The wig might have fooled her, but now she knew it was Colonel Kirov.

As the confusion grew general in the corridor they had quitted only minutes ago, Kirov threw her over his shoulder like a sack of meal and made a run for the broken door with Gentleman Jamie carrying Angele behind him.

Hester had been hopeful that her rescuer might be Sir Charles, who showed every evidence of wishing to save her when he discussed her with Sir Giles. But this man was one of the three she could never forgive. He was Colonel Kirov, the man who had been responsible for the worst horrors of her life.

Chapter Twelve

A slop cart and horse were pulled up in the dark angle made by the building and an addition being readied for the chambers of the law clerks and junior examiners. In Hester's ridiculous position the night world looked topsy-turvy but a patient horse was certainly waiting there to help them in their escape. He whinnied at the sound of Gentleman Jamie's running footsteps.

Kirov dropped Hester into the light cart, too busy to make allowance for bruises and battering. He swung up on the box and took the reins. In her confusion Hester could not imagine why the Russian risked hanging in order to save a woman whom he had delivered to her fate with a shrug and complete indifference. There must be another motive, monetary perhaps.

If Colonel Kirov had given her a comforting smile or even offered her his hand days ago when she stumbled as the guard Patterson led her away, she might have understood this escape attempt now.

In the cart Hester found Jamie beside her, with Angele a slight burden huddled within his arms, her face pressed against his chest. Then the horse and cart jerked into motion, moving off at a surprising pace, and urged on by a rifle shot from the doorway of the slops passage.

While the single guard reloaded, the horse galloped out

of range, around a corner, into another alley and onward, past a long wall festooned with ivy. There were trees inside the garden, growing close to the wall, some with the branches hanging over the little unpaved square of ground that was like a *cul de sac* with no way out.

The situation reminded Hester of something she had almost forgotten. A gypsy woman running away, betrayed to her death long ago by the owner of that garden, Lord Stamsbury, or his wife, or one of their guests.

Beside Hester the highwayman straightened up slowly, calling to Colonel Kirov.

"Take care with the sharp turn to the left. There's a river nearby."

Kirov seemed not to hear his suggestion.

Hester touched Angele gently and took up the girl's wrist, remembering the heavy feel of her own father's flesh before she realized he was dead. Though she had never been Angele's close friend, she experienced again a desolation at the discovery that death could so instantly follow on vibrant life.

Gentleman Jamie turned back to Hester. She could only see the vague outlines of his face in the fog. She said, "I'm sorry. She is gone."

He nodded. "But she didn't die in that hole. She'll be pleased at that."

"I am sure she will be."

Kirov paid no attention to them. He brought the horse up sharp. When Hester looked around she was astonished to see a coach and four belonging to Lady Pomfret pulled up in the heavy shadow of a church tower.

So the explanation was simple, after all. Lady Pomfret,

her only friend, had bribed the Russian and the highway-man to save Hester. Was there ever a better friend than Jerusha Pomfret?

Within a few seconds an agile youth had hopped up onto the box beside the colonel. Kirov leaped to the ground, groped for Hester and lifted her out of the cart.

Tugged along by his iron grip she stumbled after him across the ground to the coach, hardly knowing what she did.

Gentleman Jamie followed, carrying Angele's body wrapped in his travel cloak.

"Should have left her," he apologized. "But I couldn't. Not 'til she's got a decent burial. In the ground like."

Kirov said, "Get in." He explained to the anxious Hester, "Her Ladyship's Joshua is the coachman. Jamie and I will be your footmen. Put on one of the furred capes you will find there and cover your hair."

Weary, aching, still icy with the dread of recapture, Hester nodded and got into the coach. She had scarcely settled herself with Angele lying shrouded at her feet when Lady Pomfret's horses set off. She had no notion what would happen next. She could see that both the highwayman and Kirov now looked fairly respectable in the black and red upper livery of the Pomfret Estates.

Hester tried to concentrate on what must be done as the old coach bounced from side to side. On the seat beside her lay the ermine-trimmed hood and cloak. She raised the hood over her hair and wrapped her body in the folds of the black velvet evening cloak.

After that she could think of nothing left to her and the others but urgent prayer.

It seemed only seconds but was undoubtedly longer when she first heard the hoofbeats pounding hard on the road behind them. She tried to look out but Angele's body lay across her feet and she did not like to move it aside as though the dead girl were a bundle of dirty clothing.

If their pursuers were after the escaped women, Hester could only hope they had not been among the guards of the Cells. They would certainly recognize her.

She heard Lady Pomfret's coachman shout a warning curse at his flying team and they drew up short, jolting Hester until the body on the coach floor rolled over upon her feet. She reached down and with shaking fingers covered Angele's body again.

Staring at the covered body she tried not to think of her fate, nor that of her rescuers, if she was recaptured. And what of the women she had left behind in that gloomy prison? Half an hour ago Angele had been alive. At this minute Bess and Old Sarey and Tilda and the rest must be trying to sleep with no thought for what the ominous morning might bring.

Several horsemen signalled Joshua, rode up to the coachman, then retreated to both sides of the coach. With her nervous hands buried in the many velvet folds of Lady Pomfret's cloak she waited for her two 'footmen' to open the coach door. Neither Kirov nor the highwayman let down the coach steps for her. She was evidently expected to play the elegant aristocrat and remain inside the coach.

She leaned toward them with as much cool arrogance as she could muster.

"Yes, what is your business with me?"

Colonel Kirov, in his livery and the grey, wispy wig, bowed to Hester and made the introductions.

"Milady, these men are on the King's Service. Searching for felons who have escaped from detention while they wait their trials."

Hester's pale eyebrows raised.

"Very well, then. Let them be on their way."

The men exchanged uneasy glances. The King's Justice might very well be a social acquaintance of 'her Ladyship'.

"Ay, ma'am," one of the younger men objected carefully. "Might we be inquirin' why your Ladyship is a-travellin' with no carriage lamps lighted?"

Kirov started to speak but Hester had already begun, trying not to make her explanation sound anxious.

"Certainly, you may inquire. We have had an accident to our lamps, thanks to some of your wretched children tossing pebbles at them. If you don't wish your children to add to the prison population, I advise you to train them better."

Kirov looked so surprised Hester, took care not to glance at him again for fear she would laugh. She was just congratulating herself on their escape when a fourth man rode up, a big, sturdy man with rough but not unattractive features. She closed her eyes momentarily, wondering how fate could be so cruel.

The man was Patterson, the ex-seaman wounded off Trafalgar. She tried to shift backward surreptitiously into the darkness of the coach's interior, while repeating in a deeper, authoritative voice,

"I am Jerusha, Lady Pomfret, on my way home to Queen's Square in Bath. You have more business with me?"

"No, y'Ladyship," the youngest rider denied, a little nervous himself. "That is to say—"

"Lady Pomfret?" Patterson urged his mount closer. Hester saw Kirov's hand move to his back for a weapon. Then, just as she gave up all hope, Patterson repeated

155

her supposed name without inflection. He had looked squarely into her face.

"Sorry to 'ave give you the trouble, your Ladyship. Many thanks." He backed his mount and started on, his horse soon getting up speed to a gallop. Bless him!

The other horsemen followed him rapidly, and Kirov gazed up at Hester with genuine admiration.

"Bravo, Lady Pomfret, well played."

"Gad's life, but that was fine doin', ma'am," Gentleman Jamie congratulated her. "I'd be proud you was to join our lads on the High Road any night."

Her Ladyship's coachman had once escaped the noose himself, as Hester well knew, and he too peered around from his box to add his congratulations. Hester, while accepting all this praise, knew quite well that the real saviour of the situation was seaman Patterson who might have betrayed her but refrained.

She would never know what impulse caused him to deny her real identity, and nothing she could do would ever properly repay him.

In the meanwhile she would learn to be grateful to Colonel Kirov. He too had very nearly sacrificed his life for her. She realized that Lady Pomfret's money probably was an inducement, but the danger had been there, all the same. She must forget her hatred and bitterness toward him, that dreadful mistake of putting him into the same vile group as Sylvester Girard and Sir Giles Cartaret.

What other reason but money from Lady Pomfret, and perhaps the goodness of his heart, would he have for risking so much?

Kirov and Gentleman Jamie went back to their posts and Joshua gave the order to his team to proceed.

They had just travelled beyond the town and its

environs when the coachman turned off into a rutted lane, then east again along a narrow estate road which curved past the west portal of a weathered red brick manor house. The outlines of the house were barely visible in the fog. A double line of trees enclosed the estate road in darkness and the coachman was forced to slow his horses as they made their way over ground paved with wet leaves and the debris of autumn.

Before reaching the house itself Joshua pulled up in the shadow of a tree and waited. Nobody moved. After shifting the dead girl's body off her instep and gently covering her face again, Hester opened the carriage door and looked out.

During nearly a minute of heart-stopping tension she heard what had not escaped the coachman or Kirov and Gentleman Jamie. They were on the back of the coach and closer to the side road over which the horsemen pelted before wheeling around at the point where the estate road broke away toward the east.

"Dear God, what next can happen to us?" Hester wondered. She held her breath.

The horsemen hesitated, arguing, but one of them seemed to win the discussion. They all followed him back to the High Road slowly, discouraged. Even their horses, in profile, looked downcast. Hester wondered if the man whose actions swayed them was Patterson, who had proven her friend on the High Road.

Evidently, the danger was gone for the moment, and Hester shifted her position. Sleeping on the straw pallet, when it hadn't wended its way to Old Sarey, usually left her with a backache the next morning. Now the toe of her dusty, black morocco slipper struck something soft on the floor.

Not Angele's face! She apologized silently and moved away from that slight, cold bundle. She heard Colonel Kirov call to the coachman,

"Now hurry, they may return."

Joshua needed no second warning. Under his signal the horses jerked the coach forward and Hester was thrown back and forth, barely catching herself before she fell on top of the dead girl.

Within minutes the coach and team drew around in front of the two-and-a-half storey house with its brick west face that must be warm and welcome when the lamps were lighted in the many windows.

The team did not stop at the west door but, following Joshua's order, kept on around the north side and then along the back of the house toward the stables. Before they reached their destination Colonel Kirov leapt off, still in the Pomfret livery with the absurd white wig, and the coach halted. Hester could hear a rooster crow, fooled into thinking it was dawn. Kirov opened the carriage door.

"Quickly. The servants are reliable but there may be men in the fields, sheepmen or wanderers. I'll carry you."

"Certainly not. I may be a felon but I'm no invalid."

Nevertheless, it was humiliating when the steps were let down and she found herself shaking too much to descend without his help.

As the fog shifted and the rising moonlight illuminated the ground, she saw his eyes and guessed he was amused by her independence. After the events of the past several weeks few things seemed less amusing to her.

Lamps flickered on the upper floor but the ground floor appeared to be dark. To Hester's surprise Kirov pushed open a narrow door beyond the herb garden. The garden looked ill-tended in the rising moonlight.

"We will go through the still room," Kirov explained as he took her hand and led her in. "Follow me. The fewer lights, the better."

"But the other one, Angele."

"Jamie is taking her with him. His stallion is in the shed beyond the stables."

Hester looked back. Strange that she should feel deeply for a girl she had scarcely known. The horror she had shared with them seemed to make her a friend to all those women, even the vixenish Tilda Clavering.

"Goodbye, friend," she thought and then made her way into the darkness of the still room, past bottles, barrels and shelves, most of the latter empty. Colonel Kirov seemed to have cat's eyes, as he saw in the dark.

He opened a door at the far end of the room and a lamp somewhere caught Hester and Kirov in its dim light. He closed the door behind them at once and she realized they were still in great danger. Nobody must see her from outside.

This persistent danger further ruined her nerves. Was there no end to it?

A gruff, welcoming voice greeted her almost before she noted the small, elegant red and gold salon or the rangy female carrying an oil lamp. Lady Pomfret held her lamp high.

"Ah! That is better. You're a man of your word, Colonel. You got her out safely."

Kirov grinned.

"We may thank your highwayman friend for that. Your Ladyship has a wide acquaintance among the criminal class. I congratulate you."

159

Lady Pomfret was not in the least offended. She shoved the lamp into Kirov's hands and looked Hester up and down.

"That'll be Joshua's doings. He knows everyone worth knowing. . . . Really, Hester, I've never seen you look worse. You shake like a leaf. You should have had more confidence in me. Your colour is quite drained. And you – frankly, you need a hip bath, upon the instant."

It was a humiliating thought but she banished it. All was well with the world. How good it seemed to hear Jerusha Pomfret's rough good sense, her complete disregard for the polite nothings heard among the society of Brighton and Bath. Forgetting her long habit of reserve, Hester groped for her Ladyship's hands and kissed them.

This was far too much gratitude for her Ladyship who pulled her hands away quickly.

"Hoity-toity, miss. One would think I've contrived all this for you. Not at all. I need a companion, someone to hear my complaints and run my errands. Go along now, and heavens! Take that bath."

Hester forced back the tears of deep thanks and turned to Colonel Kirov. He wasn't the hero she would have preferred to rescue her, but if she could not have Sir Charles, she could at least be grateful to the man who had redeemed himself by this rescue.

"I owe you more than I can repay, sir. I don't understand any of this but I won't forget it. Am I truly safe?"

He shrugged. "If they do not search the house." He took the hand she offered and held it in his warm fingers. He added in an unexpectedly gentle voice, "All should go well now." She warmed to his smile. "Though you may not recognize yourself when we are done with you."

That sounded alarming, but no doubt he and Lady

160

Pomfret knew what they were about. Her Ladyship added, "I have leased this house for the season, but we shan't need it for that long, I trust. As for you, Colonel, you must remain here until your task is done. We will plan how best to remove Miss Leland at the first opportunity."

"Remove?" Hester echoed.

"And in quite another masquerade. The Colonel and I will see to it. Now, off with you. Molly, a hip bath for Miss Leland."

Dazed, Hester followed Lady Pomfret's pert little maidservant, Molly Agnew, up the dark staircase at the far end of the room. She turned back once, longing to know why the Russian Colonel risked so much in saving her when he had gone to all the difficulty of turning her over to Sir Giles Cartaret. She leaned over the heavy bannister.

"Thank you again, Colonel. There is nothing I can say now that would be enough."

As she started up the stairs again she heard Lady Pomfret's loud, crackling voice.

"You see, Colonel? You were mistaken. She does not dislike you."

Hester wished she could hear Kirov's reply.

Half an hour later she was certain that nothing had ever felt so deliciously satisfying as the hip bath in which she sat with her knees bent and her bared limbs dripping with hot, scented water.

The bedchamber was out of fashion, its furnishings of age-darkened oak, a huge clothes-press, a chest of linens between the dormer windows, a milord chair with solid arms and a high back, a lowboy, and the overpowering bed, heavy with crimson tester and curtains.

Young Molly continued to praise Hester's golden blonde hair which was skewered on top of her head with hair pegs and not nearly so thick or easily managed as Molly's mouse-brown hair. Hester sniffed joyfully at the Attar of Lilac that Molly passed beneath her nose. The maidservant got on very well with Hester whom she had briefly known in her Ladyship's house in Bath. Now, after Hester's experience, Molly felt they had a great deal in common.

"Well then, miss, this is better than a dreadful prison cell, I'll be bound."

"It is. I never knew how much better until I found myself there." Hester looked up curiously. "Why? Have you ever seen the inside of one?"

"Ay, that I have." She straightened her plump shoulders proudly. "None but the best for Molly Agnew. Newgate it was. I'd been had up for taking a knife to a female that had her claws in my own lad."

A month ago Hester would have been shocked, or even alarmed. Tonight she was more interested than disapproving.

"How did you escape the rope?"

"I'm a player, I am. They believed me, I'm right good. Her Ladyship, she said I'm the best when it come to playing up a part." She looked smugly satisfied. She reached for towels and when Hester had rubbed her flesh until it was pink with the exertion, Molly assured her.

"You've the body for the theatre. Nice and slender with the right curves. Ever think to join Doctor Waldenburg's Display of Living Marbles?"

"No. I don't think I ever have."

162

Molly rolled her big eyes.

"It's ever so fine. They do say that's how Lady Hamilton come up from the stewpots. And she got Lord Nelson." Molly considered. "Not but what I'd prefer to have a man with two eyes, if I'd got the choice." She held out an old-fashioned dressing gown too large for Hester but gratefully received.

Molly Agnew was brushing Hester's hair, making flattering remarks on its lustre in the candlelight when her hand paused in its long, pleasant strokes. She had almost put Hester to sleep when both women heard the same sounds: horses' hooves beating the ground along the estate road.

Hester was gripped again by icy dread. Molly dropped the brush, went to the dormer window and looked out.

"It's horsemen, miss."

Hester found it difficult to get the words out.

"How many?"

"Three. No, Four. Oh, miss! They'll not be after you?"

Hester's mouth felt dry. She had to swallow hard before she spoke. "I'm very much afraid they are."

Chapter Thirteen

Barefoot and cold, Hester looked around desperately for a hiding place. The most obvious was the clothes-press. Fully the height of a man, it would accommodate Hester. She started across the room on a run, headed toward the tall press, but was stopped by a heavy hand that certainly did not belong to Molly.

"It is the first place they will look."

Colonel Kirov was interfering again. In her half-dressed state she should have felt the proper embarrassment, but her only hope now was that his devious mind would conceive of some hiding place that would save her.

"Where, then?"

Holding her tightly against his body so there would be no chance for her to escape him, he looked over her head at Molly.

"You've prepared the bath for her Ladyship. You understand?"

"That I do, sir."

Then, without the slightest notion of what he intended, Hester let him manoeuvre her over to the heavy chest beneath the window.

"Get in." It seemed likely she would be smothered but nothing was as bad as a return to the Holding Cells. With his help she climbed in on top of several lengths of faded gold velvet that appeared to be portières.

He dragged the velvet lengths out from under her and laid them over her, warning her not to sneeze. She was on the verge of doing so, as the velvet was frightfully dusty, but she managed to stifle the impulse and lie absolutely still under a dozen layers of cloth.

Kirov thrust something between the heavy mahogany lid and the chest itself. It proved to be a heavy quill pen which, she assumed, would give her the necessary breathing space. She lay there trying to hold her breath, aware that her body grew more stiff and chilled by the minute. No matter, she might owe her life to Colonel Kirov a second time.

Vaguely, she heard Kirov giving orders to Molly Agnew. Then the room was silent.

Minutes went by. She wondered where the Colonel had gone. If he should be seen in a strong light several of the men who had worked about the chambers of Sir Giles Cartaret would certainly recognize the Russian who had escorted the female prisoner to Taunton.

They came then, at least four men, trouping up the staircase, apologizing to Lady Pomfret. The latter must have been hurriedly draped in full night regalia because one of the men begged her pardon for the third time:

"It is far too late, I grant, your Ladyship. We've no wish to interrupt you at this hour. But there is a grave possibility that the thief, Leland, may be hiding on these premises."

"Pish-tosh, sir!" That would certainly be Lady Pomfret. "I am not involved with theives and felons. I merely took this house in order to recover from the social whirl of Bath."

166

In any other situation Hester would have found this highly amusing. Bath's 'Social Whirl' had been replaced by the Prince Regent's fantastic Pavilion at Brighton, as the centre of Georgian Society. Despite its ageing elegance, Bath was fast becoming the haven of rheumatic invalids who sought a 'cure' at the well-known Baths.

The men from the prison went on along the corridor, opening and closing doors. Hester breathed deeply. She was startled then by the noise of several pitchers removed from the floor beside the hipbath and set on the lid of the mahogany chest. Molly Askew leaned close to the small open space which kept Hester from suffocating.

The girl whispered, "They just peeped into this room. They may not come in again."

Hester devoutly hoped Molly was right. She could scarcely feel any life in her limbs, and wondered if they had turned to ice.

Footsteps in the corridor made her hope against hope that the guards had gone and she could begin the difficult process of extricating herself from this mahogany coffin.

But the first voice she heard was clearly one of her pursuers.

"Ay. This is her Ladyship's bedchamber. Ewen, try the clothes-press over yonder. That's the natural place for the vixen."

Hester remembered Kirov's warning and was grateful that he had insisted.

"Rubbish!" Lady Pomfret barked. "Has it come to this, that I may not bathe in privacy?"

"No, ma'am. But we think a servant must've got her in. They'll do that. Can't trust 'em."

Her Ladyship persisted valiantly.

"I see I must have a word with the King's Magistrates

about this insolence. By Gad, I shall! Molly, have you seen a felon lurking about in any of these rooms?"

"Certainly not, ma'am. I'd be 'most dumbstruck if I had. The water for your bath seems to have cooled. Shall I fetch up some more from the kitchen?"

Lady Pomfret sighed. "If you must, you must." The girl apparently left the room and Hester heard her Ladyship address the guards in her frostiest tones. "Search where you like. But I most solemnly warn you, if one of you rascals lays a hand to my person, I shall have you all remanded to the cells and much good it may do you."

They may have been uneasy at her threats, but they went about their business, examining furniture, shifting chairs and even making a great to-do about shaking the portières at the two windows.

Hester lay in the chest stiff and unmoving, as she tried to guess what was going on around her. Inevitably, she heard the floor creak under heavy weight near where her head rested in the chest. A stream of light poured in upon the piled linings and velvet lengths as the lid of the chest was raised.

She had just time to take a deep breath as a shadow crossed the light above her and someone peered in.

A horrendous shriek from Lady Pomfret seemed to shake every bone in Hester's body. Luckily, it also startled the guard who had been about to examine the chest. Her Ladyship followed the shriek with the furious demand,

"I warn you, do not touch my bed. I will not have it contaminated by your hands."

"She's under the bed!" someone shouted.

There was a stampede across the room and Hester did not doubt that her Ladyship's piercing cry had kept the guard from examining the chest more thoroughly. The

168

guard dashed toward the big canopied bed with his companions. Lady Pomfret followed with more complaints and grim threats, but this would be played offstage, so far as Hester was concerned.

Her momentary relief at the closing of the chest faded rapidly, as the quill that supplied a faint draft of air slipped off and the chest became suffocating.

Hester tried to ration what remained of the air, barely breathing, holding each breath for endless seconds, wondering whether the searchers had left the room or were coming back to the chest again.

Thinking they must have gone, she tried to lift her arms. They resisted like dead weights. She wriggled her hands, first the thumbs, then the fingers. A prickling kind of life flowed back to her fingertips, but her little fingers remained numb. The struggle took her breath and she had to rest. She tried again, pushing the palms of her hands against the ceiling of her tomb. Her lungs felt drained.

In the darkness she drifted back and back. She was on the pallet in the Holding Cell. One of the women was trying to smother her. Not Bess or Angele, surely. Not Old Sarey? Perhaps Tilda. Or one of the others. No! They had become her friends.

Then she understood: We are all entombed. They are burying us alive. Cheaper than hanging. . . .

She could never after remember the final, desperate effort that balled her tired hands into fists, to pound on the lid of the chest.

This time she heard something. A grinding of wood on wood. They had returned – she was on her way back to a cell, this time to join the condemned. Would any of her friends be there? Angele, of course. And maybe others found guilty of High Theft and murder.

169

The grind of wood on wood ended in a roar as the lid of the chest was flung onto the carpet. Hands reached through the velvet layers, fastened around the numb flesh and lifted her out, dripping dusty materials from the chest.

"Gently. Breathe," the male voice commanded and she tried to do so. Every breath was cutting. But she was certainly not dead and Colonel Kirov's face, close to hers, with its harsh bronze skin and Tartar eyes, did not in the least look like one of her prison guards.

He glanced behind him, muttered something angrily in an exotic language that she took to be Russian.

Poor Molly Agnew kept excusing herself nervously. "I didn't know she couldn't breathe, sir. Whatever you put on the chest to keep the lid from closing – well, it must have slipped. She could hear me at first. There was air coming in until the prison man slammed the top of the chest down. I'm sure I'm that sorry, miss."

"A glass of water," Kirov ordered. "And hurry."

Molly looked around, obviously waiting for orders from her mistress, but her Ladyship had not appeared. She must be still seeing out her unwanted visitors. The girl scuttled away, looking back sidewise as she left the bedchamber.

"Breathe," Kirov ordered Hester.

She tried a flickering smile as she followed his orders. He couldn't be soft and gentle, even when he knew what it cost her to breathe. She managed a hoarse, croaking whisper.

"You are strange."

"How so?" But she didn't seem to annoy him.

"You wanted to see me hang; yet, here I am."

"That is a singularly stupid remark."

"Probably." She tried to moisten her lips. If they were

going to have an argument, as usual, she would need to recover rapidly.

"I told you. I had my reasons for delivering prisoners, especially those to the Taunton Assizes."

"Why?"

"Because I want to unmask a murderer's face."

She shivered, not having the faintest idea what he was talking about.

"What will you do then?"

"Here is the girl with the water. I'll hold the glass. Now, slowly."

She drank, choked, obeyed his suggestion and sipped a little. The flat, brackish-tasting well water sickened her. She waved away the delicate Waterford wine glass.

"Enough."

He gave the glass to Molly Agnew just as Lady Pomfret swept into the room, swathed in a velvet night robe that rippled majestically over the carpet. Her greying hair was all askew, and it was enormously reassuring to see her.

"What's this Molly tells me? Have you all lost your senses, suffocating the girl? May as well hang her and have done with it."

"Oh, no, please. I'm quite well, and I am alive."

Kirov laughed. "There, madam. She is alive, although she seems to have lost that sharp tongue of hers. I scarcely recognize her."

Hester refused to be taunted. More important matters occupied her.

"Have they truly gone, Lady Pomfret? Am I free of them?"

"For the moment. However, we must throw them off the trace, permanently, by one means or another."

Hester realized that although the Colonel had already

171

lifted her out of the chest he was still holding her in his arms. "You may let me go. I am quite well, now that I can breathe."

Kirov turned to her Ladyship. "Ah, that's better. The vixen is herself, I see." He asked Hester, "Can you stand?"

"Certainly." With an effort she proved to him that she could stand, but he held one arm out behind her, as though he did not trust her boast.

Lady Pomfret was relieved enough to be, like Hester, her cross self.

"Well, I do thank heaven for your safety, but I must say, this whole affair was badly managed. I'd have done better had I sent myself. Obviously, you led those wretches to this doorstep."

Hester caught the Colonel's rueful expression and was amused. Her chest and her head ached, but as she had said, at the very least, she was alive and out of the clutches of the Holding Cell.

"Ma'am, I'm afraid we've both been ungrateful to Colonel Kirov. When I think of that place I left, and this box that I thought would be my tomb, I feel I cannot thank him enough."

Lady Pomfret chuckled at this view of things and Colonel Kirov bowed to Hester with his florid but not unbecoming grace.

"Many thanks, I am appreciated at last."

"Just so." Her Ladyship immediately took command of the situation. "True. We are not done with them, but I have a notion. First, we must all be hungry for a meal that isn't served by those wretched jailers. Molly, fetch up Cook, give her instructions, and tell Joshua to serve us in my boudoir."

"Joshua?" Kirov repeated with raised eyebrows. "A most remarkable coachman."

"Not at all. The fewer persons who know of our little plot, and especially our guests, the better."

Kirov agreed with some amusement. "Admirably put, ma'am. I wish I had had you at the front against Bonaparte."

Hester, well aware of what she owed to her patroness, could not resist bending to kiss the back of her Ladyship's somewhat veined and gnarled hand.

The older woman drew back as usual with a gruff, "Now, now, I detest sentiment. Run along, Molly. As for you, my girl, I suggested you stop looking like a brazen hussy barely dressed and find some respectable garments. Try my clothes-press there."

"A pity," Kirov murmured.

Hester tried to ignore his implication as she made her way across the room to her Ladyship's clothes-press, but she was uncomfortably aware of Kirov's interest in her disreputable appearance.

Her throughts were still chaotic. The horror of the Holding Cell and more recent events tonight might not have ended yet.

It was Lady Pomfret's notion to serve champagne.

"This is a form of celebration, you know. Then I must retire to my beauty sleep. Lord knows I shall need all my wits tomorrow. Not to mention my beauty."

Lady Pomfret caught Kirov's eye and said roughly, "I can see you smirking, and I beg leave to remind you, Colonel, you're no beauty yourself."

Colonel Kirov laughed and her Ladyship held out her veine and gnarled hand. "You may salute it in style."

"With the greatest pleasure, ma'am."

He bowed and lifted her fingers to his lips.

Perfectly satisfied, her Ladyship set down her glass and motioning to the maid, sailed out of the room with a parting shot.

"I trust you two will behave with the decorum for which I am famous. And never forget, my girl, you are betrothed to that good fellow, Charles Willoughby."

"A good fellow," Kirov muttered when she was gone. "What an epitaph! Is that all you ask of life?"

She was confused by the champagne after her weeks of near-starvation and blurted out, "What else is there to hope for? I saw what passion did to my mother. She was a lady before she met Papa. She was respected, and might have lived many years. Yet she died almost in girlhood, with nothing to shroud her poor body but my father's passion. And he was far off at the wars."

"She had you," He reminded her quietly.

It hurt and she hated the admission as she jeered, "Me? A dependent child? An intruder in their lives? Don't talk nonsense."

The champagne was going to her head. She knew she shouldn't be blathering away her most intimate thoughts like this.

Fortunately, the supper which arrived could have graced a love tryst by the Prince Regent himself. Nevertheless, it was set up, in a fury, no doubt, by the cook, interrupted during a rendezvous in the scullery maid's tiny room. The lobster, the creamed sweetbreads and the patés were like a foretaste of heaven after the dark days she had known.

"Try another paté," Kirov advised her as she opened her mouth.

"Will you please stop ordering me about?" She got no further. He stuck the paté between her lips.

She was in no mood to argue. She ate it, found herself thirsty and let him pour more champagne.

Gradually, her mood lightened. She was free of the Holding Cell, for the moment. And she felt a growing excitement she had never experienced before.

All this luxury, the comfort, and the food that she had dreamed of night after night in the Holding Cell, worked its magic on her body through a champagne haze. When Colonel Kirov offered to carry the object of the celebration to her hidden bedchamber under the mansard roof she made no objection.

She was at least a connoisseur of men enough to know that the throb of the pulse in his hard, muscular throat signalled his own excitement at the close warmth of her body as he lifted her.

Hester knew how much she owed to the Russian and there was no doubt in her mind that he fascinated her in a physical way. This made her more uneasy. She still associated him in her mind with the most nightmarish experience of her life. He had admitted that his persistent hounding of her until he delivered her to Sir Giles Cartaret had been for one secret and entirely selfish purpose which was unconcerned with Hester Leland. No doubt, in true gypsy fashion, it was all due to the vengeance he sought against someone.

Gradually the champagne had blurred her uncertainties about the future when she found herself so easily borne in his arms. With two fingers on her chin he had turned her face so that her lips touched his cheek. His hard flesh against her mouth aroused in her body a heat that made her hunger to share that passion with him.

175

It was the champagne, she thought. That on top of her haunting fear that had been with her so long. Now, she was falsely stimulated by this expensive wine which was so uncommon to her.

"Set me down" she insisted. "I can walk."

"I've no doubt you can." It was not the answer she expected to hear.

"Lady Pomfret can be most persuasive, so I won't ask your motives in rescuing me. But no matter what she promised you, I am deeply in your debt. I wish I might repay you."

"Dare I hope you are offering to repay – as they say at Drury Lane – with your pink and white Anglo-Saxon body?"

She flushed, as much at his sarcasm as at his suggestion She wished her wits were sharper. That damnable champagne!

"Don't be crude. I only meant. . . ." What? She wasn't sure. "Never mind. Just leave me here and pray they don't get this far in their next search."

He set her down abruptly so that she almost lost her balance while he pushed open the door of what appeared to be a closet for linens and unused silver. He reached behind an old, standing salver and pushed hard against the wall. It was a priest's hole and revealed a little bedchamber barely furnished, and with a lighted candle reflected in the wood-framed mirror on a shaving stand. There was a stiff little bed whose faded coverlet and blanket did not add to its attractions.

Oddly enough, it was Colonel Kirov who complained. He sat down on the bed, tried to bounce, and said, "You won't get much sleep here."

176

She laughed. "It's plain you've never slept in a Holding Cell. It will do very nicely, thank you."

"True." But his oblique, faintly slanting eyes searched her face. He added brusquely, "And it is only for one night."

She started to ask where she was going but he reached up, caught her hands and pulled her forward, against his body. As she stared into his eyes, he said on a sudden rough note.

"Let us say this is Drury Lane. The lady and the Tartar soldier fence with each other over her debt. Will she pay him? What do you think?"

There was something alien, hypnotic about the way he looked at her in that unblinking way. She could already feel the heat that suffused her body under his stare.

"Well?" His hands moved over her arms as he drew her onto the bed.

She managed to confess, "I don't love you. I could never—"

His lips twisted a little and she wondered if she had hurt him, but obviously such confessions meant little to a man with his experience. He laughed but his hands continued to caress her in a disturbing way.

"What has that to do with anything? I don't make eternal commitments. They are absurd. But I am willing to accept your form of payment. You may even find it pleasant. Come! No more teasing."

She was still protesting, unsure whether she really had promised to 'pay' him, when he pulled her into his arms and had her body pinned under his on the hard bed. She felt the heat of his sensuous hands through the silk dressing gown Lady Pomfret's maid had given her. He slipped if off her bare shoulders and before she could shiver in her nakedness, the heat of his lips warmed her flesh.

She became aware of sensations she had never known before, leaving her breathless, yet craving more, always rising to something, some passionate climax that maddened her by its delay.

Her body seemed to rise to meet his so that she was ready even as his lips lingered over the tender whitness of her loins.

Release came with throbbing sensations that blurred even his violence as he invaded her body. She held him to her, her finger clawing hard at his hips, holding his strength within her.

Then it was over. The passion faded, and the knowledge of how far she had degraded herself came to remind her of a terrible fact. This sexual freedom with a strange, alien being who had none of Charles Willoughby's moral integrity, could devastate her life as surely as the Holding Cells.

The man who had chosen her and with whom she wanted to spend her life, if she had a life to live, was Charles Willoughby, gentle and kind and deserving of a good woman. Better than Hester Leland. Some day they might still be together, but tonight she had betrayed him.

And she had betrayed her rescuer, Colonel Kirov, by giving her body to him when neither of them loved the other. He had shown her a forbidden delight, an excitement that nothing else on earth, surely, could give to her, but he admitted himself that it was given for the grossest of reasons, mere physical sensation, not even a small but genuine love.

She shifted away from his touch. He got up and looked

178

at her for a long, silent minute or two. Then he was dressing. He appeared very much as he usually did. Such encounters must be common to him.

She covered herself with the blanket and reached for his hand. "I cannot feel right about this. I was not reared to make love to a man who was not my husband. I told you how it was, in the beginning. But I am truly grateful to you."

He grinned. "You have thrown the dog a bone, and he will not bark at you. Go to sleep now. You will be safe if you follow orders tomorrow. A little surprised, perhaps, but safe, for the moment."

He left the room.

She puzzled over him before falling sleep, wondering if perhaps, somewhere far beyond the sight of anyone, including herself, he had genuine feelings that had provoked their lovemaking tonight. She would probably never know, but try as she would, she was sure she would never forget what they'd just shared.

Just before dawn the fine, tender features of Charles Willoughby drifted into her wild dreams. She was deep in the new mood of rising hope, thanks to Kirov's last promise, when a hand shook her shoulder and Molly Agnew's voice called to her nervously.

"Miss, wake up. There's someone waiting to see you."

Hester sat up with a start of terror.

Molly shook her head. "No, miss. He says he's her Ladyship's fine friend. He told Lady Pomfret he hopes to marry you one day when your troubles are behind you.

Hester caught her breath. Dear, loyal Charles! So even her sordid prison experiences had not turned him against her. She briefly felt that what she had done last night, was

179

a greater crime against Charles, and so vowed to always remember his loyalty.

Molly said, "So you're to come, at once."

If Lady Pomfret approved of Sir Charles' presence, it must be safe. Hester wrapped her borrowed robe around her. "And his name was Charles Willoughby?"

"As if I wouldn't know Sir Charles! He's ever so handsome. I heard him tell her you'd made a dreadful mistake and he means to save you. Those were his very words."

Chapter Fourteen

Molly studied her.

"I best brush your hair, miss. You'll be wanting to look pretty for the gentleman."

A goblet and pitcher were near at hand. The goblet struck Hester as very like some possession Lady Pomfret might own, no dainty glasses for her. Hester reached over from the bed, poured herself a water and drank it down. She had no doubt her thirst was due to the champagne last night, and everything about that last half-hour with Colonel Kirov shamed her, but she tried to think of the important matters which occupied her now.

She admitted to Molly, "I'm in a dreadful state. Sir Charles must be very disappointed by my running away from the cells when he would have perhaps freed me." How he would despise her if he knew what had occurred between her and Kirov! To someone like Charles it would be more deeply degrading than even she felt it to be. It would soil her forever. She added aloud, "Sir Charles told the Magistrate he meant to have me freed legally."

"True, miss. Then you wouldn't be hiding the rest of your life. It's a bitter shame, so it is. My Lady says you're innocent as a babe."

"Thank you, Molly."

With her hair forming a mantle around her pallid face

Hester stood up and started toward the door. She did not look at the stand where a man's shaving glass in its frame would reveal how thin, worried and unnerved she was.

When she reached the head of the main staircase above the reception hall, on the ground floor she saw a movement along the East Gallery leading to the staircase. The gallery was illuminated by the morning sunlight that touched on family portraits belonging to the Marquess from whom Lady Pomfret had leased the property. The sun touched also on Colonel Kirov. The contrast between this barbaric figure and the stiff, solemn family portraits was amost laughable.

The Colonel still wore breeches, a homespun shirt and exotic embroidered slippers, which surprised her. She had thought he would try to look the gentleman for Lady Pomfret's sake. But at least he hadn't put on the absurd, wispy white wig again.

She waited to warn him of the visitor. Misunderstanding, he looked pleased and would have taken her hand to salute it with a polite kiss, but she cut him off anxiously.

"Hush, a visitor."

He wasted no time but drew her back, out of view of anyone below.

"Who is it?"

"Sir Charles Willoughby."

"So the damned busybody knows."

"Only about me. Her Ladyship sent for me." She noted the tension and readiness this aroused in him and added quickly, "He means me no harm."

He looked so sceptical she felt he deserved a setdown. "He explained to Lady Pomfret that we are to be married."

It appalled her that he might be thinking of last night, and she now read in his eyes what she thought of as a malignant gleam. Hester turned away toward the stairs followed by his low-voiced taunt.

"I would not wager on it if I were you."

"But you are not me."

She went rapidly down the stairs, half-afraid he would stop her. She did not hear his light, slippered steps behind her and assumed he had given up their quarrel. So much the better. How restful, how safe she would feel with Sir Charles! Even though he felt she had made a mistake in flouting the King's Justice, she remembered his vow to Sir Giles in the prison corridor:

"I will not give up my efforts . . . if I must plead for her in London, or before the Prince Regent himself."

And unlike Colonel Kirov, his motives were pure. He wanted only Hester's freedom. He had not acted as her captor or freed her in connection with some private vengeance.

No one was in the reception hall. Lady Pomfret was cautious about that, for which, among other things, Hester would be eternally in her debt, but she heard voices in the small salon, a heavily gilt and decorative room that opened out of the reception hall and was probably used by the old Marquess's female relations. Hester waited outside the door, took a deep breath, looked down at her torn and unflattering night robe with a sigh, then lowered the brass latch.

The rasp of the latch made both Lady Pomfret and Sir Charles look around. Hester's attention was unavoidably captured by the gentleman who had spoken of her as his future wife, the man she had wronged last night in the most grievous way.

183

He had never appeared nobler or more handsome to her. His light hair gleamed like gold in the sun, adding to the gentle strength of his features. He looked serious, even stern as he spoke to Lady Pomfret but when he saw Hester in the doorway he broke off and crossed quickly to her, holding out both hands.

"My dearest, what you must have suffered!" He took her own hands, brought them to his lips, then, looking into her eyes, chided her as he would have scolded a child.

"How could you be so foolish? You knew I would never let them hang you." She shuddered, wishing he had not spoken of her fate so unthinkingly. He insisted, "No, no. I have legal minds, magistrates, judges of the Taunton Assizes, working at your case. We need but prove your intentions were pure, whatever you might have done. That is all."

But she had not stolen the emerald, even accidentally, as he seemed bound to believe. He was so innocent of the law, so supremely sure of the powers available to an aristocrat that she almost wished he would avoid the subject. Still, he meant well and his gentle embrace temporarily banished the chill fear, making her feel that she was in the arms of someone who genuinely and unselfishly cared for her.

Her guilt over her behaviour the previous night almost overwhelmed her. She had a terrible desire to confess the whole of it.

Lady Pomfret looked from Sir Charles to Hester and sniffed. "Well, it is clear that I am not needed here for the moment. Say what you must to this unfortunate child and have done. I will return presently." She stalked out as Hester was murmuring,

"How good she has been to me!"

"I know, my love." His lips caressed her hair as he reminded her, "One day, all of this will be over. You must think of our future, when you are released. Think of those magic words 'Not Guilty.'"

When you are released – but I am free now. . . .

Not free of remorse for last night, however, or fear of recapture. Confession might relieve her conscience but it would burden him with a painful decision. In all likelihood it must destroy the very vestige of his tender feelings for her and there was no one else in her bitter, constricted world who still had this respect and gentle concern for her.

"How did you find me, Sir Charles?"

"Charles, remember. I knew when I was told Lady Pomfret had let a house in the vicinity that you must be concerned in it."

"You did not tell them? The authorities at the prison?"

"No. I felt that I wished to rectify your error myself. You had listened to bad advice. Those shocking criminals who took you out when they removed the highwayman's mistress. A murderess, you know. There are other poor creatures who deserved your compassion more than they. A highwayman and his doxy? Certainly not your sort."

"They were my friends."

He reminded her warmly, "Your tender heart does you credit. He attempted a little teasing joke. "You will be my own prisoner afterward. My dearest possession. We will work together to aid the innocent victims. Not the guilty. You simply were too innocent to understand about such people as those you met in the Cells. The accident of that accursed emerald will be forgotten some day."

Not by me, she thought. However, she did not say this

aloud, and felt the sincerity of his reassurance. She smiled, but knew the effort was faint and tired.

"I can't return to that place, Charles. Not even to please you."

As gently as possible, he refused to accept her words or the firmness behind them.

"I know, dearest. It must be appalling. A respectable young lady among those animals. And they are little more. Who did this to you, helped you to commit this crime against the King's Justice? A highwayman. You were wrong to let persons of that kind sway you. They only made it worse for you."

She frowned. "They are not animals who shared my prison. They are human beings who were not fortunate enough to have someone like you to care for them."

"I understand. Your compassion does you credit." He didn't seem to understand, though. He had no conception of such a life-in-death. "But it should only be a matter of months. Perhaps weeks. I am determined to make Sylvester Girard recant."

She shook her head. If Lady Pomfret had failed by bribery, the means most likely to sway a creature like Girard, then Sir Charles would fail even more dismally. She pulled herself together and told him as kindly as she could,

"Please understand how grateful I am. But I cannot return. My escape last night will be another crime charged against me. It is even more serious than the theft, and they refused to believe me there."

His hands slipped from her shoulders. She saw the disappointment and deep concern in his eyes.

"There is no hope for you if you refuse to give yourself

up, Hester. I will be with you. I swear I won't leave you until you have made your statement."

"What statement?"

"That you were taken by this highwayman because you witnessed his doxy's escape. Don't you see, my dear? You will be safe in the Holding Cell until your trial. The highwayman can't hurt you."

"And does Lady Pomfret approve of my return to the Holding Cell?"

"That is not our concern, Hester. You must be freed in a legal fashion. Otherwise, there can be no future for us."

It was tempting. It might even be the only means of freeing her legitimately. But the lies about Gentleman Jamie and the horror of the return were too much.

"Come," he urged her anxiously. "We will ask Lady Pomfret." He walked to the door with her. She was still reluctant, and as they reached the door she had a sudden mental image of the dank, foul Holding Cell and the despair that appeared to seep out of the walls.

She drew back, terrified that he would force her to return. "Please, Sir Charles, I can't go back to that place."

With his back to the open doorway he held out one arm accompanied by the stern reminder, "You must. It is the only honorable thing to do."

He doesn't know, she thought. He couldn't conceive of what it was like. He insisted again.

She shook her head. "No. I can't give myself up. They will hang me."

At the same time she was aware of something happening behind him. A hand raised, the heel of the hand visible behind his head. She screamed.

The hand came down hard across Sir Charles' neck,

just above his immaculate white shirt. He collapsed into Colonel Kirov's arms. The Colonel dragged him into the small salon and laid him on the Chippendale sofa. He was still unconscious.

Hester pushed Kirov aside and knelt to attend the unconscious man. Sir Charles looked unnaturally pale and breathed so faintly it frightened her. She was cautious enough to whisper her fierce complaint to Kirov.

"What are you, a monster? You may have killed him. He meant no harm. He only wants me to give myself up legally. He will have me freed."

"Then you are as big a fool as he is. We've no time to lose." He lifted her under the arms and got her onto her feet.

Lady Pomfret stood in the doorway shaking her head at this violence.

"Heavens, Colonel! You are so impetuous. Have you no sense of decorum?"

"Decorum be damned! I must get her out of here before this fool regains consciousness. When we've left the house ring for cold water, a cloth and vinegar. That should bring him round. Tell him you came upon him in this condition. You have been trying to keep Gentleman Jamie from capturing her."

Her Ladyship said calmly, "Then it was Gentleman Jamie who committed this outrage under my very nose? Well, hurry about your business."

Last night, thanks in part to the champagne, Hester had betrayed this kind, well-intentioned man who genuinely loved her. Today, she was asked to betray him again, in another sense.

"I am not going," she insisted.

"Don't talk rubbish. Of course you are."

188

"On the whole," Lady Pomfret agreed after considering the matter, "I think you had best do as the Colonel says. It need not be for long. His gypsy friends will get you out of the county and deposit you where you may be hidden until we are able to prove your innocence. Quite simple, really."

As might have been expected, all this intrigue enlivened what her Ladyship always complained was a dull life. It was she who would have been happy when carried off by gypsies.

Hester was still protesting when Kirov urged her away from the sofa. "I can't leave him like this."

The Colonel turned to her Ladyship. "If you have messages for me, you may trust my housekeeper in London. The Prince had Kirov House made over as Russian property. A favour to our Emperor Alexander. Have your man, Joshua, enquire for Prince Kirov's residence. He often entertained guests, friends of the Tsar, and some English as well. Your Prince Regent was there upon occasion. He was much taken by the Russian beauties he found there. My father called them 'his cousins'."

"Hmph." Lady Pomfret considered this, shrugged, and agreed, with the rider, "I suspect your gypsy friends are more worthy of acquaintance."

He laughed at that. "Probably. But you will remember?"

"Certainly. I am not in my dotage, you know." He laughed and she reminded him without mincing her words, "If you harm this lady, I will personally have you hanged, drawn and quartered in front of your still-conscious face. And I am a woman of my word."

Colonel Kirov surprised Hester by taking her Ladyship's hand and kissing her bony fingertips. "I believe

189

you, my Lady. I give you my word I have only Miss Leland's best interests at heart. I have no intention of seeing that lovely neck stretched."

"And have I nothing to say about it?" Hester demanded, knowing quite well she had not. They both ignored this as childish mumblings.

Ten minutes later she had been bundled into an old cloak and told to get into the cart behind the manor house, where she must dress herself in the clothing she found in the pile of straw.

She would have held out more firmly if her Ladyship hadn't supported Kirov's tactics. Hester still felt that her own indecent love-making with Kirov last night, and now this appalling business, might break her ties with Sir Charles forever. She mentioned the matter of her running away again, and what it would do to Sir Charles, while Molly occupied herself over Sir Charles with warm, wet cloths, Attar of Roses fragrance and *sal volatile*.

Molly winked at Hester. "Never you mind, miss. The gentleman will get the best of care. And as for any rattle of tongues – well now, what the Colonel's been about is 'twixt her Ladyship and me. We see nothing, we know nothing. Innercent as babes, we are."

"Thank you, Molly. And do be gentle with Sir Charles."

Lady Pomfret saw Kirov's signal through the long front windows and said abruptly, "Agnew understands, my girl. Leave the business to us. We will simply say Gentleman Jamie came and snatched you away. You had best not be seen by anyone in this country. Charles was wrong and the Colonel is right. You must be kept away from the Taunton Assizes. Even in London they would not know you by sight, but here, you are always in danger, until we can shake the truth out of that abominable jeweller. Now, off you go."

There was a sly twinkle in her eyes. She was enjoying herself.

Hester embraced her with nervous but sincere haste which her Ladyship dismissed in her usual brusque way.

"Here, here. If you know me at all, you must realize how much I enjoy this. By Gad, if I were a male what a highwayman I should make!"

"Dear ma'am!" Hester whispered, then she blew the unconscious man a kiss and ran from the little salon. The last thing she saw was the first tentative stirring of Sir Charles as her Ladyship and Molly Agnew made a great to-do over him, assuring him,

"That horrid highwayman is gone now. Poor Miss Leland. I'm afraid she is as good as dead. Imagine! Carrying her off to the West Coast of Ireland. What madness!"

Hester did not stay to discover what Sir Charles' reaction might be. She rushed through the kitchen and down the back steps past the Herb Garden. Colonel Kirov, in a gaudy red jerkin with a wide-brimmed field hat and black breeches, helped her into the straw covering the wagon.

"Change as quickly as possible."

While the staunch old farm horse ambled off under Kirov's signal, Hester rummaged around in the straw, locating a badly faded blue velvet skirt and violet bodice. They had seen numerous rough washings and been turned inside out besides. All the inside hems were on the outside.

A gypsy's clothing. She wondered who had worn them. They smelled of horse hides, wood smoke and grass.

191

Beneath the skirt she located something furry that made her recoil. Taking a big breath she tried again, reaching in to bring up a soft ball that proved to be a wig of black hair.

She looked up at Kirov on the box in his fairground gypsy disguise. He had his mind on the travellers the old wagon passed all heading toward Taunton, especially the West Country public stage which rattled and swayed past the gypsy wagon before vanishing around a bend in the High Road.

The Assizes would be opening soon. If she had listened to Sir Charles she might be a free woman after her trial. But if he had been too optimistic in his hopes. . . .

Urged by that pervasive fear, she pulled the wig on, scratched her forehead with hair bodkins cunningly hidden in the wig, and pulled them out, fastening them again through the wig and into the blonde hair until the transformation felt complete. As she followed this with the bodice and skirt she wondered where he had got the wig from. Had he really planned her rescue to this degree?

She was shamed by her own suspicions (did his momentary passion have anything to do with it?). Considering the boldness of this second rescue, she didn't quite believe her freedom was the sole object of his criminal efforts. Perhaps some other man might have gone to these lengths but in spite of their lovemaking last night Kirov seemed very businesslike. The explanation must lie in his curious remark recently about finding the face of a murderer. But if this was so, he had turned his back on the West Country where, it had seemed, he expected to see this murderer.

It must be some private vengeance of his own.

She had no idea where they were going and if it was likely they would be pursued. For a number of reasons she prayed that Sir Charles would not be one of her pursuers. He was much too honorable to help her run from the King's Justice. But would he betray her if he discovered how she had escaped and with whom?

Worst of all, he must not know either that she herself had collaborated in that escape or the nature of her highly theatrical disguise.

Every time a coach and team, or especially men on horseback, passed during the morning Hester was forced to duck her head and bury herself in hay. Each time was more humiliating than the last.

She was in no way reassured when she heard the rattle of harness and the squeak of wagon wheels behind them in the afternoon. She was about to hide again when she heard the Colonel call to someone approaching. He spoke in a strange tongue unlike the Russian she had occasionally heard him speak.

Hearing a heavy male voice call out a reply, she raised her head. The wagon jingling up along the side of them appeared to be a wooden house on wheels. Several other wagon-houses followed it along the road, each house heavily overhung with cheap utensils, toilet articles, knick-knacks and other objects usually sold by travelling tinkers.

This was a gypsy band carrying their worldly possessions as well, and looking more jolly, less menacing than those she had seen before on the roads to Dorset Heath and other favoured camping fields free of trouble from the authorities. Obviously, the sight of Colonel Kirov stimulated this surprising change of moods among the gypsies. Kirov might be Russian but he certainly had gypsy blood.

He pulled off the road, rattled along the wagon ruts to a row of waving bushes that apparently masked a stream from the High Road. Hester watched uneasily as the first gypsy tinker's wagon followed Kirov's lead. The others dutifully came after, tilting first to one side, then the other as the big wagon-houses tried to balance among the wagon ruts.

Hester had experienced so many dangers since the day she was accused by Master Girard that she knew she should ask herself what Kirov and his apparent friends had in mind for her, but she found herself taking this latest shock with more curiosity than fear.

These people were probably outlaws, but then so was Hester Leland!

Chapter Fifteen

As the product of an undeniable lady, and of a soldier who was far below his wife in station, Hester had always been conscious that she herself was only half a lady. She had spent her life bringing herself up to her mother's level, never, except as a child, imitating her father in manner or speech.

Yet, in some ways, she had found it a relief to make herself accepted by the females who became her friends in the Holding Cell. As a woman wanted for High Theft she was hardly in a position to look down her nose at free and independent gypsy tinkers.

She shook off bits of hay, touched her full and curly wig to be certain it was secure, and sat up with as casual an attitude as possible, prepared for almost anything.

The rutted field took on a more forested look and the mare came to a halt at Kirov's signal among the willows, carefully avoiding the brook that meandered along toward distant grazing sheep.

Hester looked over the splintering wooden side of the wagon. In spite of her best intentions, she was still wondering what would be her immediate fate amid these alien beings, so she took out her uncertainty on Kirov.

"That was clumsy. One more turn of the wheel and we'd all be bathing among those reeds. What if the owner of the fields finds you? Isn't he afraid they will rob him? Or steal his sheep?"

Kirov shook his head. "He knows Marko and the band. He is their particular *gaje*. They wouldn't rob him. In return, he protects them."

"Very sensible, whatever a *gaje* is."

"You, and other Christians. These gypsies are far older than Christianity. They are Romany. Come, give me your hands. Over you go. Let me look at you. You need something for your ears, a pair of gold coins perhaps. How are these?"

She stared at his palm. Her eyes widened at the flash of gold pieces which had been shaped to wear dangling from her ears. When he reached in among the ringlets of blue-black hair to find her ears she admitted to herself that the mere touch of his fingers as he tied the ear-bobs in place once more aroused her senses to a surprising degree. She knew she must take care not to be so easily swayed by a mere physical touch. It was the one quality of her mother's that she did not want to inherit, that destructive love of the flesh.

Kirov was busy removing the harness from the old mare when the big, very dark man leapt down from the first of the gypsy vans. He began to issue orders to those following who also piled in along the brook and fanned out to gather feed for their animals while the first of the women busied themselves with broken sticks, ground debris that had dried out, and anything else for their fires.

Children appeared from inside the wagons, running about either helpfully or in play, sometimes both at the same time. Their bronze faces flashed with light and teeth until they caught Hester watching them. The light went

196

out of their eyes at once and her tentative greeting meant nothing. Despite her clothing, she was clearly one of the 'others'.

Hester could almost read their minds: "She is not one of us, so she must be one of them, our enemies." Curious. She had known many foreigners, but never anyone from whom she felt so completely alienated.

She tried to help out, looking for sticks, dry brush, anything that would keep her arms full and make her look as though she was contributing her share to the encampment. It did not help to win their approval. The women looked even more forbidding than the men whose ink-black eyes looked Hester's way now and then with a flash of interest.

Once the women had stones, twigs and sticks set they got out tripods and hung kettles over the low, careful fires. They were all so well-organized Hester did not dare to add her contribution.

Kirov found her that way, standing helplessly on the grassy edge of the brook with her feet sinking into water and her arms full of wood. He laughed at her efforts but took the pile from her and added it to the closest fire.

A strong-faced woman of forty or so thanked Kirov in Russian and he presented Hester, speaking English which the woman obviously understood. She nodded to Kirov, her thick braids of black hair shining like golden stars, thanks to what appeared to be genuine gold coins dangling from her ears.

Kirov introduced the uneasy and fascinated Hester with a few words that seemed to impress the gypsy whom he called Sanchia.

Sanchia switched a muddy, half-naked boy once with a leaf branch before turning her attention to Hester. She

197

stood with legs apart, her three stained satin skirts, pink, yellow and green, making her look far bigger and more imposing than she was.

"This one who looks like a water-reed took the Emerald Flame. You see, we heard of it. But you want us to laugh, Taidje?"

Annoyed, Hester whispered to Kirov, "I am not a thief and you know it."

But he frowned at her and she was wise enough not to argue. She remembered that her popularity in the Holding Cell had grown from the women's belief that she was guilty of High Theft. An enviable social height to which others could only aspire.

Sanchia circled Hester, walking all around her, ignoring the watery mud that oozed into her cracked and open boots, across her strong, dark toes. She approved. She did not look any less dangerous to Hester, but she said to Kirov.

"She is your *Gaje*; so she is ours. But this name Esher? No, she will be Emerald Flame. Does she have the Emerald Flame about her now?"

It would always remind Hester of the emerald and she hated the name, but she said nothing.

Kirov grinned. "She doesn't have the Emerald Flame with her at the moment. See that the word is spread."

Sanchia did not seem disappointed. She said casually, "I will do it."

Hester couldn't see that this new phase of her life would further the efforts to pronounce her Not Guilty. But the irony struck her and she laughed.

She received no returning laugh nor even smiles from the band. They accepted her, but basically, she was alien, not one of the Romanies who traced their ancestry and their language to the ancient worlds before history. For a group who laughed, played, and joked among themselves, they were astonishingly secretive.

Worried over this and wondering if she could trust them not to betray her, Hester suggested to Kirov.

"It is my skin, my eyes. They are all wrong."

Kirov pretended to study her face. His dark forefinger started at her forehead, then travelled down over the bridge of her nose to her lips, lingering there while she tried to stifle the shameful thrill of pleasure that she wanted to conceal from him. Then the ball of his finger traced her chin and her white neck.

She both desired and feared that he would go further. The swell of her upper breasts lay within a finger's breadth of his touch.

He removed his hand. "Don't concern yourself, Yuri is a master at disguise."

"Yuri?"

"Sanchia's cousin. He is a bit of a rogue, but useful."

Feeling an unexpected freedom, she smiled at him. "Do you often disguise people to hide them from the King's Justice?"

He shrugged. "This tribe trades and sells goods. My mother's father was a gypsy tinker in Ireland. She had an Irish mother but her soul was with her people."

Then he was one-quarter gypsy, one-quarter Irish. This, combined with what appeared to be Russian-Tartar blood was a formidable combination, indeed. She had been reared to think of these exotic creatures, such as gypsies and Tartars, as if they came from far Cathay.

She must not let herself find him too fascinating. How shocked her mother would have been! And it might have been even more shameful to her father. His people had barely escaped from the poverty of the London poor. Ironically, their prohibition against other races would be even stronger.

She must always remember the affection she felt for Charles Willoughby. He had done nothing against her but attempt to free her honestly, legally. And he believed her innocent.

How different from Colonel Kirov who boasted of her crime!

During the next hour any number of children found excuses to venture near Hester who was permitted to stir the savoury meat and vegetable contents of the stew pot dangling from a tripod. Hester tried smiling at the children, then speaking, but nothing of a friendly nature worked. Then, disgusted, she wrinkled up her nose and stuck out her tongue at one urchin whose eyes, opaque as peat, seemed to bore holes in her.

To her astonishment the boy broke into giggles. He slipped up to her, reached out a hand coated with mud and lamb's grease. He pulled her wig. She cried "Ouch!" and swung the big wooden spoon at him, dripping as it was. Giggling madly, the boy ran away while she tried to set her wig in order with just one hand.

When the women decided the meal was ready and gave a signal this brought the vicious watchdogs barking and snarling but obedient to orders from their masters. The men sent them back to their posts at the perimeter of the camp before themselves settling around the small fires distant from the women. They sat cross-legged, drying their boots and talking loudly in their strange tongue. No females shared their meal. Once the males had been served, the women returned to the area near Sanchia and Hester who were joined by the children.

Hester accepted whatever strangeness seemed to surround her. It came with the escape from the Holding Cell and perhaps from this race that was so alien and exotic to her. But she was accepted, the way a stone in a man's boot was accepted.

She caught Colonel Kirov watching her occasionally and she determined not to heed his advice or assistance. The food was succulent and welcome, but since it was eaten with the fingers, it certainly required napkins or kerchiefs. These did not exist for her, although many of the men at the fire wiped their hands on the kerchiefs they wore at their necks or as headcloths. Others wore brimmed dark hats and removed them long enough to wipe the lamb's grease on their thick black hair.

Hester was secretly appalled while she watched the women as well as the men deliberately run their greasy fingers through their own hair. They evidently assured each other jokingly that this was good for the hair. Perhaps it was, as it certainly looked lustrous enough, catching the light of the campfires.

Suddenly, panic appeared to set in. Everyone stopped eating to stare at Hester. Kirov came over to the women's fire, took her arm and got her to her feet. She whispered, "What is it? What have I done?"

Already, the gypsies were clearing away everything that showed any sign of her presence at the feast.

"Nothing," the Colonel explained, hustling her to the nearest wagon. "Up the steps, make no sound. Their friend is coming to join them at supper."

"What friend? What do you mean?"

"Inside, quickly. He is a sheep farmer. He protects them from the other gentiles. This is his land. He may recognize you. If he does, the story is sure to get back to Sir Giles."

Her puzzlement turned to terror. She hadn't gone this far only to be dragged back to her fate. She opened the door of the strangely practical wagon-house and looked back. He whispered,

"No need to worry about them – they are saving themselves. If you are captured, they will be taken as well, and there's little mercy for them, I can tell you."

He turned to make the leap to the ground but stopped long enough to say, "They like you."

"Because I stole an emerald?"

"No, not that. One day, I'll tell you."

Then he was gone. She closed the door and made her way through the dark interior, between what probably were mattresses of straw and bags of property, from needles to kettles, which they used in their business as tinkers. There were windows on either side and one of them, facing the small camp fires, was only partially darkened by a piece of dirty pink satin material with many rents in it. She could see the entire greasy print of a child's hand and found the idea more endearing than repulsive. This was curious because she had never been a passionate lover of children in the aggregate.

But this was a strange and oddly intriguing world to which Colonel Kirov had introduced her. The Colonel himself behaved oddly, borrowing a wide-brimmed black hat from one of the men and pulling it down over his eyes so that he looked much like the others.

She watched the farmer striding across the field toward the brook, with what looked like a long-rifle over his shoulder – it did not strike her as a good omen.

The gypsy women stood where they were by the fires, watching the gentile's approach, while they sent the children off to bed. The children obeyed with impressive promptness. The men of the tribe showed a good nature that surprised Hester. Evidently, they trusted their own particular friend.

There were greetings all around as the farmer reached the brook. Some of the men offered to give him a hand across but he waved them away and splashed his way to the gypsies' side of the brook where he shook hands with two of the leaders and gave the others a mock salute. He addressed them in English with a strong, West Country accent.

"Any trouble lately?"

The men shrugged and disclaimed. One of the grizzled older men who seemed to be Sanchia's husband, added, "Near Bristol. They came at us with dogs and pitchforks."

Sanchia waved the farmer to a place at her man's fire. Somewhat to Hester's surprise, he accepted and dropped to the ground on his haunches. He reached into a pot beneath the tripod and drew out a lamb shank whose rich grease and sauce dripped between his fingers as he ate. Sanchia moved away, leaving room for the men but she tilted her husband's hat-brim rudely forward and muttered something.

The gypsy took the hint. He asked if their friend had been troubled by any of the band.

The farmer grinned, "Only your wife's cousin Yuri. Stole a sheep and my wife's silk petticoat. Best not let her see you this trip."

He must have guessed how this would arouse the band. They exchanged glances, narrow-eyed and promising trouble for the absent Yuri.

Sanchia's husband gave her a sign. While Hester watched from her concealment, Sanchia reached between her capacious breasts and drew out a silver coin which she polished on her outer skirt before handing it to her husband. He, in turn, offered it to the farmer who took it with what sounded like a ritual response:

"It shall be yours, Marko, when a lamb is returned to me. This is my word."

Meanwhile, Sanchia had disappeared behind the wagon in which Hester was concealed. When she returned she threw a much stained full skirt of deep green satin to her husband, Marko. He delivered this to the farmer with a formal bow.

Once again the farmer made his ritual response and everyone went on eating.

Hester felt that she had entered a strange new world. She was not yet sure she liked it. There was something too exotic, too alarming in all these rigid courtesies. But she found it more fascinating than anything she had ever known.

Suddenly, this idyllic, exotic world closed in upon her. The farmer reached for what she had supposed was a rifle. It was a long-handled ax and with it, several wooden boards.

"Now, I redeem my pledge to you, my friends. I promised to repair the door of Marko's house." He laughed. "But I must fortify myself first."

He reached for a large spoon, dipped it into a blackened pot on the coals and came up with a smoking spoonful of what appeared to be vegetables. Hester gasped, wondering how he could swallow the hot contents, but he pursed his thin mouth and after blowing for a moment or two, began to chew.

Meanwhile, Colonel Kirov had disappeared. When Hester heard a grating noise at the door of Marko's wagon, she was ready for him. He got an arm around her waist, lifted her to the ground, ignoring the steps, and ran with her into the wooded area beyond the open ground.

On a moist bed of leaves and brush, well hidden from the activities in the gypsy camp, he ordered her to lie flat, not to shift her position, and to remain absolutely still until the sheep farmer had left the camp. Hester was not aware that she had been shaking until he promised her in a low but audible voice,

"They won't betray you. Their honour is as important to them as yours is to you."

More, she thought with irony and truth. She would sacrifice honour to free herself from the horrors of the last month. But she was ashamed to admit this to him before he left her and went back to join the others around one of the little campfires that could not be seen from the High Road.

She knew now, having seen and briefly shared the life of his people, that they really were a different kind. The sophistication of her gentile life was at the far end of the spectrum from the lives, honour and habits of these primitive, fiercely independent people.

Her gratitude toward them and Colonel Kirov was enormous, but it must remain simply a brief, exotic moment in her real life. That specifically included the sensations Taidje Kirov aroused in her.

Hester did not like to admit even to herself the effect this gypsy-Tartar's closeness had on her senses. It was not what she hoped for or dreamed of in her life. But then, she had not dreamed of being condemned for theft either.

Meanwhile, after considerable pounding, along with a deal of unsolicited advice from members of the band, the farmer did whatever had to be done to the wagon door.

She tried to follow Kirov's orders to remain motionless but she was very much aware that other life besides her own, including insects and small furred creatures, shared the tiny spot with her and thought nothing of crawling over and under her.

Gradually, she became aware of another presence. The slight figure behind her dropped to his knees and she tried to scramble away from his groping hands. One of the campfires snapped and sputtered. By its flicker of light she saw the teeth gleaming in his dark face. He put a finger to his lips and warned her in a whisper, "Say nothing. I'm wanted."

She had a strong urge to say, "Not so much as I am, I'll wager," but she remained silent.

He knelt beside her and closed his hand over her bare upper arm with impudent freedom.

"I'm Yuri. And you?"

Remembering what she had heard about this thieving cousin of the band, she carefully removed each of his fingers but did not answer his question. Something about his insolent grin warned her that he was not a man to be trusted, even if she hadn't heard the tale of the stolen sheep and the petticoat which had to be redeemed by his 'cousins'.

The sheep farmer finished his work, with the help of the formidable Sanchia who made suggestions while her husband, Marko, discussed a horse trade at which he had gotten the better of a keen-eyed Cornishman.

"Bah! I'd get the better of Marko at any game," Yuri confided in the ear of an annoyed Hester. She waved him to silence. She was terrified that the sheep farmer would

206

recognize him and, indirectly, get a glimpse of a gentile female among the band. She had very little hope that he would keep the news from the authorities in Taunton.

But the sheep farmer left at last, splashing through the brook again and going home with the tokens of what the gypsy band owed him.

Sanchia saw Yuri first and nudged her husband. Others in the band gathered around. Hester did not like the look of all those knives catching flashes from the low-burning coals of the fires.

Yuri backed away, like a mischievous puppy who knows he has gone too far. He rattled off excuses, and no doubt lies, to his tribe, with all the easy charm he could muster. But it was Kirov who stopped what threatened to become a bloody affair. He spoke in English, perhaps so that Hester could understand.

"Yuri, you are an artist when you choose to be. I will repay Marko—"

"My friend! My loyal Taidje!" Yuri babbled, trying to embrace him. Kirov shook him off.

"— if you can do me a service with that stain on the skin. Walnut, or whatever it may be."

"What?" Yuri's eyes widened. "You are not dark enough?" But then he looked at Hester and understood. She was not the only one who read cynicism in his agreement. "Of course. We are not satisfied with one who is only half Romany, but we now add one who is—"

He broke off, seeing something in Kirov's face that was promised nothing good for the renegade.

"I can do it. For you, Taidje, I will do it." He considered Hester from her dishevelled wig to her muddy slippers. "And what shall I call my masterpiece?"

207

"She is called Emerald Flame," Sanchia put in roughly before Kirov could speak. "As with an emerald."

This aroused a new excitement in the 'artist'.

"What? This is the female who stole the Emerald Flame?" He looked around, all enthusiasm. "But don't you see? She is worth a fortune to someone."

Chapter Sixteen

Hester was tired and cold and dispirited, but she wasn't surprised. The only thing that shook her out of this lethargy of despair was the sight of Colonel Kirov moving with deliberate steps toward the little artist, flanked by stout Marko and another of the band whom she didn't recognize.

The two gypsies fingered blades they used for slitting the throats of their live meat, but Kirov's thumb traced a pattern on a curious blade with deeply serrated edges, and a hilt by which he might have gripped it for chopping purposes.

Yuri shrank back against Hester, waving his hands wildly.

"Funning. Only to see you laugh, only—"

Hester too put her hands out as a barricade. Perhaps this rogue would recognize the truth, shameful as her confession might be, and realize she could be a victim, like the gypsy band. She addressed Yuri, not the others.

"The jeweller lied. He tricked me because he wanted to take me to his bed. He offered to free me if I became his property."

Yuri stared at her, his mouth open. Then he glanced at Kirov, "Is it true? Will they make property of their own kind?"

Knives were lowered slowly. Only Kirov remained at the ready.

"Why not? My *gaje* friend was thrown into the cell where they threw my mother a score of years ago. They shot my mother. Are they any more kind now?"

A score of years, surely this could be the story Angele had told.

Kirov's tone was deadly in its lack of excitement or passion. But this time it was not directed at Yuri.

"I do not yet know who at the Stamsbury House betrayed her to the warders. I have questioned Lord Stamsbury. I have questioned many in Taunton and in the cells. Either they lie or they do not know. But I will know, one day." His strong fingers ran over the blade in his hand.

"Was that why you rescued me?" Hester asked quietly. "I was not told the identity, though I have heard the story. Have you searched all these years? You must have been a boy then."

Sanchia reached between the men and pulled at Hester's arm.

"This is the men's concern. Come, Emerald Flame, you look tired." She explained as they walked between the files of men. "Taidje did not know how his mother died until he came to London last year with the Russians. An old woman told him."

Kirov was still looking at Yuri but his explanation was for Hester.

"Nettie Bindle told me, you remember her. She was my mother's friend when I was a child."

Hester understood very little of this except that it seemed these gypsies had a blood feud against his mother's betrayer. It sounded primitive, but after her own experiences with the law, she could scarcely find it in her heart to condemn them for it.

Sanchia found a mattress of straw for Hester but did not think a pillow necessary. However, a heavy coverlet that appeared to have been a parlour portière at one time, plus someone's huge, well-worn cloak was necessary if she was to sleep on the ground.

This was a new notion for Hester but she had the murky sky for a roof and all the out-of-doors for the walls of her bedchamber. The idea was far superior to the stone walls of the Holding Cells.

How were the women getting on? Bess and Old Sarey and the others, including that kind-hearted warder Patterson?

She prayed silently to the great, murky night: please, please don't let my friends in the Holding Cells be found guilty when their trials come up!

Hester lay on a dry bit of ground half protected by one of the gypsy wagon wheels and the floor of the wagon over her head. She was surprised by her own acceptance of the situation here, but some small use in repeating to herself, as she had several times, "It isn't fair. It isn't fair."

Absurd statement. What was fair for innocent people in this England of the Prince Regent and his fabulously rich friends?

She could scarcely remember that only this morning she had awakened in Lady Pomfret's house, to be greeted by the news that Charles Willoughby was waiting for her. Would he know it had not been her fault that he was attacked, and by Colonel Kirov whom he certainly would not trust?

He might think she was a part of the plot. He was comfortable, trustworthy, everything a female could want.

What a pity such men did not excite women in quite the way she felt when she found herself in Taidje Kirov's company!

If there had been no emerald, what the gypsies called Emerald Flame, she might have looked forward to a contented, happy and unexciting life with Charles.

She was roused by the snap of a twig underfoot and sat up, instantly alert.

"Who is it?"

"Who else would it be?" Colonel Kirov asked, dropping to the ground beside her. "What were you thinking about?"

He was so sure of himself she couldn't help blurting out the truth.

"I was thinking how happy I might have been as Sir Charles Willoughby's wife."

Whatever his true feelings, he reminded her with a nasty twist of humour, "Sheer bliss. And you need never be alone. There would be Willoughby's sainted mother breathing her Attar of Roses perfume into your ear."

True enough.

"And probably a knife blade in my back too."

He laughed and she found his unexpected good humour contagious. She began to laugh as well, but softly. She didn't wish to awaken Sanchia in the wagon over her head, if, that is, the good gypsy woman hadn't already been awakened by her husband's loud and tuneful snores.

Kirov patted the ground, removing a stick with a few moist leaves from under her hand.

"I have a message for you."

She was all eagerness. "Does Sir Charles understand?"

"No! Not that addle-pated saint."

Before she could get angry he added, "From Lady Pomfret. Her coachman was the intermediary. She has very nearly convinced that dried-up old vinegar-cruet named Enderby that she saw the emerald in the jeweller's hand as he reached into your reticule."

Surely, this was the beginning of rescue.

"Oh, how glorious! Thank you, thank you." She took his hands and squeezed them in her enthusiasm. Even in the dim light of a distant star she was taken aback by the glitter in those oblique dark eyes and wished she hadn't been so wildly demonstrative.

He said something that sounded like a curse in another language and would not release her hands.

"Don't play games, you little hussy. Unless you are willing to forget this elegant lady pose."

"What? You must be mad. I only meant to thank you."

"You think I cared only for the great lady's thanks?"

"That and something a great deal more important to you. You had your mother in mind. You were using me as your spy in the Holding Cells to discover what happened to her in Lord Stamsbury's garden. That is why you escorted the other prisoners to the Taunton Assizes before me. You were hoping to find the truth."

For a few seconds he looked a little stunned. In that reaction she knew she had hit upon the truth. It was curiously disillusioning to find she had been right.

There was a painful silence between them. When he broke it he had recovered his usual sardonic manner which seemed to tell her that there were a good many other things in life that came before his interest in saving her from the gallows — she could hardly blame him for that.

"You are more clever than you look," was his dubious compliment.

She felt that the least she could do was to show him how understanding she could be.

"If your mother was betrayed, then I was conceited to blame you for any motive you had. I lived in those cells, and without you I would still be there. I am very, very sorry. I spoke without thinking."

They were interrupted by a loud thump over their heads. She was startled but the Colonel grinned. Nevertheless, he lowered his voice.

"That would be Marko. We interrupted his snoring. . . . Go to sleep. At sunrise you are going to be transformed into a gypsy, like the others."

"My transformation is at the hands of your thieving cousin, of course."

"Cousin is a courtesy title, but yes, Yuri is the artist of our band. You can't keep running about the countryside with that absurd wig on and those pale hands. Not to mention a face like yours."

He put his fingers out, following the lines of her profile in his sensuous way. She was aroused by his touch, but there was discouragement in her thoughts, too. That was nothing new. Would there never be any return to the self that once was a respectable young lady named Hester Leland?

Perhaps he guessed her troubled thoughts. He leaned over and kissed her mouth which she had forgotten to close.

There was no doubt of it. His touch, and especially his lips, made her pulse beat faster, though she was afraid to let him know. Then he slapped her shoulder in a friendly way. She felt the sting before he got up and left her in her curious, warm cocoon under the gypsy wagon.

She knew she could not sleep. Too much had happened. Her brain whirled with wild thoughts, most of them bits and pieces of the long, incredible day she had lived through since she left Lady Pomfret.

Pictures of the day and the gypsy camp tonight. The memories seemed to whirl faster. Then she was awakened by the booted footsteps of Marko overhead in the wagon. She was about to sit up with a start but just remembered in time how close above her the floor of the wagon actually was.

The chilly dawn light looked golden and beautiful. Hester crawled out from under the wagon, shook herself, wondered if she was beginning to smell quite as pungent as the gypsies who used their thick, glossy hair as a towel and seemed to wear their dark but cheerful clothing until it fell away in rags.

The odour of campfires, burning wood, and stale grease from some deliciously grilled meat blotted out her first revulsion at the smell of strong, muscular bodies.

She wasn't sure whether it would seem intrusive if she reminded the band of her presence. She had noticed the night before that the women did not eat with the men and she wasn't sure what the etiquette would be about an uninvited stranger like herself who shared their hard come by meals.

They seemed more foreign and strange to her than any French, Spaniards or even Russians whom she and her father had met during her youth. She was not so much afraid of them as she was anxious not to infringe on their privacy. Except for Lady Pomfret and the women of the Holding Cells, they had been the only human beings who accepted her since the charges were made by Sylvester Girard and his so-called witnesses.

She huddled into the faded and dusty portière that had kept her warm in the night and made her way down the bank of the stream through prickly weeds and willows. She washed her hands, then cupped them, filled them with cold water and drank, wondering if this would be her breakfast.

Footsteps in the weeds behind her were startling and she spilled the rest of the water, only to be given a big chunk of savoury bread that Sanchia had brought her. It had been toasted over last night's still glowing coals, apparently on the end of a stick. It was heavenly to chew and Hester thanked her, still with her mouth full. Also on the morning air was the sweet, mouthwatering smell of roasting onions.

The woman waved away her thanks. Something in her manner seemed to suggest to Hester that outcasts together shared one another's good luck or bad.

"Come to the women's fire for onions and coffee," she suggested in her very fair English. "And wine? You like hot wine, Emerald Flame?"

"Coffee and onions would be wonderful," Hester said quickly and got up to follow her.

They passed the wily, sloe-eyed Yuri with his serpent grace and Hester tried to avoid staring at him, but he held up brown-stained hands, a cloth and delicate brush, obviously intended for her.

She hurried to join Sanchia who took long steps in her boots, like a man. Her satin skirt, the seams all inside out, gleamed as she moved into the rising sunlight.

Hester spoke just above a whisper, to avoid Yuri who

seemed uncomfortably anxious to make her over into something so far from her familiar self.

"If I am not to be seen, must I still be completely changed?"

Sanchia looked back, her black eyes opaque and unreadable. All the same Hester was sure the woman was angry, or maybe disappointed in her.

"You do not wish to be like one of us?"

"Oh, certainly. Absolutely. It is so good of your people. But I meant . . . taking your valuable time."

"Time?" The word seemed unfamiliar to the gypsy. "For you *Gaje*, may be. Do you know how long we existed in the world before your kind?" She raised one hand, the long forefinger describing a semi-circle around them. "We do not change. Our world is the same all the thousand thousand suns. You Gentiles, you come. You take this water, that tree, the grass. Yours, you say. Not ours. Yet a thousand, thousand suns from now, you are gone. And this world that we do not hurt, you have left dead to us. No, Emerald Flame. Do not be disgraced because we make you one of us."

"I didn't mean—" Hester stammered.

Sanchia's forefinger stabbed Hester's carefully covered breast, different from Sanchia's great, half-exposed breasts. The pressure eased, but Sanchia's curious words remained with her longer.

"You are today, but we are always."

Hester knew she had made a serious mistake, one she deeply regretted.

"Tell me what I can do to thank you."

"It is arranged. When a favour or a wrong is given, we must pay. It is our custom. You will tell fortunes tonight at the fair."

The idea was both intriguing and alarming. Hester devoutly hoped someone would give her a few hints, but despite her lack of skill as a fortune-teller, she meant to do her wholehearted best. As Sanchia said, she owed it to them.

The men of the band were finishing their breakfast and Colonel Kirov was among them, sitting on the ground cross-legged. He always seemed very clean around Hester, or at least, as clean as she was in what she thought of as her costume. But here he was, eating half a leftover cold chicken between his strong, white teeth and enjoying it without napkin or handkerchief. He licked his fingers when he finished and looked up at Hester as he did so.

She felt just a shade disappointed. She had got used to his smoothing the way for her. She smiled at him, including his male companions. She thought his eyes answered her, amused, but the gypsies gave her neither approval nor disapproval.

Undoubtedly, they realized her presence among them would draw trouble to their band. She suspected that trouble came to them easily enough without the complications she brought.

While she drank the coffee and tried to grasp a fire-hot onion, sunlight spread over the glade. The children began to play tag and running games, the dogs barked and chased rabbits. But when one dog splashed into the stream to pursue sheep in the meadow across the stream he was called back sharply.

The meadow belonged to the farmer who had called on them the night before. As Sanchia explained to her, it was always wise to have a friend among the Gentiles.

Although everyone seemed ready for Yuri to make

218

Hester's great transformation, she thought it much too soon, but the peculiar, unblinking look of Sanchia and others in the band told her not to argue. She had hoped momentarily that Colonel Kirov might put up some objection but when Yuri, the artist, slithered up to her with his bag of artistic weapons and she looked around, the Colonel was nowhere in sight.

One of the exotically handsome younger women, interested in the coming transformation, guessed where her real interest lay, as she informed Hester.

"Taidje is off with Marko to settle for our fairgrounds tonight. They give coins which may be taken back if a good trade is made with the townsfolk. They have no time for you. Sanchia, this one is a troublemaker. Why do we take her? She will bring the *Gaje* police."

Hester was startled to see Sanchia remove a knife blade from the roll of cloth that formed a belt around her still trim waist. She cut off the heel of a bread loaf while the blade shone in the sunlight, very like Angele in the Holding Cells. She studied the blade without glancing Zia's way.

"Go practice your wire walk, Zia. You are clumsy as a turtle."

Zia shrugged and retreated, looking sullen. The gold coins across her forehead and dangling from her ears accentuated her barbaric beauty, and Hester thought again of the women in the Holding Cells – sisters under the different skins.

"And I am one of them," she reminded herself, bolstering her courage and lowering her pride. She turned to find Yuri so close that his breath was warm and moist on her throat. She remembered that she had always wondered what it would be like to play a role before the footlight candles, and now she would find out.

She pretended to be as tough and hard as these eternal wanderers whose home was a wagon forever moving and a heath that was never theirs.

"Well, Yuri, make me like yourself, and no nonsense."

His dark eyebrows went up in an inverted 'v'.

"A pleasure, O Lady of the Sun. Yuri will make you Queen of the Night."

"Never mind that. Hurry about your business." She also thought it wise to keep him doubly occupied. His eyes were much too busy over her body. "While you work, explain what I must know if I am to tell fortunes and foresee the future."

He was getting out the ugly mess that must be walnut stain, and her order seemed to surprise him but he accepted it.

"What Taidje says, Taidje gets. But one day the wrong person may whisper a word in the ear of the police." He removed her wig and threw it on the leaf-strewn ground.

She began to be more anxious but tried not to let him guess. He struck her as a kind of person whose object was to keep others off balance with sly threats that might, or might never be carried out.

"Why do you think you would be spared? Your people always pay their debts, I was told that by Sanchia."

"Ah!" He had been about to dip her head into a black concoction that looked revolting. He stopped, looked across the tripod and dying coals where Sanchia and Zia were removing the kettle and tripod with a cloth and a heavy-handled knife blade. He laughed. "Well then, when Sanchia talks, I advise you to listen. Even Marko knows who is truly our chief. . . . Now, under! What a shame! All the golden threads turning as dark as Sanchia's bottom."

It was not a happy thought.

At least, he was so busy at his work of turning her from light blonde to swarthy brunette that he spent little time on those sexual caresses he had at first anticipated.

Hester had no idea how long this radical disguise took, except by studying the sun as it moved overhead, but it must have been mid-morning when she was permitted to see the change for herself.

"No looking glass," Yuri told her. "See yourself in the water."

It was only then, as she made her way down the bank among the willows, that she realized Sanchia had been watching much of the proceedings. She wondered if the woman had done this to protect her from Yuri's eager fingers, or because Colonel Kirov had asked her to watch over Hester. Perhaps both.

The woman nodded with satisfaction.

"Yuri has talent. The theatre in London would be glad of him. But he is too lazy and the four walls of a house, even a theatre house, are not for him."

Yuri made an elaborate bow, then began to put away his tools. He had not yet washed his hands and didn't seem to care. Hester reached the brook which ran slowly through a little pool above the camp. She saw a big-eyed, swarthy gypsy's face peering up at her and looked over her shoulder nervously before she realized this insolent looking, none too friendly woman reflected in the pool had once been Hester Leland.

Surely, those voluptuous red lips and black lashes were

221

not hers! Meanwhile, she must rehearse the fortune-telling tricks Yuri had told her about, emphasizing that her chief asset would be the ability to read her subject's mind, to guess what troubled or obsessed them.

"Do you tell each other's fortune?" she had asked as Yuri tangled and curled her long, blackened hair. He scoffed at that.

"Some, but only the fools, like Zia who loves Edris. He walks the wire with her and pretends to return her love, but he is indifferent. Not like me."

Hester had drawn back but she knew she would have to react in a less proud and revolted way. She could not risk offending the band. Besides, Yuri immediately began to teach her the reading of the Tarot. This would be necessary.

She knew that with so much to learn it was impossible for her to remember the proper laying out of the cards, as well as their meaning in relation to their placement. The only answer would be a powerful imagination, expressed with great authority.

Colonel Kirov returned in the afternoon with Marko who went at once to Sanchia, obviously to report on their luck or otherwise with the town authorities. The Colonel found Hester on the edge of the brook laying out the Tarot cards once more on the grass while she repeated phrases she was making up from Yuri's earlier hints.

She found it rude of the Colonel to laugh at her while he tood there with his hands on his hips enjoying the absurd scene she presented. To stop his annoying attack of humour, Hester tried to change the subject.

"Yuri told me that Sanchia rules the band. Did you notice that her husband went directly to her with his report? Yuri was right."

Colonel Kirov looked back toward the wagon shared by Sanchia and Marko. He still seemed amused but reminded her teasingly, "Well then, I came directly to you. What does that prove?"

She picked up a card at random. "Are you asking me to tell what fate has in store for you?"

He glanced at the card. "Not that fortune, I hope."

She looked down at the card in the palm of her hand: the Hanged Man. She dropped it in a sudden, cold horror.

Perhaps the Hanged Man still waited for her somewhere. Or even for the Colonel who had helped her to escape.

He kicked and scattered the rows of cards. "Aren't you ashamed to yourself? I do believe you are superstitious. And you, a fine, highborn English lady!"

She pretended to be cross because he had scattered the cards and he knelt to help her pick them up, observing her as he dropped them in the folds of her worn silk skirt which was the colour of burning coals in a campfire. It and her low-necked black blouse had the advantage of casting her light eyes in shadow. Her painted and stained face was fairly disguised by a fringe of hair across her forehead and the black lace mantilla, whose forehead band shone with gold coins.

"I didn't want to be responsible for them," she apologized. "But there is no arguing with your cousin Yuri."

He grinned. "My cousin by courtesy only. And the coins are Russian. They belong to me. Try not to lose them. It might help if you could babble some Russian now and then. You don't know any Russian, by chance?"

"Will French do? After all, they were in Russia not so long ago."

"Don't remind me. However, a little French will

do, if necessary. How are you coming along with the fortune-telling?"

With a glint in her eyes she prophesied, "You are about to be attacked by a creditor demanding payment."

He frowned at the abrupt lightening of her mood. Then he looked around to find Yuri standing with one palm outstretched, clearly expecting it to be filled.

"A masterly job, wouldn't you say, Taidje?"

Colonel Kirov looked Hester up and down. "Tolerable." While Hester was disgesting this dubious compliment, he reached into his breeches' pocket, took out a shining, polished guinea piece which was far more than her transformation deserved.

Yuri blew Hester a kiss and loped away, satisfied.

Kirov lifted Hester to her feet.

"Now, you pay your debt. The fair is being talked about in several villages. I shouldn't be surprised if the takings are good tonight."

Hester reminded him, "They do say there is an occasional theft at these country fairs."

He refused to be offended.

"That is Yuri's department, the fool! Sanchia and Marko, and Edris, our wirewalker, may return to these places in years to come. Then too, before we put up our equipment, we put up a ransom for our behaviour."

He took her arm. Feeling her tremble, he shook her playfully. "What? Our fortune-teller has lost her courage? Is this the girl who braved the Holding Cells? Put a good face upon it and hope you don't meet some old acquaintances."

Chapter Seventeen

Hester Leland had been to many fairs, some of which included gypsies because, as she had discovered, Lady Pomfret reserved a soft place in her heart for the exotic people of Romany. It was probable that she had never outgrown her first love for a young gypsy on the Dorset Heath.

Hester even remembered how she had secretly smiled at her Ladyship's belief in the fortune-tellers whom she always sought out. They were not hard to find in their tents that were open on one side to admit the superstitious. Bright pennons snapped in the breeze from the peak of the tent, attracting attention along with the gaily spangled cloth thrown around over unseen objects and the carpets that formed the floor and often the walls of the fortune-teller's mysterious lair.

That evening Hester realized why such places smelled so odd, half repulsive, half intriguing, with their strong hint of grilled meat, wet grass, age-old dust hardened by the rains, and occasionally urine.

As the wagons rattled and creaked along over dusty, dirt-packed roads, Hester tried to remember everything Yuri and Sanchia had taught her. She rode beside the sensual beauty, Zia, on the wagon owned by Zia's quiet, slim lover, Edris, who walked the wire above the fairgrounds from a pole to the peaked roof of a barn. He looked almost frail but Hester noted his fingers, guiding the horses with heavy strings of rawhide, and she decided that there was steel in those thin fingers as well as the muscles of his well-trained body.

She took care not to observe the high wire man very often, since it was clear that Zia adored him.

The almost cleared field selected for the fair had often been used for such a purpose and this, combined with the close-cropping of grass by flocks of sheep, meant that the field was now ready for them. Hester marvelled at how much had to be done each time in order to set up all these booths, tents, high poles, stilts, and rings for small domestic animals to amuse the children.

And what part would Colonel Kirov play in all this? She couldn't imagine. Finally, as she helped Zia carry the equipment for Edris's balancing act, she remarked casually to Zia.

"It must be very pleasant to sit back and watch your people work so hard, as Colonel Kirov seems to do."

Zia gave her an impatient sidelong glance.

"He has his own tasks, has Taidji. Sometimes he walks the stilts. He is very funny. The *gaje* little ones, they like him and their mothers pay us. He plays music too, for my dancing. You know the mandolina of Italy, the Spanish strings? His music is Tartar strings on a long, wooden base. Calling to the passions."

Edris stopped by with a pair of strange, supple shoes that he used in his walk.

"You talk of Taidje? When we are in trouble with the Gentile police he saves us. When we starve in the Irish country, he brings a tinker's wagon and we survive. You are a fool, Zia. You think the dance is

226

everything. The dance, and love. It is better to eat than to love."

He went off toward the pole which was the starting point of his walk and which had their bright pennons flying in the sunset breeze.

Although Hester's mind was occupied with worry over all she must remember tonight, she spared a minute now and then to ask herself what she could of the future, assuming she had one.

Why had Kirov forced Sanchia and her band to accept a Gentile, and initiate her into their customs, perhaps even their secrets? Why didn't he simply leave her in some hidden place on the understanding with Lady Pomfret that she could return to her normal life when the truth about her innocence was either forced or tricked out of Sylvester Girard?

Surely, it was not Kirov's object to degrade and humiliate her, to make her into the lowest of the low. . . .

Why had that flashed across her brain? Was she still convinced of her superiority over these people? Hadn't she learned a little humility yet?

She was surprised to note her own pride when Sanchia took her to the fortune-teller's tent which would be Hester's property until the fair closed, sometime after midnight. Zia stuck her curly head between Sanchia and Hester.

"And she must take it down. That is the hard part, eh, Sanchia? Carrying all those carpets and the swinging lamp and that accursed crystal. Heavier than you think, Miss Emerald Flame."

Sanchia snapped, "We all do our part. No one knows better than you, Lazy One."

Zia stuck out her tongue and ran off barefooted, to meet

227

her beloved Edris. Hester wondered why she didn't get slivers or cuts on the soles of her feet but little seemed to trouble her.

The thought of those toughened extremities made Hester aware of her own hands and feet, now dyed to a peculiar shade, neither brown nor grey but with a hint of green like unpolished brass. Luckily she had been given sandals, but even her fingernails and her palms were not those she had been familiar with for a lifetime.

All the same, when she was within the fortune-teller's stuffy carpet tent she reigned supreme. As she got used to the dim, flickering lamp that swung from the little entrance under the carpet roof, she realized she could make out all the features of her visitors but they could see only the glitter of Russian coins across her forehead and the flecks of gold sewn into the lacy black gauze scarf that fell gracefully over her head and hung below her shoulders.

Besides, the Holding Cells had taught her briefly to see in the semi-darkness. She would have a definite advantage over her clients. Surely, a little careful observation would help her to read the fortunes of those others who were not Romany.

How odd! Had she thought of herself in that moment as a real gypsy? What made Hester Leland so much better than Emerald Flame?

Always aware that Colonel Kirov was nearby, though she hadn't seen him since they left for the fairground, she thought: "Is this what you are trying to teach me? That your people are my equals?"

With some shame she remembered her attitude toward Colonel Kirov at the Blassingame house in Bath. He had been outraged because she seemed to feel superior in some way, but now she was learning.

The carnival noise spreading across the fairground did much to cheer her. She could hear the shrieks of laughter and pretended fear as children on ponies trotted by, but the greatest challenge for Hester was the argument between some giggling young woman and her sweetheart, or between two girls discussing whether they should have their fortunes told.

Most of them held their discussions at the entry under the carpet roof or beside the carpet wall, the girls inisting that it was all too absurd but "it would be such fun". And, as one girl said, scoffingly, "You'll ask if Hindly loves that MacLeitt creature with her horrid big teeth and her silly grin."

This was easier than Hester had expected. She hoped the two girls would move around to the entry and come in, half shy, half bold, for each other's benefit. They came in.

Hester must look more horrifying than she thought. One of the girls uttered a little shriek.

"It's so dark and horrid. Why does she glow all over like that?"

"It's metal pieces on her shawl and her head, you goose." The taller and heavier of the two girls was the one who had teased her friend about Hindly.

With her heart beating rapidly Hester waited in her ancient, backless cerulean chair, her face and figure illuminated only by the flickering flames of what appeared to be ruby light beneath the crystal. The tiny, darting lights flicked through the crystal like serpent tongues, further scaring the girls and a man and woman, a local sheepman and his wife, who were also there, and proved surprisingly gullible. The wife whispered:

"It'll be the devil fire. See how it licks its way through the crystal."

It was obvious to Hester that the crystal was hollow underneath somewhere, and blood-red liquid flowed through the little paths carved in the crystal. The light itself must be a tiny, shielded lamp in the base of the table.

Really quite clever enough to fool the unsophisticated.

In her deepest, practised voice Hester held out her hands, palms up, and recited the famous password,

"Cross the hands with silver."

The man and woman backed away, temporarily leaving the scene to the girls. The tall one was still a non-believer.

"They always say that," she claimed, but dropped thrupence into Hester's palm.

Hester resented this low rating of her art and decided the girl would get what she paid for — a bad fortune.

The girl's pretty friend who wanted the boy called Hindly paid sixpence and, in a manner of speaking, Hester gave her the precious Hindly. She traced an 'H' on the top of the crystal and said in her deepest, most ominous voice:

"Into your life once more comes this one . . . Hen – Hemp . . . No, Hinden? Not so. Hindell?"

The girl clapped her hands. "Jess, it's Hindly. My own Otho Hindly."

"But take care," Hester warned her. "There is another in the crystal."

The two girls peered in. Jess said stoutly, "Where? I don't see it at all."

"Otho Hindly," the love-smitten girl repeated, enthralled.

"I can see his eyes in the crystal, and that awful MacLeitt creature behind him."

The girlfriend said, "I don't see either one," and they started away, wrangling. Hester called to the non-believer:

"Your fortune, miss? Or your silver?" She offered it to the heavy girl who looked surprised but snatched it up and hurried after her friend, boasting, "First time I ever got even ha'penny bit from a gypsy."

"Well," Hester thought, "I made a mistake there!"

It was a double mistake, as the sheepman muttered, "Come away. It's all tricks."

Hester sighed. She had not done too well on her first transactions.

Things picked up later, although it was hard to keep her mind on fortune-telling when so much excitement was going on outside. From the comments she heard in her cave-like tent, she judged that the wire-walker, Edris, had performed skilfully, balancing himself from the pole which he climbed by wooden steps, to the rooftop across the main concourse of the fairground. Several drunken watchers and a child or two tried to disturb him, doubtless hoping he would tumble down the two-storey distance and break his neck. But he seemed to be used to this sort of persuasion from his audience.

After several customers Hester was jarred later when she thought she recognized the voice of a highly painted woman of an indeterminate age somewhere between youth and thirty-five, who persuaded her gentleman friend to have her fortune told. Hester was more worried over not being able to judge the woman's age than if she had known her. The uncertainty troubled her so, in order to gain time, she murmured in a gutteral voice:

"It is dark. . . . It is not night, but it is dark. I cannot see the past of this one. It is dark." She added for good measure, "And cold," wondering why she had said it. Creeping into her consciousness was a vague picture that suited the querulous voice of the woman but she couldn't identify the face, probably due to the heavily made up features. The woman's male companion did so for her.

"Tildy-Girl, she's got you there. Ever seen a gypsy in that hole where they sunk you?"

Tilda Clavering. Good God! One of the few women in the Holding Cells whom she had actively disliked.

"Don't you talk of it, Ned. I'm free and out, and I've a paper to prove it. Not guilty, they said. I'm innercent as a bird. . . . The dirty gypsy's guessin', that's all."

Dirty gypsy, is it! Hester lowered her head further, pretending to study the crystal, thinking: "I'd like to give you the Hanged Man, you tale-bearer!" It would be very like fate to have hanged Bess and Sarey and freed this one.

Tilda and her man finally left, but not before Hester had promised her "Something mighty fine in another part of the country. The North, deep in the Penines." Let Derbyshire worry about her.

But they were gone, although there had been a near-danger at the end of their visit to her tent. Tilda's man said as they were leaving:

"She had funny hands for a gypsy. Nails looked painted darker."

"All them gypsies paint," Tilda informed him wisely.

Along about the middle of the evening Hester began to think about something to eat and went to the entry of the tent, still in shadows. She was there in time to see an absurd pirate on stilts having great fun with the children running after him. She recognized those bare, bronze legs with the breeches tied at the knees and the pirate's breast only half covered by a sleeveless leather vest.

Taidji Kirov, of course. She joined in the chorus of applause when he passed Edris on the barn roof and both men saluted each other, then Kirov leaped down from his great height, seeming to bounce on a pile of leaves and hay.

He threw aside the stilts which the farm children tried vainly to mount, and came striding along to Hester. He reached around behind her for a cloth which she had used to dust her ancient cerulean chair. He wiped his body which gleamed with sweat.

"Enjoying yourself?"

"Very much, unless someone recognizes me. In ordinary circumstances I might be uneasy around your friends, but I almost feel like one of them."

"That was the notion." He draped the cloth around her neck and while she was trying to get it off, he leaned forward against the tent pole imprisoning her between his outstretched arms.

She felt daring and moistened her lips, her gaze fixed on his mouth. He was not a man to refuse a dare. He leaned a little nearer and his mouth caught hers, his lips hard over her own, as if he would draw her within his body, his willing prisoner. She closed her eyes, her hands around his bare neck. He held her close to his hot body and the pulse beat between them excited her as always.

She heard his voice at her ear, a ticklish sensation that made her want to giggle, but she refrained with an effort.

"No more sleeping on the wet ground," he promised her, but there was a sting in his promise. "Come, share my bed tonight."

She stiffened with fear of her own weakness. She was afraid her body might yield to him again under such circumstances. Clearly, the passion was in her blood, as it had been in her mother's. Hester might have been born a lady, but her love had made her a camp follower.

Charles Willoughby offered a respectable life filled with normal, everyday good works, such as were already a part of his own life. Their children would feel they shared in that love, the joys and the sorrows.

But a brief, passionate idyl with this strange gypsy would destroy the rest of her life, if anything of that life was left to her. Besides, she had no assurance that she could ever be anything more to him than a camp follower of sorts, a woman whose body he used on a few occasions and then abandoned.

As her brain warned her, she felt her muscles begin to withdraw from him. He knew he had lost whatever was in his mind, and released her abruptly. He looked grim in spite of his smile.

"Still the aristocrat, still the tease."

She started to deny the despicable charge but he was already leaving her. She went back into the fortune-teller's tent. She felt a trembling through her body and hugged her arms to restore what she thought of as her self-possession.

She reminded herself wryly, "At least, I've won the battle with myself over lust and desire. If that is any comfort."

Straight backed, she settled herself in the cerulean chair, careful to lean forward just far enough for her features to look as sinister as possible above the blood-red ribbon of light glowing through the crystal.

Since the hour must be near closing, she was surprised

at the business her dubious fortune-telling ability began to generate. She did not make the mistake of promising very many ominous developments. She told people, especially the females, what they wanted to hear about love, fidelity, and proposals. The males, most of whom had drunk more than their share of ale, were interested in money and a good deal in some business of their own on the morrow.

Once, in a daring moment, she advised a horse coper to "beware of trading with unknowns".

"Don't ye be afeared o' that, Witch – Old Matt knows yer people right well. Mind that."

She thought he was a trifle overconfident. He wouldn't be the first horse trader to make a brilliant trade and find, too late, that he had got a spavined horse.

She was relieved not to see any more of Tilda Clavering and her observant companion, and more than relieved when she heard what might be the breaking up of the fair. Poles, tents, frame and equipment began to come down. The visitors sauntered down the length of the fairgrounds on their way past gypsy wagons to the pony carts, horses, wagons and a few stylish curricles whose well-cared-for teams were guarded by men in the livery of the owners.

Hester ate the last of the cone full of thick and savoury lamb, drank the sour wine, and decided it was time to put the crystal into its pocket of lamb's wool and take down some of the wall hangings. She wondered where the swaying, top-heavy wagons would carry her tomorrow.

Suddenly the sound of running footsteps past her tent and cries of "A fight, a fight!" brought her to the front flap of the tent. In the distance she could see the wire-walker, Edris, stalking toward the cleared centre of the grounds. With his back to the fortune-teller's tent Yuri, the troublemaker, had been holding the flirtatious

Zia tight against his body. He was laughing as he shoved the girl away from him and held up his empty palms to the oncoming acrobat.

"Funning, no-but funning. Ask Zia."

A crowd gathered fast and many looked to see the climax between the main characters in this perforemance. Zia shrugged her bare, dark shoulders. Hester suspected that she would like nothing better than to watch Edris and Yuri fight over her.

A thrill of excitement swept through the crowd as Edris drew a narrow, gleaming blade from the light sheath at his hip.

Behind Hester another witness appeared. Kirov asked, "What the devil now?"

"Stop them!" Hester whispered, guessing what trouble, including the authorities, this might bring to the band.

Kirov waved aside her plea as if she had said something ridiculous, or perhaps unnecessary. He pushed his way through the crowd which was already betting on the outcome of the duel. It was obvious from their comments that they considered this a typical gypsy entertainment.

The high wire performer had his weapon out in plain sight and made threatening passes with it, but what alarmed Hester more was the way Yuri pretended to be unarmed, retreating with jokes and pleas for understanding while one of his hands crept around to the back of his blue sash where his stiletto was concealed. Kirov had moved toward the grounds but Hester was near enough to see that Yuri would try to surprise Edris with a quick and bloody stab from the stiletto. It looked like a woman's weapon, though no less deadly.

She cried out a warning but her voice was drowned by the shouts of the audience as they wagered Edris against Yuri. There were disgruntled complaints from the bettors when Kirov gave some order to Yuri in their own language but Yuri only laughed, making a joke as his fingers groped and found the stiletto at his back.

Kirov said something to Edris who looked at Zia. The girl blew a kiss to him, apparently satisfied that this would end his belligerence. She knew him well. Edris stood there in the flickering torchlight surrounded by deep shadows. He lowered his arm with the knife just as Yuri sprang forward, stiletto thrust out. The crowd was once more edgy with excitement, yelling encouragement to one or the other of the two gypsies.

But this time Kirov was between them, stalking Yuri, ordering him in their own tongue to surrender the stiletto. Still grinning and well aware of his audience, Yuri cried in English,

"Come, Taidje, try me. Take it."

Meanwhile, Marko lumbered into the crowd, his thick, white moustaches quivering. He elbowed himself into the cleared circle where Edris, having turned his back, swung around again but the players in the duel were now the unarmed Colonel Kirov and Yuri, still in his bloodthirsty, playful mood.

"Take it, Taidje," he taunted. "Or are you afraid of a little nick in the arm, a little bloodletting?"

Marko started to interfere heavily. Edris stopped him, an act that terrified Hester for Kirov's sake. Yuri was still in retreat, though facing Kirov. Since he was armed and Kirov was not, he felt free to wave the lethal little blade back and forth tantalizingly in the air between himself and Kirov's face. But nothing seemed to stop Kirov.

With the suddenness of a striking cobra Kirov shot out one bare arm, his flesh glittering in the light. He grasped Yuri's wrist above the knife blade and twisted hard.

Edris laughed shortly, took Zia's arm and left the scene.

Yuri was screaming, trying to turn the blade upon the hand that held his wrist in a vice. His leg jerked forward, probably to kick at his assailant. The enthusiasm among the male watchers increased.

Bets were exchanged but already Kirov had thrust one knee out, catching Yuri in the groin and he went down hard, groaning. The stiletto dropped to the ground as Yuri clutched his body and lay huddled at the Russian's feet.

Among the bettors in the crowd there was a brisk exchange of coins while those closest to Yuri heard him muttering in English,

"I'll have you for this. Don't think you'll not suffer. I know things, I do."

Just as Hester elbowed her way into the ring, seeing Kirov grip his own bloodstained right arm with his left hand, Marko reached down, slung the groaning Yuri over his powerful shoulder, and tramped off, probably to the wagons. He passed Sanchia on the way and she came running to the scene of the fight, her red skirts flying.

Hester had reached Kirov and was feeling on her own body for cloth that would serve as a bandage. She did not think her worn and dyed skirts would help. Kirov was amused by her efforts.

"Do you think I've never had a knife scratch before? Here is Sanchia. Let me have her kerchief."

The gypsy queen obligingly removed her sweat-stained yellow scarf and Hester, folding it with the worst stain underneath, bound it around Kirov's arm above the wrist.

The cut was bleeding in spurts but, as she might have expected, he scoffed at her efforts.

"Tell her, Sanchia. There is a deal more blood where that came from. Now, shall we give these good friends some more entertainment for their money?"

Seeing the end of the most exciting entertainment, the crowd scattered to look for other wonders on the fairgrounds. A dozen women were waiting at the tinker's wagon for Sanchia to return and bargain with them for household supplies. Sanchia hurried off to her business.

Hester had finished tying the yellow scarf and ordered Kirov severely, "Don't use that arm for a few hours or the blood will start again."

Small wet patches were forming on the outside folds of the scarf but Kirov was cheerful as ever. He seemed to enjoy her attentions, however. His good hand reached out to tighten on her wrist. She winced and joked, "Now, I understand Yuri's pain."

He laughed but did not loosen his grasp.

"I would have you tell my fortune if there was more time. But I know the quick fingers of those gypsy children among that crowd. We had best decamp before their drunken victims wake to find watches and silver pieces missing."

She said nothing to this calm talk of thievery but could imagine what Charles Willoughby would think of her if he knew the worst. Since she was consorting with thieves and, in Yuri's case, perhaps worse, Charles might wonder if she was worth saving.

Kirov took her into the fortune-teller's tent. In front of the curious, glowing crystal, half in and half out of its soft pocket, he said abruptly, "Sit. You look as though you would fall down."

She smiled faintly, with an effort. "Thank you, I will. Do you expect more trouble from Yuri?"

"I always expect more trouble from Yuri. However, there are ways of keeping him quiet, even if it is impossible to keep him out of trouble. He is a coward as you saw tonight. He only fights when the odds are in his favour. He won't cause too much harm, so long as he is afraid of the band."

"Thank heaven for that!"

He reached over and put his palm against her forehead. "Cold sweat. You need a little toughening."

"Oh, splendid! Don't you think I've had enough toughening these last few weeks to make me the equal of your Zia and the others?"

He laughed. "Not *my* Zia. I believe you really are interested in my health. I heard you scream when that little toad nicked me."

Her tired, nervous spirits were raised by his teasing. "Why not? I count upon you to save me from the hangman.

"I ought to leave you in the hands of your beloved milksop, Willoughby. You are bound to appreciate me more. At least I don't ask you to be tried and possibly hanged before I save you."

It was quite true. The one thing about Charles that did frighten her was his insistence on having her freed legally. He refused to allow for the possible miscarriage of justice.

Kirov pulled her up onto her feet with his good arm, complaining, "Now, you have spoiled our relationship. It was much more stimulating when we quarrelled all the time."

She laughed at that but demanded as they left the tent, "Under which wagon do I sleep tonight?"

"Tonight you have earned the inside of a wagon. How much money did you make with your fortunes?"

"Not a fortune certainly," she admitted, offering to him the grease-stained velvet bag given to her for the purpose.

He pocketed it in those baggy Tartar breeches he wore and took her hand. She wondered how she would ever cope with living her own life again without his overwhelming assistance.

They walked out of the tent together, Kirov carrying the lamp that burned in fitful spurts of light.

A man and woman passed at that moment, the female loaded down with trinkets either won or wheedled out of her companion. The woman pinched her companion's arm at the sight of Hester.

"I do know that girl."

Hester hurried her steps as she had recognized Tilda Clavering's shrill voice. The woman stopped.

"But Patterson said she was dead and buried the night of the escape."

Kirov nudged Hester, shook her and burst out at her in the patois of the Romanies. His deep voice sounded curt and dangerous, but utterly incomprehensible.

Not knowing what to say in reply, Hester lowered her voice a good octave and defended herself in her own mediocre French. For good measure she threw in some gutteral language her father had used on occasion and to her enormous relief Tilda's gentleman friend said, "You never hear that tongue in no Holding Cell. That's real Romany, all right."

Tilda grumbled and admitted, "Well then, they do say for sure, the highwayman that got Angele out of the cells did bury the dead body of that other female;

241

so this can't be Leel. But I would-of swore – no matter."

The two walked on. Amused, Kirov turned to Hester who was well aware of her danger.

"Do you agree that the West County is none too healthy for you?"

"I know. I must get away. Somewhere in the opposite direction, where they would never look for me. Wandering around here I am forever likely to be seen by the Tildas and the odious Girards. If I could hide where there are fewer people. . . ."

"And stand out for the beauty you are?"

She was not flattered. "Don't talk nonsense. What is your notion? Smack in the middle of London, I suppose."

"Why not? One of my raven-haired, dark-skinned cousins fresh from the imperial court at St Petersburg? Living in luxury in the house where my father was famous for entertaining beautiful cousins. Or nieces, depending on the age."

"I can imagine."

"No," he insisted. "You can't. I am not my father and I actually do have cousins who visited me during the festivities after Waterloo. Matter of fact, I have been known to house two aunts and an uncle."

He considered. "Though now that I think of it, Uncle Sergei was a bit of a bounder."

She could not help laughing.

"And of course, no duennas, no chaperones."

"There is my housekeeper. A stickler for the behaviour of the Kirovs. She has been trying to marry me off since my father died. I've no doubt she will choose you as her latest candidate."

Was he sincere? Or was this more of his absurd and dangerously attractive teasing?

She tried to borrow his light manner. "I see I must behave with more decorum than I have shown so far."

He glanced at her. She thought he might indicate that he had read an agreement in her remark and be pleased, but he said indifferently.

"By all means. It will be expected of you. Mrs Fifield, my housekeeper, tells me I am enough of a rogue for one household."

"Like father, like son, in fact."

"Unfortunately, no. My father would ride his Tartar mount up the staircase and into the ballroom if he chose. But I am not permitted the same liberties."

She could hardly believe that a few minutes ago she had been cold with fear, wondering if there was any refuge left to her in the world. Now, he was making her laugh.

"Let us hope it doesn't come to that."

He walked with her to one of the darkened wagons that appeared to be deserted.

He sighed elaborately. "No. I doubt if you've the courage to play the part, even in perfect disguise."

She refused to rise to the bait but when he left her at the wagon, she gave him her hand and thanked him for all he had done to save her.

"I shall never forget it."

Looking sardonic, he put his hands on both sides of her waist and lifted her off the wagon steps, holding her in midair, two feet off the ground. She made no protest. He deserved that, at least. The way his strange, Tartar eyes looked into hers troubled her.

Evidently he could not see what he looked for there, but only the warm gratitude she had expressed.

"Well then," he said finally as he set her back on the steps, "It's the North Country, not the bold London masquerade."

She stood a few seconds watching him stride away across the now empty and darkening fairgrounds. She thought she saw Yuri far across the grounds, rounding up the horses with Marko but the troublemaker did not look her way. She turned, went into the chill, dusty wagon, and lay down upon a heavy cloth coat which she recognized by the touch as belonging to Colonel Kirov. She would like to have undressed and taken a bath while someone poured delicious scented warm water over her, but the gypsy world did not seem quite the place for those luxuries.

She patted the collar of Kirov's coat where her head would lie and wished the Russian might have been a gentleman like Charles, or that trustworthy Charles might possess a little of Kirov's aggressiveness to go with his own honourable intentions.

The troubles of the day had left her tired enough to sleep very shortly and for once her dreams failed to be shadowed by a masked hangman.

She was awakened roughly by a heavy hand shaking her. She sat up, tense and ready. She had no doubt this was bad news.

In the low voice of authority that no one ever questioned, Sanchia said, "Quick! Taidje is waiting. Tuck your hair into this hat. Put on the coat and, fasten it. The boots are Zia's. Too large, but no matter."

Numb with cold but ready for action, Hester followed orders, whispering, "What happened?"

"Two *gaje*. The woman thought she knew you. The man disagrees. But Marko heard them arguing. The squire's men will look for you on the High Road north. Quick."

"Do they know the Colonel – I mean Taidje – will be with me?"

"They know nothing of that connection. But the North Road out of the county will be the easiest and most obvious way for you to escape. They'll send out men in that direction. They think you are alone. Hurry!"

"Then, where are we to go?" She was busy dressing, and she could see that in spite of her natural anxiety, Sanchia was rapidly losing patience with her.

"It must be London and Kirov House. Taidje is sending a message ahead to the housekeeper, who is faithful. The Russian house is not like to be touched by those pursuing you."

Yes, Hester's spirits rose at the thought. Even the Bow Street Runners and any others sent to bring her to Justice would be in serious difficulties if they stole a prisoner from the property of the Emperor Alexander's associates. And there was Hester's own gypsy disguise. That should help.

The Regent's world had not seen her since her girl-hood in the stews of London. She had no intimates in Bath who made London visits except Charles and Lady Pomfret. No others were likely to recognize a black-haired, well-rounded, sensuous-looking Russian heavily rouged, with eyes rimmed by black kohl. Lady Pomfret had said that the Russians who accompanied the Emperor Alexander to London for the celebrations were a bit noisy and occasionally vulgar. So be it. She would play the voluptuous exotic. Or anything else, if it would save her neck.

There was ironic amusement in the fact that she must

245

now take refuge in the very centre of the world that wanted to hang her.

At the last minute, as she moved stealthily past the dark and silent wagons to meet Colonel Kirov who was saddling the horses, she realized that she would be rather sorry to leave the gypsy camp. For a very short time she had been almost a part of them, an exceedingly rare privilege. And she was certain she could trust them more than the fashionable world of London.

Chapter Eighteen

After a bright, sunny dawn three days later, Kirov and his prisoner made what the Colonel called "their triumphant entry into London."

Having shed forever her gypsy title of Emerald Flame, Hester found herself missing the bright, barbaric name at times. But at least, she had more to think of now than her dreadful memories of the word emerald.

Hester and Colonel Kirov travelled in some style. As she told the Colonel, she half-expected to be met by the unforgotten Netti Bindle, drunk as a lord, and ready to escort them to the Kirov mansion.

Instead, however, Alfey Fifield met them at the first posting house, a remarkable example of Taidje Kirov's command over boy and beast. Young Alfey, grandson of the Kirov's London housekeeper, brought Kirov's own black team, splendidly groomed, to take them the last stretch of their journey. Alfey played the part of coachman, though he seemed, to Hester, much too young for the role. But like the almost forgotten Jody who, had taken Hester and Kirov on the first part of their long Hegira, Alfey loved Kirov and presumably would lay down his life for the Russian gypsy.

Alfey was exceedingly efficient and was introduced to Hester as his housekeeper's grandson. All in the family, thought Hester with dry humour. Still, it seemed safe, since Colonel Kirov's employees appeared to be remarkably loyal, for the most part. Even the gypsies had not betrayed him or Hester, except the odious Yuri, and you had to expect at least one rotten apple in a barrel, she reminded herself.

Kirov explained while they dined on the usual savoury mutton one day's journey out of London, that he had ordered some of his late father's equipage, complete with the Kirov arms and polished brass, to impress the Londoners.

"Not that we will," she remarked with a cynical smile. "I do know that much about my fellow townsmen."

But she was grateful, owing him everything. He had also taken care not to make any advances during their journey, treating her, in fact, like the young cousin which, he said, she would be known as in the Kirov household, "Until we get the little matter of your guilt or innocence settled."

By now she assumed this was his odd sense of humour, a trait which she had begun to notice was easily rubbing off on her. But there was always the nagging doubt that this entire flight – into the very jaws of the King's Justice – was just another example of his humour?

As if his humour were not alarming enough, he ushered her to her bedchamber at the busy inn and made a little play of attempting to take her in his arms while his fingers were unlocking the door with the huge key.

She felt the now familiar excitement of his body pressed against hers and was warned of its effect on her. She tried to stiffen her flesh against the heat of his own but when his lips lingered over her throat and the globe of one

248

breast, she surrendered thus far in spite of herself. The wild exultation that consumed her as his mouth lingered on her flesh would certainly have led to another of those unforgettable nights in his arms. But in his maddening, tantalizing way, he let her go suddenly and she almost fell, catching herself against the half-opened door.

She stared at his eyes, bright with his own excitement, and breathing hard, slammed the door in his face. So much for his maddening jokes!

Her hands were shaking so much she could hardly pull the sleeve and neck of her gown up to cover the still-moist flesh of her breast.

When she crept into the bed, which was surprisingly clean – did Taidje Kirov have powers over everything in the kingdom? – she lay there for some time wishing his bodily touch, the pressure of his thighs and groin in their tight pantaloons had less effect on her. She sensed that this was how her mother had been trapped into surrendering all her own life and her personality itself into the selfish hands of her lover and husband.

And what of her parents' child? The by-blow of this dreadfully confined passion? Hester thought, I wouldn't want my child, male or female, to be a mere by-blow of that sexual passion.

But here she was, her pulse beating heavily in her throat, her loins on fire for his embrace. . . .

No. She had chosen the gentle, ideal man for her, a man who did good for many persons, not just to attain his own ends with her. He was a man whose love would be divided equally between her and their future family, and whose irresistible passion would never consume all her own private feelings. Passion be damned.

She slept ill for the first hour or two that night, but

awakened at dawn after a dream that seemed to convulse her entire body. To her relief Colonel Kirov was very much his assertive, sardonic self though, hurrying her through her breakfast, paying little attention when anxiety over her impending arrival in London cost her her appetite.

When they were driving along, their equipage surprising a number of good citizens, with its princely Kirov crest (but no postboys or footmen and no proper coachman), the Colonel seemed fascinated by the environs of the great city. Once, after she had made a friendly attempt at conversation, she found herself disappointed when he gave no answer or seemed not to hear.

She realized she missed his humorous sarcasm, his interesting knowledge and comments on almost any subject.

Well, I can't have it both ways, she reminded herself, and thought it was the worst form of treachery to encourage his sexual interest and her own carefully smothered desires, just to accept his friendship.

The coachwheels rattled over the stones of London on their way to Portman Square, led by a very much admired team, about which there was considerable speculation among gentlemen stepping out of their own equipage on their way to their favourite coffee houses. Peddlers shifted the loads on their shoulders and backs and stopped to look after the wondrous fiery Russian steeds, and Hester laughed.

"I was wrong. I do admit it, Colonel. London is impressed."

He studied her face, only partially covered by her saucy, tilted morning hat and veil, and his black eyebrows went up.

"They'll be impressed by my gypsy-faced cousin, or I'm a Dutchman." This was hard to imagine but he actually didn't give her time to imagine it, continuing "Dear cousin, you act like a gypsy, you often look like a gypsy, but beneath it all, you are one of the numerous royalty of Russia and an aristocrat to the marrow of your bones. Remember that."

"Yes, sir."

"Best stay with the French language when you must speak a foreign tongue."

"But they've just finished a war with France."

"My dear cousin, do you think we Russians are barbarians? We speak French, war or no war. And we even speak it in Moscow and St Petersburg."

She laughed again and shook her head. "I'll never understand the ways of war."

"Let's hope you need not be asked to."

A scrawny youth was winding a coil of rope by his shoulder and elbow as they passed and Kirov's easy remark was banished when that rope conjured up for Hester a sudden picture of a wooden platform and a hangman's noose that haunted her beneath the outward hope of vindication. She was sober and shaking a little when the Colonel leaned forward, pointing out the more or less symmetrical houses, some of them mansions, that surrounded neat and quiet Portman Square at this hour of the morning.

She had occasionally walked to this area with her father in his later days, hoping he would find something in the bustle of genteel life around Upper Berkeley Square to revive his hope of recovery.

But her father grumbled all the way, even when she used their meagre shillings to get him home again. When

251

he didn't grumble, he invariably pointed out that under this lamppost, or in the shadow of that grand, fine mansion he had kissed her mother, and now there was nothing left. Nothing, and none to care.

"There's me, Father," she had said several times, meekly and humbly. "I care."

But he had simply given her a scowl and dismissed this as a pointless remark. "Naught the same, girl. And so she'd say if me darlin' was here." True enough.

Eventually, she gave up her attempts to brighten his spirits. She wouldn't admit it then, but she knew now that it had become a chore.

Thank God for Lady Pomfret. In her muddled or imperious way that blesed woman had occasionally been like a mother to her.

Hester closed her eyes to the rope in the boy's hands and asked brigdhtly, "Are we here? You didn't tell me it was so very – so—"

"In such good taste?" he asked without sounding any more sarcastic than usual.

"Well, I mean to say—" She broke off her apologies to add with enthusiasm, "I like it, it's rather classic. In awfully good taste."

"Yes," he agreed, getting her down to the paving stones. "Once in a great while, we Kirovs do surprise the civilized people of London with our good taste. Not often, of course. We don't like to give ourselves a false impression."

"Say what you will, I think it's splendid. Much nicer than the silly mansion across the Square."

The Kirov House was a big, solid building of four stories, including the garret floor whose unfashionable casement windows were actually furnished with fresh

252

looking white curtains. That must be the doing of a good housekeeper.

The long lower windows on the Square were framed by thick, impressive green portières on one side of the entrance, and on the other side by heavy gold drapes that suggested great expense.

The Colonel said quietly to Hester, "Cover the lower half of your face. You are what I shall refer to – hoping I deal with none who know better – as a semi-Muslim. Tartar influence, you know."

She managed to cover her mouth with the black Siberian fur of her coat collar, hoping for the best as she descended the carriage steps into the Colonel's arms.

He let her go at once. No dallying here under the eyes of passers-by who would be certain to spread the news. His smile for the stout little female who met them in the street told Hester that this must be his trusted housekeeper, a female whose black gown was relieved from severity by the neat white cap that crowned her greying hair, and by the absurd weapon, a candle-snuffer, that she wielded to direct the boy coachman, her grandson.

During Kirov's presentation of Mrs Fifield to Hester, the housekeeper was giving orders to her grandson. He must take the team around to the stableman who would managed the rest of the task. The boy must return at once, "if not sooner," to take up the luggage of Her Highness, the Princess Livadia, and the Colonel. The princess, somewhat to Hester's own surprise, was herself.

This splendid title impressed Hester so much she almost corrected Mrs Fifield but caught herself in time.

Afterward, having obviously heard every word of the Colonel's introduction and greetings, the chubby little woman bobbed a respectful but not overdone curtsy and led the way along a little walk of flagstones and a few bricks to the front step and the formal entrance, into the Reception Hall of what she called proudly "The Kirov Mansion."

Hester was fascinated by the look of that interior, with its heavy but dazzling Slavic decor along the Reception Hall, though not, she was happy to see, with the Slavic motif carried out in a small gold and gilt salon, just inside the street door. A staircase led up to the ballroom and dining salon on the first floor, and presumably the bedchambers on the floors above.

Hester wondered a little when Mrs Fifield ordered her coachboy grandson, Alfey, up the stairs with the travelling cases she referred to as "Her Highness's wardrobe". But this was at a sign from Kirov who stopped beside an inlaid table with a matching pier glass above it in the Reception Hall. Here he sorted out several mysterious folded and sealed letters that had apparently been delivered during his absence in pursuit of Hester.

Even after all their experiences together, Hester stopped on the staircase, looking over the heavy bannister anxiously, to see whether this was bad news.

Kirov glanced up at her, then tore open each sheet of what appeared to be scratchy but important news. He raised his head again and reassured her: "Excellent, my suspicion was correct. I may always depend on Paris." He turned to other pieces of mail franked by very impressive officials.

How good of him to reassure her with his optimistic remark, though what Paris had to do with it, she couldn't imagine.

She followed the figure of Mrs Fifield with its dumpling shape, but found nothing ridiculous in that female. Better yet, there was a quality of confidence and usefulness about her. She certainly looked capable of running a household complicated by doubtless foreign ownership and requirements.

The woman looked back, motioned Hester to join her and then went along the upper floor past the formal ball and dining salons to the narrower stairs which led up to the private chambers on the floor above.

Hester felt that the woman was loyal to Colonel Kirov and polite to his guest, but her recent experiences still made her uneasy about being betrayed.

She did not dare to explain that, as she herself was distinctly of the new class which had not yet reached the preferment of high gentry, she might behave in ways that did not fit the portrait of a princess at all. Mrs Fifield seemed to understand though, even without the confession.

"Indeed, miss, Your Highness, that is, I was in no case to choose when the Colonel's father, Prince Kirov, brought me here to supervise the household. Perhaps, like you, I expected wild-eyed Cossacks and Tartars pictured across the walls. But as you can see, the Russkies – Russians, that'll be, proved to have more taste than Prinny has, by far."

She lowered her voice in mentioning the Prince Regent, but the roll of her big, round eyes clearly told Hester that the Regent held little fears for Mrs Fifield.

"He comes here on occasion," she explained. "Was used to be seen more frequent-like when His Highness, Prince Kirov, visited London with his—" This time she confided with a knowing nod, "his fancy pieces, for all he called them his nieces. Ha! Likely." She coughed, adding with some dignity, "I am somewhat familiar with your own situation, miss, your Highness, that is to say. And I do not include you in that class, you may be assured."

Hester felt her cheeks redden but had only the comfort of knowing that the gypsy-dark stain on her face would probably hide her embarrassment.

"Thank you, Mrs Fifield." It was all she could think to say, and she meant it with all her heart. After a moment, consumed by curiosity, she added, "I daresay, Colonel Kirov also entertains his lady-loves here. Like father, like son?"

Mrs Fifield looked surprised but said merely, "The Colonel's had his moments, but nobody's sent him to earth yet. Perhaps because of his mother, the gypsy woman whose fate he was tracing in the West Country. It is the thought of her, I am persuaded, that made him so excessively kind to me and to others he has helped." She looked Hester over. "It may be, wedlock wasn't ripe for him, so to speak. Not at least, until—" She broke off. "Come this way, miss – Highness."

Hester was convinced that Mrs Fifield did know the whole of Hester's story. She could only hope the woman believed it, as she could make disastrous trouble if she didn't.

Or if she betrays me, Hester thought. Her life had not made her believe very strongly in her fellow man. Or woman, when it came to that. Except for dear Lady Pomfret and the women in the Holding Cells, she had not too much experience with females she could trust. But when she looked at the housekeeper again, she read something in that round face that surprised her. It looked very like pity. This was soon banished however by the housekeeper's common sense manner.

"Your Highness will feel herself immediately within

256

her own St Petersburg apartments here, as requested by the Colonel."

She opened a door at the end of the corridor and Hester was both horrified and amused to see the heavy, overdone pretence of oriental splendour revealed to her among velvet cushioned fauteuils, a *chaise-longue*, an elaborately carved tea table, armoire and mirrors all dominated by the high bed with crimson velvet curtains, fortunately dusted and shaken.

The light from two modern sash windows, one on the south and one on the west, gave the room at least a suggestion of fresh air to combat the general feeling that she had stumbled into a Tartar encampment by mistake.

Hester heard her voice saying weakly, "Very impressive, Mrs Fifield, you are too kind."

"Nonsense, Your Highness. It was Prince Kirov's apartment, reserved for his – cousins."

I can imagine, Hester thought.

"As you say, ma'am, impressive for visitors here while Your Highness remains. Not quite what one would expect of an English young lady, now is it?"

Belatedly, Hester understood and her spirits rose. She looked at the housekeeper whose expression of calm good sense hadn't changed, though Hester thought she read a slight twinkle in those large round eyes.

"How very right you are, Mrs Fifield! I shall certainly dream of my native Russian steppes and of distant Tartar encampments while I am here."

"Just so, ma'am."

Her busy and industrious grandson came hustling along the hall, loaded with travelling cases. He seemed happy and proud in his work, his sandy hair ruffled by the morning breeze, his frown of concentration belied by his eagerness.

His grandmother said, "Alfey, set Her Highness's cases down here. I will personally unpack them."

Since the housekeeper seemed to be in on the secret of Hester's identity, Hester had an idea that the good woman would certainly know more about the contents of those bandboxes and cases than Hester knew.

At the same time Hester glimpsed her own reflection in the standing mirror across the room, and was startled as always by the changed, even shocking image she saw during the days and weeks since the jeweller's charge against her.

She was wondering what might be expected of her, now that she had reached safety amid the deadly terrors of London's Bridewell, Newgate and the scaffold when young Alfey looked out the south window toward the carefully planned and now moderately busy Portman Square.

"Granny, do come and see! That rackety big carriage trotting around the Square on its way to Kirov House."

"Scarcely trotting of itself, Alfey," his grandmother corrected him calmly as Hester swung around, aware that three days without fear had been all she might have expected.

"Well," the boy amended, "The team is pretty fair, not truly matched, and no champions, but still—"

Hester paid no attention to this gabble. From behind the heavy crimson portières she studied the equipage Alfey had pointed out and was just slightly relieved. The entire carriage and team had been brought to London by Lady Pomfret's ex-jailbird coachman who, with her Ladyship, had first rescued Hester from Colonel Kirov on the highroad. To have gone from Kirov to the Willoughby House might not be said to have improved her luck, but that could hardly be Lady Pomfret's doing.

In her rented house near Taunton Lady Pomfret had more or less said she would go to London, but good-hearted as she was, when her presence was added to that of Colonel Kirov, she might very well lead the authorities direct to Hester.

Mrs Fifield saw her face. "Is it an enemy, miss?"

"No, no, my employer. But everyone in Bath knows she is my dearest friend. Someone in London may possibly know as well."

Mrs Fifield's mouth twisted and she exhaled sharply, but she was by no means defeated.

"Then the lady understands how dangerous it would be for her to recognize you. Colonel Kirov will manage very well."

She turned to leave the room, motioning to Alfey who observed with satisfaction,

"Ay, Grandmama. They've drawn up handsomely. . . . I see a female head. What a bonnet she wears! Was you expecting such a lady, ma'am?"

Hester learned over Alfey's head and then drew back quickly. "It's Lady Pomfret, right enough."

"Is there some way you can trust her?" Mrs Fifield asked hopefully. "I mean to say, trust her to hold her tongue?"

"It is as I said. The best of hearts, but indiscreet."

"The lady might not know our princess dressed as she is, like this," Alfey suggested.

Hester and Mrs Fifield looked at each other. The house-keeper shook her head. "It is too easy to talk, by mistake."

259

It was true. "I cannot appear for her inspection."

Mrs Fifield thought about it. "Let's be saying, only as a last recourse. So long as Colonel Kirov is present, we should have nothing to fear. The Colonel will know what to do. He's got a rare understanding, that man."

Hester swung around and stared at the peculiar sight she saw in the long, standing mirror across the room. Adding to this Tartar female she saw in that reflection would be a veil of some kind, a great aid to the little jewelled wings in her dyed black hair.

Plus a change of voice, of course. Better yet, very little to say and only in French. If Kirov were present, she just might carry off the masquerade.

Nothing else presented itself, except to remain here, ready for anything, but not taking deliberate chances. Mrs Fifield read her thoughts.

"Let us not fly into the lion's den. Remain here, looking your barbaric but charming self. With those eyes so heavily disguised – all that dreadful black kohl, and a veil, I'll find one, just trust to Providence. Remain here unless absolutely necessary. What do you say?"

"Unless, of course, the Colonel doesn't admit the lady, or worse, if he should leave us to our own devices. Not that I can give him any blame for that."

Mrs Fifield was looking just a bit apprehensive, though she told Hester, "The Colonel's not the sort to let anyone stand in his way. Not when he's a mind to carry it off. Shall I be on my way and see how he makes do with this Lady Pomfret?"

Hester smiled. "I would appreciate it, if you've a mind to. And even more, Mrs Fifield, if you can give me fair notice before I must go down to face her. She is a dear, but she does talk, as I say. Yet, I know I ask much of you."

"Tell them that owes nothing to Taidje Kirov, ma'am. If you've ever been in Bridewell, you'll know what I owe to Prince Kirov's son. My daughter – she was taken to Bridewell, this little rogue, Alfey, not yet born. I'd lost her when I was taken up for the theft of two oranges, Spanish, they was, years gone by. The Prince found my girl and got her out of Bridewell and bought me off as well."

Hester felt a growing closeness to this jolly looking little woman. Mrs Fifield had turned out far luckier than Hester's companions in the Holding Cells, but then, they hadn't the benefit of help from the Kirovs. Was all of the Kirov humanity due to the long ago love of the senior Kirov for Taidje's mother, and the memory of her fate?

Hester knew very little about Bridewell except that women taken off the streets, and many other females with no resources were taken to the prison holding rooms. Mainly, Hester supposed, to remove them from the sight of 'decent' people.

Since the world provided so few ways in which a solitary and penniless female could earn even a beggar's food or lodging, places like Bridewell must be necessary.

Small wonder that Charles Willoughby spent so much time aiding fallen women, and the Kirovs lent their help as well. It said something very creditable about both men.

Mrs Fifield opened the door into the corridor but stuck her head back in to ask Hester:

"Will you be needing my grandson, Your Highness? To help empty your cases?"

"No, no. I'll manage, I devoutly hope. But ma'am, I mean Mrs Fifield, it isn't my property, as you may have guessed. It all belongs to Colonel Kirov."

The housekeeper gave her a saucy grin. "And did you think, ma'am, that what adorns this plump form was

261

mine? Indeed, every stitch of it was run up for me by seamstresses known to the Colonel. And there's my pay as well, thanks to the Kirovs. I'm not a nabob, no. But I am well paid, that I promise you."

She rustled away, Alfey prancing, half running, ahead of her to the curving upper staircase. Neither troubled to use the dark servants' stairs at this moment.

Watching them, Hester confessed to herself that for all her recent appalling adventures concerning the emerald, her meeting with Taidje Kirov had been the most fortunate moment in her life. It had not seemed so at the time, but there it was.

She did not like what she saw in the luggage Alfey had left for her, all looking like garments worn at Covent Garden and glorifying rich Russians and Tartars. But there was no mistaking their ability to disguise her.

In the luggage and beribboned bandboxes (and what ribbons, purplish red!) were more astonishing colours: gold and autumn brown with a lacy silk jacket, short and Spanish in style, the colour of Seville oranges, plus delightful golden brown little boots which she half expected to be worn with filmy net trousers. Luckily, these, at least, had been forgotten.

She was smoothing all these net, lace and shimmering silken garments for the armoire when young Alfey burst in without rapping on the door.

"She's gone on her way, Highness. No bother or trouble. She left you a letter." He offered her a folded paper, unsealed. "That tall, ugly lady, she was funny. She gave me a wink. She's a game one, that lady."

"Thank God! I didn't want her to be angry. She means a great deal to me."

Alfey put his hands into a pile of clothing not yet put

away in the side drawers of the armoire and stood there admiring the flashy brightness.

"Then I shan't have to see her today," Hester pursued the matter, rescuing her clothes from Alfey.

Alfey said happily, "You've at least 'til she comes back again. The Colonel, he's off 'cross the Channel to Paris today, returning soon as ever he can."

This was a new danger. Paris was a complicated journey these days, who knows how long it would take him. There need be only one betrayal in London meanwhile, one recognition and Hester would be in Newgate and unreachable before he returned. Alfey was watching her, curious over her anxiety.

"Don't you go pale, ma'am. It'll mean the walnut stain all over again."

She laughed on a note of hysteria, "And we musn't have that, Alfey, must we?"

"Sure not, ma'am. You leave all to the Colonel."

Clearly, he had Taidje Kirov confused with the Almighty. There were moments when Hester almost made the same mistake.

When she was alone Hester opened Lady Pomfret's note. It was very like Lady Pomfret, useful and helpful and very much to the point.

'Another recruit, my dear. Charles Willoughby overheard words between his mother and her wretched companion, the Pankridge woman. He is now convinced you are innocent of the Willoughby House theft and from this he leaped to the Girard Emerald.

'Your innocence on the one charge must include the possibility that you were falsely accused on the other. I did not argue with this reasoning. The result is what counts.

'He is at our service in London now and I am told by our excellent conspirator, Colonel Kirov, that Charles may be of use if matters threaten trouble while he is gone to France.

'Charles will be at hand, should he be needed. He has even offered to tool this coach of mine, should my Joshua prove unable to remove you without difficulty. All this until the Colonel returns or the odious Girard is trapped.

'I tell you the above because it is only fair that when we have you all right and tight and free, you must know, dear Charles wishes to prove that his loyalty is as great as that of our gypsy friend.

Jerusha Pomfret.'

The news of Charles Willoughby's about-face was better than she had dared hope. Good might yet come of it, and Hester thought again that Charles truly loved her.

If all went well and she was eventually vindicated, she could marry him. All would be as it had been intended. Dear Charles. . . .

But in that case, would she never see Taidje Kirov again, after her freedom? As she was not yet free, it was not a decision she had to make.

In London she was nearer the gallows than ever. She mustn't be too free with her belief in the future. If she should set foot outside the Russian territory of Kirov House, the danger remained as long as Girard and his witnesses were upon her trail.

Chapter Nineteen

There seemed to be no help for it. Every moment of her life had been at risk since the fatal visit to Gerard And Hailsham Jewellers' establishment. Hester braced herself for another risk now, and perhaps the greatest one yet.

It might be that a miracle of good luck would occur. Surely, no one was likely to recognize the brass-skinned black-haired Princess Livadia of some Russian province or other, especially if she remained strictly within doors during the time of Colonel Kirov's absence in Paris.

When Kirov came up to her room to explain, some two "Emerald Flame" hours later he seemed sure of her being cleared of the charge. She met him as respectably as possible in a silk gown adorned by a short, fashionable Spanish jacket, the latter woven of what appeared to be gold cobwebs, as well as slippers with curving toes that looked for all the world as if they belonged in a Turkish harem.

Kirov did not seem surprised but the sight of her did impress him. He took her hands, held them away from her gown and pronounced her "a breathtaking creature".

"In borrowed finery," she reminded him, but she couldn't help being pleased by his look as he considered her.

"Let us hope Prinny doesn't take a fancy to pursue my

father's latest 'cousin'. Apparently, even after my father's death, your beloved Regent still finds the Tsar's citizens creatures to be dangling from his belt of conquests."

She stiffened. "What do you mean? Not while you are gone to Paris, surely. You know I cannot leave this house, or I am done for." She might need Charles' help, after all.

"We must be quite certain to spread the word that you are laid down with something he will dislike excessively. Typhus? Or merely a childhood disease, something with spots. He has a gift for showing Russian princesses about Carlton House, incognito, so to speak, comes upon them quite by chance, as you might say. I daresay, you would be the first to avoid him. No harm done, if the ladies manage to turn his attentions elsewhere."

"Dear God!"

"No fear. I don't recall his ever seeking a lady wanted by the King's Justice."

"You are not amusing me," she said hoarsely.

Why he chose to tease her in this fashion she could not imagine. Maybe he merely wanted to instill a little courage in her.

"Please," she began again, hoping to change the subject. "You will be returning soon? You will!"

"I promise you this, I will do my utmost."

Damn him! Why must he continue to make her suffer? He must hope to make her more beholden to him than Sir Charles who might turn her over to the authorities, but surely Charles would not do such a thing after all she had gone through!

"Do you honestly believe someone in Paris may help us?"

"I honestly believe it."

266

That was better. He shook her hands, teasingly. "After all this time, have you still no confidence in me? The message was in my mail this morning, from a shop on the Rue St Honore in Paris. I had questions delivered to Paris several days ago, before we left our gypsy friends. I intend to bring back my answer very much in my own person. We have only to be patient."

"Unless someone betrays me."

"Be quiet. Life is full of ups and downs. Your turn on the wheel upward is very much overdue."

She did not know why, but the very way he talked to her gave her renewed confidence. In spite of his jokes and sarcasm, he could always bring her around, at the very least, to share his self-confidence.

She did not mention Charles Willoughby. Perhaps Lady Pomfret had not told him of that development.

Still, her confidence in Taidje Kirov reinforced a corresponding fear.

"While you are gone, I know I must keep very much within doors, see no one, refuse all callers, but a visit from His Highness, the Prince Regent – I mean, a visit from one of his aides. . . ."

He looked down at her hands in his. "True. Very much in Prinny's style, since he has managed to entertain some of my father's 'cousins'."

"But how can I avoid him?"

"Look as unattractive as you may. A pity you look – as you do. Much easier in every way if you had been an acid-faced ninny."

"Perhaps I should blacken my teeth and wear a scullery maid's cap and gown."

He grinned. "Good. Your spirits are improved."

She took a chance. "Sir Charles Willoughby is in the

City. It is quite possible he will discover my whereabouts. He will not betray me this time, I am certain."

He frowned, drew her closer, looking into her eyes. "And you wish to see him, of course."

"He is a good man and it might be quite another thing if I had been free of these charges. But at this moment, no, I thank you."

He raised his hard, dark fingers to her chin and then bracketed them around her face. "If I should bring back rescue for you, am I to provide that ridiculous creature with a loving mistress of Willoughby House?"

She hesitated, adding after a little pause which did not escape him, "That would hardly be possible. There is already a Lady Willoughby. I am persuaded she would accept her replacement with less than complete enthusiasm."

He laughed, pinched her right cheek brusquely and then pulled her close.

"We must hope she will soften her rigid propriety and accept you."

He was taking her ambivalence with a calm that piqued her a little, but before she could free herself from his painful grip, he bent his head and his lips touched the side of her throat. It was almost as though he tasted her love and knew she offered a return of his passion. She had expected his kiss before his departure but not his aim. She moved slightly in his grasp and responded to his warm lips with an urgency that surprised her.

Hester knew a brief moment when she wondered what life would be like if she were indeed freed and forgiven by Charles Willoughby. But Taidje's kisses brought back all the memories of his body that had shaken her in the past and filled her senses with a passionate desire to return his lovemaking as she had returned it before, thinking it was under duress.

But though the great bed was within a length of them, this was obviously not the time for dalliance. She was both sorry and urgently relieved, considering the shortness of time, when he let her go all too soon.

Despite the sudden strengthening of her feelings for him, she sensed that he was less sure of her than he had been during those strange and passionate moments beside the gypsy wagons. Perhaps it was because of her inexperience in passion, her lifetime of denial. No matter. When he returned, if she was finally freed of all fetters of every sort, she would show him that her love could be as strong as his.

Still, the oblique slant of his eyes did not hide the glitter in their depths. He even shook her a little.

"All's well. No sad airs now, I won't fail you."

"I know that. If—"

"Yes?"

"Keep yourself safe from harm, I do pray."

He inclined his head formally, with a polite air that was almost a caricature of Charles Willoughby.

"For your sake, madam, I give you my word. And all for that damned Charles Willoughby."

He turned and walked to the door while she stood there motionless, wondering if she would see him again.

Anything could happen in the meantime. If her identity were discovered, even Taidje Kirov could not save her. No long waits here in holding cells. There was quicker action in London.

But something else was involved. More than physical passion, more than the excitement of his lovemaking, she had enjoyed his company, his conversation, his moments of friendship, sardonic as he might be. He would never bore her. Perhaps she would never know him entirely if she became a part of his life.

But looking back, she knew that during these last days with him she hed felt his deeper care for her that transcended the physical bond between them.

He never doubted her. If only Charles Willoughby, kind and good-hearted and charitable, had also expressed a little faith in her earlier. But that was probably not in his nature.

She shook herself out of these dreams and rushed to the open door, calling after Colonel Kirov.

"Do not regard Sir Charles, do not regard him."

Too late – he was already halfway down the stairs.

Chapter Twenty

Hester had once felt deeply the lack of privacy in the Holding Cells. She was long used to sleeping alone and quite sure she could survive better alone than in the company of the strange women she met at Taunton.

But that notion had soon been banished. At the time of her escape she hadn't believed how often in the following days she would think of those women and wonder if, at their trials., they would have any luck. She devoutly hoped so. By the time she arrived in London as the preposterous Princess Livadia, she knew that a part of her would always find herself one of them.

Her anxiety to rise from the dubious status as a dependent of a father who did not care a shred for her, and even as a dependent of Lady Pomfret, had faded a little. Her hope of establishing herself as a gentlewoman had certainly gone awry.

In the depths of her great and absurd bed at Colonel Kirov's house, she felt the awful loneliness of the state in which she found herself. Even her luck in not having to deal with callers at Portman Square did not cover the fact that another gloomy autumn day would dawn shortly and very likely bring with it several visitors, each more dangerous than the one before.

Her recent adventures, the nerve-wracking twist to her

271

emotions, now finding herself less enthralled by a quiet, companionable life – assuming she had a life in the future – kept Hester from sleep until well into the depths of night. As a result she awoke the next morning to find a hazy, smoky sun well up.

The nature of Mrs Fifield had led her to expect a tea tray and later a breakfast brought to this wild Russian Tartar room, but that the little housekeeper herself should bring it was an unexpected kindness.

She sat up, washed quickly from the fragile French bowl, with the delicious violet soap and beautifully embroidered old linen all brought by young Alfey. She took care not to disturb her dark-skinned disguise more than necessary. Alfey, having gone with the bowl and its contents, she appreciated the sight of Mrs Fifield who personally delivered her tray of breakfast together with the latest chapter in what Hester now regarded in her wryly humorous moments as the hair-raising adventures of Hester Leland.

Her first sight of the scrambled eggs, tea and bread was pleasant to look at but the little housekeeper's low, confiding tone made her less hungry than she had thought herself to be.

She had just raised the eggshell-thin china cup to her lips when Mrs Fifield told her,

"We are being watched, Miss – Your Highness, I do believe."

"Watched? Who by?"

Hester swung her bare feet over the side of the huge bed, starting to descend the three wooden steps beside it.

Mrs Fifield protested, "No, no. He hasn't approached the house itself, although he stopped our poultry woman and asked how many guests occupied Kirov House."

"What did she say?" Hester pushed the curtains open slightly and tried to look out the window without showing herself but she did not locate the watcher.

Mrs Fifield said, "The woman merely shrugged and ordered him out of her way. I believe she said 'None but the Kirov family members'."

"Good. But who is he? I can't see any but a young lackey carrying a chair on his head, and a gentleman tooling a curricle. The Square is almost empty."

The housekeeper hesitated. "He seems odd, in any case. He is – or was – a gypsy. We don't see them often in these streets."

Hester scarcely dared hope. "Could it be one of Colonel Kirov's people?" The housekeeper's face cleared. "Ah! Just so. It must have been someone sent by the band as a guard. A protection. He has no enemies there."

Much relieved, Hester breathed deeply. "You must be right. What was his description?"

"Youngish, I think. And slender. Well – thin. A rogue's eyes, the woman said. But I don't doubt all gypsies are rogues to her sort."

"A slender young rogue," Hester repeated with growing concern. She said slowly, "Colonel Kirov does have an enemy. A blood-enemy, outlawed by his people. He is called Yuri. But why hasn't he reported me to the Watch, or someone higher up?"

Mrs Fifield digested this, seeing the brighter side of the discovery.

"It's clear as a pikestaff. He doesn't know you are here."

That might be, but Hester was by no means relieved. Yuri was the one person in the world aside from this household who would know her disguise and the capital charge against her. She leaned back against the bed in a growing fury she hadn't known she possessed.

"What is this accursed trap I seem to have fallen into? I fancy I have enemies everywhere." She laughed at a strange and terrible thought, "I seem to be a gamester whose luck is always out."

But Mrs Fifield was forever an optimist. "You are alive, miss. And Colonel Kirov will break whatever it is that hounds you, and you will be saved. I have the greatest trust in him, I give you my word. Then, too —" she looked out between the heavy curtains, "no gypsy in sight now."

Possibly he had gone off to inform on Hester, but she did not say so aloud. Instead, she set the tray of rapidly cooling food on the mahogany stand between the bed and the window and began to dress. She might as well present an appearance of decency if the accursed Yuri brought the King's Justice here in any guise. In this case, it must be Regent's warders or some such creatures.

A big, square shaving mirror on the table showed her that her complexion was still the colour of brass and the flesh of her hands was reasonably dark.

Afterward, she sat down to breakfast, grateful that though the eggs were nearly cold, with the newly baked bread and strong tea, it was more than adequate.

Pulling the heavy curtains back to let in more light, she found the Square occupied by various wheeled vehicles, most of them highly respectable, to judge by the fine horse flesh exhibited. There were also some strolling citizens handsomely attired for business in the City or the coffee houses. There were no delivery carts that she could see at the moment, and so far as she could make out, no gypsies.

274

After arranging her black, unfamiliar hair into a reasonably modern coiffure that concealed a part of her cheeks and brow, she now felt much more herself. She went carefully down the front stairs that frequently levelled off to curtained recesses perfect for concealment purposes. The Kirovs were such an odd family, she couldn't help wondering how often this old house concealed other fugitives.

She made as little noise as possible, but the great staircase creaked and made her aware that though the big house was elegant in its heavy way, everything about it suggested age.

On the last flight she was able to look over the bannister to see the Reception Hall below and luckily to see nothing that looked to be an immediate threat.

Hearing footsteps approaching from the kitchen and still room, she hesitated, one foot still on the bottom stair. She could avoid being seen if she stepped into a curious little recess where the stairs met the hall, but she recognized the rustle of Mrs Fifield's skirts. With her was her grandson, Alfey, looking proud, even important, his usual good-humoured self disguised.

It was he who saw Hester first. Before the housekeeper could speak, he raised his pointed chin and confided,

"I'm to spy out the Square, Highness. Just careless-like. A 'tossing the ball and going after it. Just to see who's got eyes for the Kirov folk."

Hester felt much of the relief of a freed prisoner. True, what the boy did find out might be of little importance, but his faith in her, like that of his grandmother, made all the difference. She had always been independent until the emerald episode in Girard's shop. But all that was changing, she hoped.

She could only murmur, "Thank you, Alfey. You'll deal fair. I know you will."

Alfey looked surprised, his tawny eyebrows raised.

"Wouldn't never do nothin' other. May I go now, Granny?"

Mrs Fifield exchanged a look with Hester and smiled. "Go along. And mind you, keep tight about this house."

"Ay, that I'll do." He scampered out through the front door and onto the stones of the Square, bouncing his ball and sweeping it along with a bundle of broom straws that had seen better days.

The housekeeper and Hester crossed the hall into a small salon that looked to be used very seldom. The formal gilt touches here and there on the decor, including the stiff, brocaded couch and wall brackets, showed Hester the excessively uncomfortable milord chairs, a long table and heavy gold drapes, which were dusty in spite of Mrs Fifield's insistence that she and one of the maids saw to its weekly cleaning.

"Since His Highness Prince Kirov died a short time ago it's had little use. Colonel Kirov is forever busy studying English laws and usage, ways to report to Tsar Alexander. That and the sudden fact that he was about to learn his gypsy mother's fate."

"So he told me."

The housekeeper nodded. "It was their Tsar himself that got Colonel Kirov onto these warder-prison guard trips. Said it was to learn our ways, and find use for them in the Tsar's land. Our Prince Regent, he give permission, but I heard tell that he said 'some parents wasn't worth the trouble'. Him thinking of our poor mad King, his father, no doubt."

"No doubt. Can we see the Square from this window?"

One window faced the northerly exit from the Square and the other gave a good view of the activities across the fairly busy Square itself. Mrs Fifield led Hester to the latter window where she pulled heavy gilt-coloured cords to part the draperies and give Hester a good view.

It was an hour for pedestrians, a few strollers, but for the most part the Square's own dwellers, dressed and over-dressed, as though they were a mere part of the decor and posing for elegant mass scenes as far from Great London's heart as if they inhabited the moon.

What would they say, Hester asked herself, how would they react, to the Holding Cells, and the workings of justice at the Old Bailey. One day trials – twenty-four hours later, the gallows. Probably, she thought, they wouldn't regard that sordid aspect of London as anything more than a devil's fantasy, and very much what those inhuman creatures deserved for the theft of a piece of lace or a thimble, or a lawn handkerchief.

She shuddered. Mrs Fifield glanced at her.

"Come, my dear, you are not to be thinking sad thoughts. If Colonel Kirov isn't delayed, he will save you."

"Thank you. Yes, I must place all my hopes, all my prayers in Colonel Kirov."

Young Alfey, meanwhile, had knocked his ball against the wheel of a closed carriage and now ran to retrieve it.

Hester watched anxiously but the housekeeper, though puzzled, did not seem too worried.

"No fear, miss. That'll be how Major Godfrey Linsfoote was used to come with invitations."

Hester did not find this reassuring. "Surely, the carriage doesn't belong to one of the late Prince Kirov's friends." But the plain, nondescript carriage and reasonably strong and well-groomed bay team might belong to an associate of Taidje Kirov. No one knew better than she that the Colonel dealt with some very odd persons, including highwaymen, gypsies, and females wanted on hanging offences.

"It was more discreet," Mrs Fifield explained. "I recall His Highness, Prince Kirov, once said it was invariably done by Bonaparte, after he discovered his wife's little peccadilloes. I suppose what served Boney was well enough for our Regent."

"You mean to say the man in that carriage transport women to our Prince Regent for purposes of—"

Mrs Fifield broke in with gentle haste. "Only if the lady is complaisant. No force is ever – well – needed. Often it is a matter of polite conversation only. The Regent is a gentleman, after all."

Hester rolled her eyes. "And the Kirov princesses?"

"One does not ask the ladies such a question." Then Mrs Fifield added, "In my own experience of the three Kirov ladies, I have often wondered if the titles are genuine. I suspect they reported interesting little facts about our government's future plans to the Tsar's ministers."

"Good Lord! Spies, in fact."

Royal harlots and spies. This realization was given even more painful immediacy by the noisy entrance of young Alfey through the front door, bellowing from the hall,

"It's our friend the Major, Granny. All's safe. He' come to see our princess about a message from Prinny I mean – well, you know."

Hester started out of the gold salon in a rush, headed for the stairs, but only just caught herself before running into a solidly built, smiling gentleman of middle years, sheathed in a modest travel cloak that concealed whatever elegance he may have sported in the presence of his master, the Prince Regent.

She begged his pardon in her rapid but certainly not grammatical French. She was grateful for his good nature and easy acceptance of these bad manners.

He had taken her arm but let her go at once, preventing her from tripping.

"Well met, ma'am. I trust you will pardon my haste to meet you, but His Royal Highness has a friendly message which he asks be personally delivered to the royal Kirov Ladies who adorned the court with their presence a year gone by. That is, of course, if Your Highness will be attending them in the course of your return to St Petersburg."

"Yes, of course, sir. When I return to St Petersburg." *When* – if ever.

He went on with his casual explanation. "He – we feared you might be off on a jaunt to Brighton or elsewhere, as Princess Ekaterina was last year."

Hester drew her arm away, seeing his pleasant, even friendly gaze fixed on first her face, then her figure.

For a moment his gaze remained on her eyes. No, The corner of her left eye. Perhaps her lashes, and she thought he frowned. But it was so slight she might have imagined it. Or was he remembering that the Prince Regent preferred his ladies excessively clean, with not the slightest sign of badly applied coloring on their faces or their bodies? Good. Perhaps she would not pass this fellow's test. There was always a chance that a bit of black kohl remained by her eyelashes. Excellent!

She raised her hand to the lower half of her face. So much for the housekeeper's plan that her features should be shrouded by a veil. Obviously, they weren't. Not that it mattered. The Regent obviously found almost any of the Russian 'princesses' worthy of a light-hearted pursuit.

With a strong desire to wring young Alfey's neck for having brought the Regent's emissary indoors, she was exceedingly formal.

"Sir, I have been forbidden by the Emperor to leave this house. But I will be happy to deliver a message to the princesses."

She knew she must invite him to remove that cumbersome cloak, which was almost the equivalent of a disguise to keep Portman Square's elegant residents from guessing his identity, or who had sent him. He would think she had been reared in a stable, but, surely, Mrs Fifield would give her the lead in that, even though she was not the mistress of Kirov House. When it came to such matters, neither was Hester.

Major Linsfoote, however, was a gentleman of considerable good nature and even charm. He knew where his duties lay. When Mrs Fifield suggested he remain for a glass of that excellent Jerez, sent over to Kirov House with the Prince Regent's compliments, he thanked her but refused on the grounds that he must return to Carlton House where the Regent himself would be showing his superbly refurbished London home to a brace of Portuguese princelings.

"His Royal Highness prefers to demonstrate his expert knowledge of the most tasteful furnishings."

His farewell bow to Hester was unexceptionable and the smile he bestowed on her was more than she deserved considering her own disgust at the post he held in the Prince Regent's household.

When he had gone Hester got no sympathy from Mrs Fifield or her grandson, both of whom seemed to hold

Major Linsfoote in great esteem and admiration. Hester complained, "How absurd that one of the Regent's adjutants, a gentleman obviously, should be chosen to deliver a mere note, warm though it may be, to a pair of Russians with whom he whiled away an hour many months ago!"

"Oh, no, ma'am," Alfey put in. "Major Linsfoote is a friend. The Regent trusts him, and he gives me a ride, now and again, right up afore him on the handsomest thoroughbred."

Mrs Fifield agreed, but on a note of caution. "If only you had been wearing a veil, even a very slight one! His report upon you will surely draw an invitation for you to be shown about Carlton House. Otherwise, we might have foisted you off as recovering from some odious, spotted, child's disease."

"I'm sure I wish I might have obliged with the real thing."

Ignoring this as Hester's form of humour, Mrs Fifield was cheered rapidly. "His Highness is a gentleman, when all's said. If you behave with great propriety, as I know you will, there'll be no harm done. That's to say, you've nothing to fear."

"He frowned when he looked at my left eye," Hester reminded her.

Mrs Fifield reddened. "I was that embarrassed for you, my dear. But it may all be just as well. There was a tiny stain of black kohl from your lashes, and the major knows that His Highness prefers—"

Hester smiled. "Indeed, I will remember that." It might serve her well.

Then she occupied herself with the problem of Charles Willoughby, her dear Charles, once her future husband. And he still loved her. If she was ever restored to her true self, her future lay before her as Charles Willoughby's wife.

Like Colonel Kirov, he had sacrificed much for her, if he had decided to contravene the law at any moment to save her.

Hester had always enjoyed being useful, first in running a tiny household for her father, then as an under-housekeeper where a cook-housekeeper lorded it over the household, and finally as Lady Pomfret's companion and glorified errand girl, a post which she found welcome and enjoyable until she encountered Girard And Hailsham's shop.

Each post kept her busy and, either by accident or design, she was often in a position requiring initiative and a good deal of variety.

But the long wait, day after day, in the Kirov Portman Square house, without daring to be seen outside the walls of the house itself, was remarkably tedious. It also added to a lowness of spirit that seized her after the third day.

On the fourth day a note was pressed into young Alfey's hand by a man in a coachman's caped greatcoat and sugar loaf hat and, having read it, Mrs Fifield discussed it with Hester.

It was from Charles, who had apparently been the man in the coachman's greatcoat and wished Hester to know he would manage her rescue.

The two women were as one in agreeing that they must give Taidje Kirov more time, perhaps even three more days, before venturing flight in the keeping of Charles Willoughby. He was not a conspirator at heart, for one thing. Even more important, both women felt that Charles had an inquisitive mother who detested Hester and might discover her son's plans.

There was no doubt, however, that Hester was grateful to him, knowing his offer and plan were not in keeping with his character, and that he was risking personal ruin as well as self-respect in committing so outrageous a criminal act.

The dreaded invitation from Major Linsfoote arrived the following day, honouring Her Highness, the Princess Livadia Kirov, with a showing of the magnificent new public salons in Carlton House, perhaps to include a brief meeting with HRH the Prince Regent on the third day hence. Major Linsfoote would be pleased on that day to escort Her Highness to Carlton House immediately after midday.

"This, I think, must be accepted if it can be done without interference," Mrs Fifield decided. "It is clearly a short tour of inspection, and not a banquet or some other elaborate affair."

"Thank heaven for that."

The housekeeper reminded her, "A dinner or ball would be most improper in any case, my dear, as you have not been presented officially."

Hester knew she must return to Kirov House without being seized by Girard or his cohorts. Very likely, he was using Runners from Bow Street by now to aid in her capture.

She prayed that Taidje Kirov would have returned by then. If not, her presence here was certain to be discovered. Alfey had confided somewhat portentiously that a slim, evil-looking gypsy had followed him from the Covent Garden markets to Upper Berkeley Street, and Hester was sure it must be Yuri.

The night before her approaching visit to Carlton House Hester dreamed of the gypsy and was awakened by the memory of Taidje Kirov's bloodstained arm and the spurting vessel of blood after Yuri's knife ripped the flesh.

She did not want to discuss the bloody dream or the gypsy with Mrs Fifield, but she was more apprehensive than ever when the housekeeper broached the subject first: she too had dreamed of a gypsy, but in her case it was Taidje Kirov.

Hester asked herself why Yuri had followed the boy if he knew where Alfey lived? Yuri had been seen in Portman Square the first day after Hester arrived. What was his reason for the pursuit now? Or was he in league with Girard, even, and her protectors keeping Hester in sight until more of Girard's hirelings arrived? It was very like a cat-and-mouse game.

Hester knew that if Kirov had not returned by tomorrow, the day of Hester's visit to Carlton House, she must accept the royal invitation and hope Major Linsfoote, and perhaps Charles Willoughby, would protect her from Girard's men.

Mrs Fifield agreed. "We must send Alfey to the Willoughby residence in Grosvenor Square and explain the need for his presence at the hour of your visit to Carlton House."

Secretly, Hester placed all her faith in the return of Taidje Kirov before that hour, but there was one comfort. Alfey brought back a message from Charles Willoughby:

'Have no fear of others. My mother has returned to the estate. We have quarrelled, which I regret, but I dare say she will receive you as I do, my dearest.
    Count upon me.
                                        C.W.S.

Hester read the note, feeling strong revulsion over the possibility of Lady Willoughby's being forced by her son to receive a woman she had wronged and betrayed. She was about to say so, when Alfey lowered his voice to something scarcely above a whisper.

"He's a-waiting in the little parlour off the kitchen, ma'am. It's used by the chef when the Kirovs are staying in London."

Astonished, Hester took the boy by his thin, bony shoulders.

"Who is, Alfey? Not Sir Charles. In this house?"

"Ay. He come through the still room, seeming to bring firewood-like. He begs to see Your Highness."

Could she ever trust him again? No, no. It would be a betrayal of Captain Kirov.

"He's that anxious, ma'am, to beg your forgiveness."

She was surprised by her own emotion at this news. It was pity.

"Very well, No one has seen him deliver this – what is it? Firewood?"

"None that grandmama could see. But I saw an odd one, looked to be a Runner from Bow Street. Hard and solid he was, and with a pistol inside his coat. Or some'ut that looked to be one. He was down by the stables beyond the old mews."

A Bow Street Runner. Doubtless in the service of the courts, to seize and hold one Hester Leland for the courts and her trial. That meant the jeweller, Girard, must be near.

At least they couldn't enter Kirov House. It had been deeded to the Tsar's trusted friends.

"I'll go down to the chef's parlour, but no further," she agreed.

285

He was satisfied and walked down the dark servants' stairs ahead of her. She had a feeling that he too pitied Charles Willoughby and hoped she would be kind to him.

She was still uncertain when they reached the long-unused chef's parlour and saw Charles' tall, trim figure hunched over and covered by an absurd old frieze cloak. The cloak was still dusty from splinters and dust of the firewood dropped in the middle of the worn drugget carpeting.

He straightened as she came into the room. He held out his hands to hers. She let him take them but gave no returning pressure as he shook them. His smile was wistful.

"Dearest Hester!" he murmured, with the old, gentle kindness. The sound made her remember, ironically, her last sight of him before Taidje Kirov came up behind him at Lady Pomfret's rented house near Taunton. Charles had just pleaded with her to return to the Holding Cells.

She smiled now, in recollection. He misinterpreted that smile.

"Is it possible, my dearest? Can you ever find it in your heart to forgive me for the wrong I did you?"

She wanted him to admit her innocence in the emerald episode, to show his trust in her word, because it had been his first wrong against her.

"Of course, I can," she told him. "I do understand." His hands were warm as they gripped hers, and she tried to release herself without offending him. "You believed me guilty because my accusers represented the law. It is natural, I suppose."

Something crossed his face, a shadow. He had misunderstood her.

"I was referring to that wretched Pankridge, dearest. You were certainly not guilty of that theft in my own house. My mother should have known it was the doing of her companion. As for the other – but that will be settled properly, legally, as soon as the courts understand that you were never guilty that second time. My mother was grievously wrong in adding that to your case."

He looked down, saw her gloved fingers move in his, and bit his lip at what he understood to be her attempt at rejection.

She stiffened with a renewed anger. He was not apologizing for his lack of faith in the emerald affair. He still expected her to stand trial and perhaps – a very small perhaps – his word in her favour would free her on some sort of probation, perhaps in his care.

He must be aware that she had emotionally slipped away from him, and went on in a hurried way.

"Long ago, I swore I would give my aid to all defenceless females who had committed crimes that were petty or committed through an unknown mental weakness. I would spend my lifetime defending them, hiring of defence counsel to protect them."

"Why?" There was little else she could say, since he had already lost her and still did not seem to know it.

He was bewildered. "Why do I defend them? I must. I have memories. They would mean nothing to you or to another who was not there at the time, but in my childhood – I was a boy of eight – the guards from the local prison were pursuing a wretched female thief. They passed the garden where I was tossing a ball. I saw the woman hide near where my ball lay beneath a rose hedge."

She raised her head. A memory pierced the candle-lit room.

"Where was this?"

He was puzzled by her sharp interest.

"In the West Country. Taunton, as a matter of fact."

"And you pointed out the thief to her pursuers."

"Yes." He added with sudden, unexpected violence, "She ran, and they shot her. It is true she was a criminal, but I have never forgotten her haunted face. The eyes like a fox vixen as the life goes out of the creature's eyes."

He reached for her again, shaking her but she scarcely felt it.

"I knew she must be guilty. If only she had surrendered, admitted whatever crime it was, she would have saved herself. You do see that don't you, my dearest? Dearest, you do understand."

She had broken away from him. This time he did not reach for her again as he saw her face.

"Dearest Hester – no!"

She stopped in the doorway.

"Have you ever told this story before?"

He was confused. His voice sounded tortured.

"Of course not. Not that shame of my childhood, never!"

She swallowed with an effort. "Swear to me you will never do so."

"Yes, yes. If it means so much to you, Hester. I would never mention it, in any case."

She nodded. "Then – goodbye."

He was still wide-eyed, dismayed at her reaction when she left him. She heard his protest as she left the room.

"Hester, don't you understand? A confession would have saved her. As it would save—"

She was going up the servants' stairs when she heard his last plea to her, "Can you not find it in your heart to forgive me for believing that wretched Pankridge, dearest?"

He hadn't the slightest notion of why she had reacted that way.

She shook her head at her thought that it was not her place to forgive or not to forgive. She prayed that the man whose choice it must be would never know, for his own sake.

Chapter Twenty-One

Hester slept little that night. She waited the long hours before dawn, wondering if perhaps Major Linsfoote, or even His Royal Highness, the Prince Regent himself, might help her. But the risk was great. Once they heard only her story it was unlikely that they would act against the courts who were acting in the name of the King's Justice.

On the morrow, a few minutes before Major Linsfoote was expected to escort her to Carlton House, Hester and Mrs Fifield were forced to agree that Taidje Kirov would not reach London in time.

In the bedchamber of the Russian princesses, Mrs Fifield circled around Hester, agreeing with young Alfey that the lady was prettier than her predecessors.

"Ay, it's elegance you've got, miss. I can see His Highness now at sight of you. He's never been overfond of that poor princess he was forced to wed, poor soul. They do say as how she was not quite so clean as she might be. Habits, you know. And manners, too. But as to other ladies, His Highness has always been the soul of graciousness. Take that Mrs Fitzherbert. As sweet a soul as ever was. There's talk he was actually married to her in some sort of ceremony, not official, that may be. But still, the intent seems true."

This might well be true, Hester thought, but somehow it hadn't stopped the Prince Regent from his royal marriage to the lady who "was not as clean as she might be". Who knew if that rumour was even a half-truth?

At all events, Hester had never seen herself as a sweet soul, but she was too nervous to argue the matter. Nor did she wish to be thought a successor to any of Prinny's women.

She was still wondering whether she dared to entrust the story of her own true background with Major Linsfoote when Alfey came away from the window to announce that his good friend, the Major, had arrived.

Hester looked out. No question about it and no postponing the inevitable. It was the black carriage, though the doors were carefully devoid of any regal crest, or any other indication that the Prince Regent's man intended to take up a Russian princess for the Regent's inspection.

Hester wondered how many other females referred to loosely as 'princesses' had made this same journey. And how many, if any, had actually shared a couch or an evening with His Highness.

Before permitting Hester outside, Mrs Fifield looked out at the Square on which fog pockets were beginning to gather, and remarked that Alfey was right. The aged carriage and a bay team of respectable lineage had just swung around the Square to pull up before Kirov House. As before, there were no footmen but only a coachman, looking as ancient as the carriage.

She added the advice, "Do not enter the carriage until you are able to see the Major. It is not as light within as I should like."

Hester closed her eyes for a second or two, prayed silently and incoherently and even to herself, and then straightened her spine, took up her black and gold satin reticule, and said as coolly as she could utter the words, "Shall we be on our way now?"

Mrs Fifield agreed. "If we wait a deal longer, we may be having the Watch come upon you when you return. And let me tell you, miss, though they aren't much to look upon and are old beside all else, they can make more noise than a half-dozen Bow Street Runners."

It was an ominous thought.

"What I wouldn't give to see Colonel Kirov come riding up at this moment!" Hester said, trying to sound brave and amusing.

"Ah, that'll be the answer," Alfey agreed.

Accompanied by the housekeeper and her grandson, with as much style as these two loyal friends could give her, Hester walked to the front door that opened upon the Square, and there made her brief, supposedly careless farewells to both of them, adding the rider that they must expect her back within the hour.

This, she hoped, was for the benefit of the coachman and Major Linsfoote who stood beside the steps of the carriage, waiting for her to join them.

"As you say, Your Highness," Mrs Fifield said loudly, adding on a much lower note, "All seems safe. None of them horrid Bow Street boys lurking about as I can see."

Hester braced herself and strolled calmly to Major Linsfoote who bowed, ushered her up the steps and into the carriage. Nothing appeared to be lurking inside, ready to leap out at her. She hadn't actually expected it, but she had learned during the last few weeks that any horror was possible.

The aged coachman gave the signal over the reins

and the carriage started to move. It was then that Hester noticed the Major was smiling. She did not find anything amusing about the day, or about this visit and he explained, evidently expecting her to join in his amusement.

"Forgive me, Your Highness, but I am not used to hearing the formidable Bow Street Runners referred to as 'boys', as though their work were a matter of childish pleasure."

"Anything but pleasure," she muttered, then hoped he wouldn't read any of her real fears in that remark.

She knew the Major was trying to discover a subject that would bring out some of the charm for which the Kirov ladies were celebrated, but she was afraid he would guess the extent of her fears for her future, once the visit to Carlton House was ended.

Would she be permitted to enter the Kirov Mansion again? Or would the jeweller Girard and the men from Bow Street stop her? How much power did Runners have? She was sure they were used by the Crown on criminal cases and Girard must certainly have acquired their help on what was now a Crown Case.

She tried to keep a set smile upon her lips but it did not reach her eyes.

Major Linsfoote watched her curiously, and saw a chance to bring up pursue the matter.

"Ah, there! I wonder if we may see a true Runner over there near Upper St James Street, where we are now turning."

She looked out quickly. The fellow was chunky-looking, perhaps – as Alfey had said, this one looked to be carrying a pistol beneath his tight coat. His breeches and boots looked well used. But more important, there was solid strength in the face that only made a heavily carved scar between his eyebrows look more terrifying.

"Probably once a pugilist, I should think," the Major remarked. "Good man for hunting down the baser sort. I suppose I should be happy he is passing the gates of Carlton House. One never knows when the fellows may be useful. Sometimes better than the soldiery, when needed."

She looked at the Runner (if, indeed, he was a Runner) and then looked quickly away, relieved when the Major's team and carriage rattled through the opened gates and the impressive walls of the Prince Regent's newly redecorated London home loomed up before her.

The Major was reminded of the great re-opening of Carlton House seven years previously, when half of London pushed forward to watch the carriages enter through the princely gates. When he mentioned this to Hester she remembered that night of the first ball here, when her father was in the midst of what proved to be his long death, the fool's payment for services to his country during the war in Spain and France.

"Yes," she said, paying little attention to the overwhelming splendours Major Linsfoote pointed out. He offered his hand to her and they moved along an elegant portico, then through the Prince's awe-inspiring Receiving Chamber, whose delicate gray hues, with a hint of sea-blue, softened the overdone splendour a trifle.

Hester and Major Linsfoote were not alone. There were voices around them, especially from a staircase somewhere high above them. Several people were speaking at once, the easy, broken-off exclamations of visitors impressed by the overwhelming expense that the Regent, once he was given official recognition, had expended on an ageing, crumbling mansion.

The original mansion was obviously unworthy of his new dignity when he succeeded to the power and glory of his wretchedly ill father, who was still very much alive. It impressed Hester less than it obviously impressed the chattering people coming down a magnificent double staircase in the care of His Royal Highness's librarian.

The Major was not happy to see the group of more than a dozen visitors pointing out the great chandelier, the exquisitely draped portières as they descended.

He muttered, "Good God! The Portuguese Party. They should have been out of here after an elaborate luncheon."

The Portuguese group passed the Major and his guests with some curiosity but, to Hester's surprise, they were too busy discussing the matter of an accident on the Dover Post Road to remark upon the elegant hall the leaders of the party were about to enter on the floor below the staircase.

"An accident?" Major Linsfoote interrupted the royal librarian, as he and Hester passed the gesticulating little man who scarcely paused in his speech to the Portuguese Party.

"— the wonders of our Prince's library can scarcely be believed until one has the inestimable pleasure of gazing upon—" He frowned at the Major's interruption. "Accident, Major? But of course. A shooting. His Royal Highness is very much disturbed. He has been unable to greet our good allies, the Portuguese Delegation because of it. This way, if you please, gentlemen. You will see, sirs, I have not lied. No, indeed."

On the floor below the splendid curving staircase, the enthusiastic librarian was now gone and so were his guests, leaving a troubled Major Linsfoote, though it

296

seemed entirely a non sequitur to Hester, whose worries were more personal.

Hester and the Major were still climbing the stairs with their dazzling circular motion, when she was astonished to see two men come out upon the top stair, the larger of the two being unquestionably the Prince Regent.

Even as she sank in a low curtsy, Hester was impressed at her first sight of the fleshy prince, once famed for his good looks, his much envied delicate complexion, and above all, his warm and gracious manners. His tall, lean, uniformed companion, seeing Major Linsfoote, hastened to reassure the Prince Regent.

"You see, Your Royal Highness, he is here just as you wished. My dear Linsfoote, we have been scouring London for you this hour. An appalling business. The attack was either upon our good Portuguese friends or a representative of another foreign government, and obviously meant as a threat to the safety of our visiting allies."

Before the Major could excuse himself, having clearly been sent to Kirov House by order of the Regent, the Prince came forward, gave Hester one of his famous warm smiles, and dismissed her with polite indifference.

"My librarian was to show the young lady about Carlton House, isn't that so? But it must be later. I only trust that nothing of today's affair will affect our relationship with her family. Linsfoote, we must do something. Highwaymen – yes, the very thing – have been shooting gentlemen on horseback. I am told there are witnesses, a pair of French travellers, known to us, who were nearby in a post chaise."

"Yes, but Sir—" Clearly, Major Linsfoote was entirely

confused. "Who was shot at? And were they robbed? And too, are soldiers in attendance?"

The Regent waved away his curiosity. "Guards have been sent, of course. As many as needed. Bow Street must be called upon if necessary, to take up the rascals. They must be seized."

"I understand, Your Highness." Although Hester doubted this. The poor Major was still looking doubtful. "Do I escort this lady back to Portman Square?"

"Emphatically. We must show every courtesy, especially now."

The Prince stared at her, then looked over her slender form from the black ringlets confined by a bandeau of gold threads, to her feet, carefully shod in bronze slippers with turned-up Turkish toes. She was surprised that the Prince did not examine her through his quizzing glass. Still, he remained polite with excellent manners, in spite of this international upset on the Dover Post Road.

"Poor child." He looked beyond her at Major Linsfoote. "My dear fellow, do escort her to Kirov House at once and return immediately . . . I hadn't believed it possible." He was back on the subject of the shooting and robbery. "So close to London, so close to me! Go, my good fellow. And waste no time in returning. You will be needed if we are dealing with dead men . . . especially to calm our friends if disaster has occurred."

Whatever the unexpected disaster concerning highwaymen shooting on the Dover Road, the Prince Regent wished to keep Hester out of it.

Hester sank again in a deep curtsy and then stepped carefully backward, down the first flight of stairs before turning at the first landing and descending the rest of the stairs in the Major's care.

She could not conceive of what would happen to her next with Taidje Kirov still in France and none remaining to speak up for her except Lady Pomfret.

Could the Major possibly be constrained to locate Lady Pomfret's London house and ask the lady's help once more in what appeared to be Hester's last chance of freedom?

She doubted if even the redoubtable Lady Pomfret would be able to save her now, with the King's Justice torn by talk of highwaymen, shootings, and other violence. This was no time to expect justice for a suspected criminal.

Chapter Twenty-Two

The silence of his lovely companion was misunderstood by Major Linsfoote as the black carriage rattled on toward Portman Square from Upper Berkeley Street, with its busy teams pulling up to select addresses for an evening's entertainment.

The Princess Livadia was undoubtedly shocked by the disappointment of not being officially received by His Royal Highness. A pity, as Linsfoote found her more than ordinarily attractive with a kind of wistful, even haunted beauty that made him wonder what tragedy had occurred in her past to so depress her.

She had decided at the last minute that the Pomfret House could not save her, but it was still possible that she could not be removed from the Kirov property without the Tsar's consent.

They came within sight of Kirov House at last and Hester sat forward, looking out anxiously.

"Your Highness may be pleased to find yourself at your destination," the Major told her with genuine regret. "But I assure you, I am not."

She smiled but it was not a happy smile and he thought it even an effort. "It isn't your company, sir, I give you my word. It is only—" How to begin? Could she actually confess she was wanted by the Crown for attempting to steal a jewel worth hundreds, perhaps thousands of guineas? A hanging offence, in fact. The mere fact that the jeweller had recovered his emerald in no way mitigated the offence, according to the law.

Meanwhile, there was the painful mystery of what had happened to Taidje Kirov. Was he dead or alive? Had he even forgotten her, or been murdered in Paris while working to save her? What this work amounted to, she had no idea. But Hester refused to permit herself the acceptance of this ultimate horror. She realised then that without Taidje Kirov, even her freedom would mean little.

"Yes, Your Highness," the Major prompted her as she made no effort to pick up the thread of conversation with him. "You were saying?"

The carriage had halted, the incurious coachman was before the carriage door and the steps let down. Hester was helped down and looked around nervously. Only the equipage and teams of Portman residents appeared to line the Square. If any of her enemies had arrived, they must be at the back of the building, perhaps in the stables.

She could only trust to fate now and she walked across the stones toward the door of Kirov House with her gloved hand on that of Major Linsfoote.

Very ill at ease, she saw the door open slowly, with an accompanying sight of Mrs Fifield, looking white and badly shaken.

The Major said at once, "Where is the boy, ma'am? Seems devilish odd, not to see the little fellow at his usual place of business, so to speak."

Mrs Fifield cleared her throat nervously. "He's been sent on an errand, sir – to Carlton House."

"There's a coincidence for you, ma'am," the Major

went on calmly. He seemed to be a man prepared for any eventuality. "We've only just come from there. Reception for the Portuguese envoys."

The housekeeper was not relieved by his obvious calm. "Come, sir, miss. Inside, if you please."

Edged forward by the Major who saw nothing wrong in this situation, Hester found herself in the heavily Slavic decor of the hall with Mrs Fifield beside her. The woman murmured, "You'll find him in the front salon, miss."

Not knowing what to expect in the Gold Salon except trouble, Hester pushed the gilt panelled door open. Four men were there but she saw only one at the far end of the room under the long window. The view of the Square was beginning to cast long shadows.

Colonel Kirov was seated in a large milord chair with his left shoulder in a sling down to his wrist, resting on one arm of the chair. Whatever his condition, she saw only his sardonic grin that made a joke of his own condition and the world.

"Well, Your Highness, am I to be greeted by nothing but open-mouthed wonder?"

Hester ran across the room, feeling herself reborn. She had been prepared for anything but this. She knelt before his chair, and said, "You are hurt. My darling, what have they done to you?"

"Shot me, darling Highness. But luckily, they're not very good shots."

He held out his good hand to her and she covered it with her hands, bringing it to her lips. Over his dark, lean fingers, closed on hers in the old, painful embrace, she looked around the room, ignoring the Major's demand to know what was happening here.

"Those rogues there are Bow Street Runners or I miss my guess. Did they shoot you, my dear fellow?"

He stamped across the worn gold carpet. "Why, damme, I'll have them removed from the Runners! Shooting innocent visitors from our ally, Russia."

Hester suddenly became aware of Girard, who was squeaking in protest. He was drowned by a husky man of middle years, wearing a tight redingote and soiled neckcloth, who spoke with the voice of authority.

"Official business, sir – whoever you might be."

Colonel Kirov leaned forward, and wincing slightly, pressed a firm kiss on Hester's forehead, and then presented his friend Linsfoote to the Runners.

"Then let me introduce you to my good friend Major Geoffrey Linsfoote, a liaison to His Royal Highness, the Prince Regent, and liaison to His Imperial Majesty, Tsar Alexander."

Hester, who had begun to hope, now realized their problems were far from over when the Runner waved away this information.

"That's as may be. But we have our rights and were sent to do our duty – Official. My partner here, Job Dayce, and me, I'm Harry Prodgers, was charged with bringing in a jewel thief, this female here and her – what you'd call accomplice in any country, emperor or not. They're Crown Prisoners, is what they be."

"Of all the preposterous charges!" Major Linsfoote then demanded, "Why did you shoot my friend? The Prince Regent's friend?"

The fat little Runner introduced as Job Dayce, coughed. "Well now, sir, we're only doin' of our duty. In Bow Street they give us the word to follow the orders of this

304

here Mr Girard. He'd point out the person what helped the thief to escape from a holding place."

"One person?" Kirov put in with what appeared to be mild curiosity.

Girard put in quickly, "Persons it was. We saw the fellow on horseback as he entered the very streets of the City from off the Post Road. I knew him for a rogue who got the female out of a Holding Cell in Taunton. I saw him raise his pistol – he was wearing a brace of them – and I ordered the Runners – the big one here – to shoot. He did."

"Likely!" muttered Major Linsfoote. "You'll never prove that story."

"Indeed," Kirov added. "Where's your witness?"

Girard swung around to the Runners. "There was a post chaise close behind this villain. They're your witnesses. We've only to find them."

"Don't reckon as I'd know 'em by sight," the big Runner admitted. "I'm willin' to try but seems this Mister Girard's word ought to be good enough for Bow Street, as it was an hour gone by."

"I always wondered. How did you obtain your jewels in the first place?" Kirov asked with what the others thought was astonishing ease at such a tense moment.

Girard drew himself up proudly. "In my native France, of course. My partners – junior partners, I must add – were jailed and executed as Bonapartists at the time the Usurper was sent to Elba. I escaped, fortunately, with my share of our assets and founded Girard And Hailshams. Finest jewellers in Bath, as you will allow."

"Ay," the little Runner admitted. "I've heard talk of them jewels. None better."

Girard nodded. "As that creature that calls herself a

Rusky Princess will admit, when pressed, she took the emerald off right before my eyes. Caused me to spill them, and made off with the emerald."

"You put it into my reticule," Hester snapped. "You put your hand with the emerald into my reticule and brought it out as it had gone in, inside your own palm."

"An old trick, I'm told," the Major said. "I've heard about such things. Some rogues a few years ago tried it with a lace collar."

"This wasn't no lace collar," Harry Prodgers said firmly. We've our duty to perform and there's a trial that ought to settle the emerald matter. Come along, Your Highness – or miss – whatever you calls yourself."

Hester tried to look around but Kirov was holding her hands too tightly. Had it all been for nothing, Colonel Kirov's painful wound, her own suffering, the belief of decent people in her innocence?

The door into the reception hall had opened and closed. Mrs Fifield had gone out into the hall, and they could hear her steps on the staircase. Hester saw Kirov glance that way and wondered.

Her Taidje, who still believed in her. His tense expression even made her wonder if he had not done with his blessed tricks yet.

Meanwhile, Major Linsfoote said in thorough disgust, "A pack of gudgeons, all of these so-called witnesses. You won't get a word of truth from a pair of drunken rogues cutting a fine pace in their mighty elegant chaise, coming off the Post Road to visit Prinny, like as not."

But his friend, Colonel Kirov, took exception to this.

"No, no. I'd be the last to deny their testimony." While they all stared at him, frowning, his look at Hester was even more reassuring than his touch. While he spoke in particular to the Runners, Hester could not resist bending over his fingers and kissing the back of his hand. He broke off to give her a smile that went to her heart, then he turned to his friend, the Major.

"Whatever this damned rogue, Girard, says of me no longer matters. There is a deal more to be said of him and frankly, gentlemen—", this to the two confused Runners, "— you are welcome in this house, even though it has been deeded to the Russian Emperor's aides."

"Well now," Harry Prodgers put in, offering his own good manners. "Any gentleman as calls our Prince Regent 'Prinny' saucy as they come, makes me wonder if a mistake's been made. If so, sir, I'm the man to mend it. Me and my fat little partner here, eh, Job?"

"Ay, Harry. You bein' one as knows these swells." Nevertheless, Job's moon face was still wrinkled by confusion. "Does we put 'em all in the dock then, or none?"

Girard stamped his foot in a fury. "You'll place 'em, all three, under the hatches, including this Major and that Russsky that you shot – *you* shot, Mr Prodgers! And the female that tried to steal my emerald."

"Now, see here," the Major began but his voice trailed off as he looked over at the reception hall door which had begun to open under the pressure of Mrs Fifield's hand. She stepped aside, making room for two gaunt and ageing gentlemen to make their way into the Gold Salon. The two were obviously related and carried their almost meatless bones with a quiet, shy elegance that bespoke enormous pride.

Neither man was dressed in the modern fashion, both wearing courtly breeches and satin coats admirably fitted, as well as heavily buckled pumps, and looking as if they were about to be presented to the late Queen Marie Antoinette at Versailles.

Hester was as dumbfounded as were the two Bow Street Runners. Major Linsfoote was surprised but pleasantly so and glanced over at Colonel Kirov who nodded.

"Just so, Geoffrey. His Royal Highness makes purchases of the finest jewels from our French friends. He considers his dealings with the DuVal Brothers among his most reliable."

"Indeed, yes," the Major agreed. "My dear Gaspard, and you, Joseph, welcome to London." The Major bowed but the tall elder brother proved his English and his manners were adaptable to any situation. He offered his hand which the Major accepted, going on to shake the younger DuVal's hand as well.

They seemed to have forgotten the jeweller Girard who had been thunderstruck and now edged toward the door.

"What, Girard?" Kirov called to him from across the room. "Don't you wish to meet your old Paris partners?"

Girard tried to save face by the breathless reminder, "They are Bonapartists, spies. I'll have no dealings with them. I'm loyal to the Allies, I am."

The Major laughed but the others were gripped by Monsieur DuVal's quiet accusation.

"The man was a clerk with DuVal Freres. Our politics have never been a problem, thanks in great part to the intervention of friends in your government, Major. But one truth this *canaille* did utter, like his sort. As a clerk in a menial capacity, he fled Paris with a number of our more celebrated jewels which we used for display purposes to certain royal clients. His name, in those days was Gerald Binet."

"A lie! A lie!" Girard cried hoarsely and reached for the door latch again. This time the younger DuVal's hand prevented him and the Frenchman said something in French to his brother.

The elder DuVal looked over at the fascinated Bow Street Runners. He continued to speak in English for Harry Prodger's benefit.

"We were in the post chaise behind Colonel Kirov, my brother and I. We are quite ready to testify that it was this thieving dog here who indicated Colonel Kirov as the dangerous man they must shoot."

"A moment. They lie, all of them," Girard protested, badly shaken. He was shouted down by Harry Prodgers who asked the DuVal Brothers,

"You've legal proof of what you say about our man here?"

The elder DuVal pointed to Colonel Kirov.

"Our Russian friend has the evidence of that rogue's thefts. Sealed and witnessed in the offices of the Prefect of the Seine. You will find a description of the emerald that caused this lady so much anguish."

The younger DuVal added in his careful English, "It was not the first time he tried this. No. In Paris during the year of the Peace of Amiens with Great Britain, he made accusation against two Anglaises about some pearls. He was not with DuVal Freres at that time and when we made hire of him, we had no knowledge of his past crimes. It is our understanding that those ladies were not well treated. All this, we found after the *canaille* had escaped from Paris two years ago."

The Major exclaimed, "Good Gad! What a monster the fellow is!" and shook hands again with the two DuVals.

Kirov removed his good hand from Hester's and drew her close to him.

"You are safe, sweetheart."

She had known all was safe moments ago when she saw that Taidje Kirov was alive and well. She kissed his lips, almost but not quite surprising him. He hugged her to him tightly.

The door slammed, arousing everyone else in the room. Girard had sneaked out. The DuVals looked troubled, but the Runners knew their duty. Fat little Job Dayce ran after the jeweller and Harry Prodgers waited only to ask of anyone in the room, "What proof do we offer in Bow Street?"

Major Linsfoote waved aside technicalities.

"Don't concern yourselves. The DuVals and I will follow you in my carriage. By Gad, we'll make that vile dog pay. Come along, gentlemen. Will you testify, Kirov, when you have both arms free?"

The elder DuVal, amused by what he saw, murmured, "That may not be for some time, messieurs."

In any case, it was necessary to repeat the question as the Colonel had not heard it the first time.

Just as the men, with the exception of Kirov, were leaving the room, Mrs Fifield came hurrying in, looking flushed and frustrated.

"Alfey has come back with three – four – half a dozen troopers. To save you, Colonel."

The men ignored her, hurrying out to the Square, but Kirov looked up from Hester's face and called out, "Tell Alfey I'll be thanking them all in person very soon. Meanwhile—", he turned his attention to Hester, ignoring his own wince of pain.

"I'll tell them we couldn't find you," Mrs Fifield said

and looked out the open street door again. "Heavens! They are dismounting. Chasing that gypsy, Yuri, around the Square. What will the neighbours think? Shall I call them back?"

"Not at all. Let them enjoy themselves."

A moment later the housekeeper looked in at them apologetically.

"Colonel, I do believe there is someone you must see. Her carriage has been across the Square for the past half-hour. It's my belief she intended to rescue the two of you if matters went awry."

Kirov and Hester exchanged looks and weary nods. The Colonel admitted, "You are right, Fifield. We really must see Lady Pomfret, though I will admit it would have been a great moment to watch the good lady single-handedly send two Runners, a jewel thief, two French Gentlemen, and Prinny's own adjutant about their business."